LOVE AND MARRIAGE . . .

Go together like a horse and carriage. But not always in that order—and not always smoothly. Now three beloved authors of historical romance have penned dramatic and passionate tales of wooing and wedding, of handsome, hot-blooded men and the women they will make their brides.

Women like Jayce Cullen, raised from childhood to become the lady of a stranger's castle, only to find that her new husband has very different expectations of marriage, leaving them as mismatched as "The Bride and the Brute." Or Eleanor, known not so affectionately as "That Barlow Woman," whose bitter experience has hardened her heart against the possibility of love. Or Pony Express rider Lou Farland, who is so used to disguising herself as a boy that she can't imagine ever becoming "A Bride for Gideon." From Medieval England to the rugged American frontier to the elegance of aristocratic Louisville, accompany three blushing brides on a journey to eternal love and happiness.

BOOK YOUR PLACE ON OUR WEBSITE AND MAKE THE READING CONNECTION!

We've created a customized website just for our very special readers, where you can get the inside scoop on everything that's going on with Zebra, Pinnacle and Kensington books.

When you come online, you'll have the exciting opportunity to:

- View covers of upcoming books
- Read sample chapters
- Learn about our future publishing schedule (listed by publication month *and author*)
- Find out when your favorite authors will be visiting a city near you
- Search for and order backlist books from our online catalog
- Check out author bios and background information
- Send e-mail to your favorite authors
- Meet the Kensington staff online
- Join us in weekly chats with authors, readers and other guests
- Get writing guidelines
- AND MUCH MORE!

**Visit our website at
http://www.zebrabooks.com**

Blushing Brides

Valerie Kirkwood
Laurel O'Donnell
Patricia Werner

Zebra Books
Kensington Publishing Corp.
http://www.zebrabooks.com

ZEBRA BOOKS are published by

Kensington Publishing Corp.
850 Third Avenue
New York, NY 10022

First Printing: June, 1998
10 9 8 7 6 5 4 3 2 1

Printed in the United States of America

Contents

That Barlow Woman

Valerie Kirkwood

For my sister, Jeanine, who is graced with many beauties, and who graces many lives, not least, mine.

One

Louisville, Kentucky
July, 1888

"So, Kit, what do you make of Josiah Bond's new girl?"

Puffing on his cigar, Christopher McCarron, Jr., leisurely glanced over his shoulder at the owner of the hand now clamping it. Behind a swirl of smoke, he gave a slack smile. "If you're referring to the young lady from Boston, Henry, I make nothing at all of her."

Henry Callard, who Kit thought easily possessed the idlest mind and loosest tongue in the Thoroughbred Club, lowered his bourbon from his lips. "Surely you can't mean you haven't formed a single opinion of her?"

Without looking, Kit flicked an ash at the amber tray in the brass stand beside him. "What I *mean* is that I've not had the pleasure of making the lady's acquaintance."

"And since when have you ever denied yourself a pleasure, Kit?" Grinning, Robert Eldham joined the conversation. "On the other hand, Miss Barlow *is* a Yankee."

Kit indulged his childhood friend with a smile despite his unceasing wonder at Robert's determination to preserve useless distinctions. "Come now, Robert. Where's the Southern hospitality you boast of as the true mark of a civilized society?"

"It's not civilization I'm worried about," Robert replied,

his pale brows shirring. "It's my wife. Lately, all she talks about is this Eleanor Barlow and what a singularly emancipated woman she is." He accepted the brandy a waiter brought on a tray. "I insist on Delia's shopping at McCarron's, of course. But she has friends who patronize Bond's, and I don't like their taxing her with Miss Barlow's strenuous notions. As you know, Kit, Delia's a mere slip of a girl."

Bringing the pommel of his fist to his mouth, Kit faked a cough. Delia Eldham was as frail as a trolley horse and why Robert—indeed, most married men he knew—cast their wives in the roles of near invalids was beyond him. Perhaps they had no other means of ensuring their manhoods would survive their marriages. "I'm sure you exaggerate, Robert—Miss Barlow's influence over our blushing belles, I mean."

"I wouldn't be quite so certain if I were you," Henry Callard replied, draining his glass and signaling the waiter for a refill. "I hear old Mr. Bond's given the gal the reins to the store. Can you imagine? A woman second in command to the proprietor. It's unheard of."

"An oversight I'm sure you'll correct, Henry." Sidling a smile as he stubbed out his cigar, Kit only then noticed that he'd been raining ashes on the carpet. He stepped around them.

Callard, apparently oblivious to Kit's jibe, followed his companions to a grouping of leather, hobnailed chairs. "Kit, shall I tell you what Marcus Spence told me?"

"The architect? You can tell me," Robert said, supplying the interest Kit was devoting to the *Courier Journal.*

Looking at Kit, Henry leaned toward Robert. "Eleanor Barlow consulted him about remodeling the store."

Robert frowned at Kit, who blithely continued turning pages. "For heaven's sake, Kit, as your accountant as well as your friend, I should think you'd find Henry's news more important than anything in the paper. After all, J. Bond's is McCarron's only real competitor."

"My father's patrons have been loyal, Robert, because McCarron's never changes." Kit's gaze remained steady on a story about MacBeth II, the recent Derby winner. "So, if you're suggesting I take a hammer and saw to the place—"

"The place is yours now, Kit," Robert said. "And so are its patrons. When are you finally going to take charge?"

Sighing, Kit folded his paper. "Philby runs the store exactly as my father ran it. I see no reason to interfere with either of their successes." Laughing, he reached out and patted his friend's shoulder. "You worry too much, Robert."

"Perhaps," Robert allowed. "But a good dose of worry now and then wouldn't do you harm, Kit."

"Nor a good dose of Kentucky bourbon." Though his glass was half-full, Henry Callard motioned to the liveried waiter for another. "Can I order one for you, Kit?"

"I never indulge this early in the day," Kit replied, glancing at the gold pocket watch his father had given him when he'd returned from a year's stint aboard a cargo ship. The elder McCarron had made it clear he expected his only heir to have satisfied his wanderlust and assume responsibilities at the store. Kit had tried, for all of a month, before bolting to work his way to California. He'd wanted to see what gold looked like before it became a pocket watch. Replacing his now, he rose, drawing the other men to their feet. "In any case, I need to keep a clear head today if I'm to bargain for a filly I've been admiring."

"I'm afraid there's a two-legged filly you may have to bargain with before long." Henry's mouth, aslouch with bourbon, failed to complete a smirk.

"Now that's one thing I never worry about," Robert said, grinning and raising his glass to Kit. "Kit's not knowing just how to handle a filly."

Henry lifted his own glass in salute. "To Kit!"

"Just a moment," Kit said. Taking Robert's glass, he

cocked a smile. "To Miss Barlow." Hoisting the snifter, he downed a swallow. Then, returning the brandy to an astonished Robert, he made a bow and his exit, secure in the knowledge that Henry's prediction would never come to pass. If his track record were any indication, the one thing he'd never have to do was bargain with a woman.

October, 1888

"Higher!" Eleanor Barlow marshaled a commanding upward gaze at the young lieutenant she'd charged with hanging the red-lettered banner over J. Bond's new bronze doors. "Travis Partee, I want every woman in Louisville to be able to read 'GRAND REOPENING SALE!' from three blocks away."

From his perch on a narrow second-story scaffold, the youth gaped at Ellie. "But, Miss B., that's clear to McCarron's!"

Though a wind gust tacked her skirts to the backs of her legs, Ellie stood firm. She knew she had to if she was to mold Travis into a first-rate assistant, starting with relieving him of strange Southern notions of fair play. "Hard as it may be to believe, Travis, we really do want the ladies to walk straight past McCarron's doors to ours. That's how we're going to become Louisville's finest department store."

Shooing Travis up the ladder that extended from the scaffold to the roof, Ellie reminded herself that like McCarron's, the Josiah Bond Emporium wasn't exactly a department store. At least not one the equal of Marshall Field's in Chicago or Wanamaker's in Philadelphia.

Yet.

Josiah Bond had a vision. One, he'd quickly discovered during their chance meeting in Boston several years ago, Ellie shared. Then and there, he'd made her a standing offer of a job and when she'd finally accepted it, he'd given her free rein to modernize his store. To make of Bond's what she would have made of Barlow's—what she'd been born to make of Barlow's—had she also been born the right sex.

Instead, for want of the male member, she'd been privileged to work in her father's store without recognition or authority while her younger half brother was afforded both without the requirement of work. She'd remained for just one reason: The store was the only thing that had ever truly thrilled her senses. Her eye had delighted in the colors and patterns of fabrics, her touch, their textures. She'd preferred the aroma of kid gloves to that of a dozen bouquets, and the plink of coins in the registers to a concert on the banks of the Charles. Although she'd never persuaded her father to her belief that merchandizing was theater, she'd always assumed he would leave half ownership of the store to her. Half a chance to make of it the pageant she'd always envisioned.

But Donald Barlow, Sr., had built his life upon presumptions that had blinded him to his children's true natures. He'd never understood them less than when he'd bequeathed to each what the other most desired. A large cash settlement had gone to Ellie and the store to her father's namesake.

To be fair, when Donald had taken control of Barlow's, he hadn't let his previous disinterest or inexperience prevent him from making his mark. Possessed of all the foresight of the last mule on a team, he'd neglected the modernization necessary to compete with fast-growing Filene's and quickly drove Barlow's into bankruptcy. In the process, he'd depleted Ellie's inheritance, of which her father had foolishly made him trustee. Then, he'd conveniently vanished, leaving her to suffer the humiliation of a public auction of the family's estate and to do what both Barlow men had believed a woman could never do—take care of herself.

She'd done that and more. She'd escaped dependence on men like her father and Donald—benighted, incompetent, and fatally arrogant. Her employer, Josiah Bond, was smart. Smart enough to have remained both a bachelor and without an indifferent, irresponsible son to destroy his life's work. Smart enough to recognize that a clever merchant unafraid of change could make a fortune in a growing city like Louisville. Smart enough to hire her.

"Miss? Couldn't we could just hang the sign from these here windersills?"

Ellie met Travis's round-eyed gaze as he clutched a ladder rung in one hand and the flapping banner in the other. Folding her arms, she tapped her foot, once. "Travis, at this very moment a customer is entering McCarron's because she can't see that we're having a sale."

"No foolin'!" The youth craned his neck toward Ninth Street. "Who?"

Ellie pressed her middle fingers to her forehead. "Travis, wouldn't you like to be able to tell all your friends that you work for the biggest store in Louisville?"

The adolescent gave her an eager grin. "Sure."

In response, Ellie merely pointed her index finger at the eaves eight feet above the boy's head.

Travis looked at the overhanging eaves, then gulped. "But I don't I think I can go any higher, Miss B."

"You're afraid to go higher, you mean!" In truth, Ellie didn't blame Travis for having a fear of heights, just for not challenging himself to conquer it. She still had to wrestle down the panic that seized her whenever she heard a windowpane rattle. Still had to force back the memories, as she was doing now. Propping her downturned fingers on her waist, she ordered the boy to the ground. She snatched the banner from his grasp, then lifted the hammer and nails from the tool bag around his waist and tucked them into the slit pocket in her three-quarter coat.

"You're not going up there yourself, Miss?"

With one foot already on the first rung of the ladder to the scaffold, Ellie saw the fright in Travis's blue eyes balloon to horror. "And why—" Reacting to the wind, she held down the crown of her hat. "Not?"

The rusty-haired youth shifted his gaze right and left, at the passersby who thronged the corner of Twelfth and Market at midday and who were themselves casting curious glances at Ellie. First sucking in his lips, as if deciding among any number of possible objections, he finally said, "It's dangerous, Miss. Mr. Josiah would skin me was I to let anything happen to you."

As Ellie was about to reply, a length of the oilcloth banner unfurled, slapping a startled expression on a pedestrian's face. Surprise became outrage when the man saw Ellie behind the banner, poised to scale the ladder and with a hammerhead protruding from her coat pocket. "Women will get the vote over my dead body!"

Ellie's gaze fell on the man's girth. "A weighty issue, indeed, sir. I'd be delighted to cast my first ballot on it. What is it you wish decided about your remains?"

The man's skin mottled purple. Sputtering at her "cheek," he pumped himself around the corner. Ellie stared after him, immobilized, as always, by the sound of that word. She frowned at her toes, then took a breath and returned her attention to Travis and the matter of her imminent peril.

"Young man, I relieve you of any responsibility for my well-being." As if she would ever again allow anyone but herself to assume that obligation. "Besides, if I could travel alone by train a thousand miles, I can certainly negotiate twenty-some feet to the roof of this building." Lifting a fold of cypress green gabardine, she raised both her skirt and her elevation a daring height.

"Jehoshaphat, Miss B.," Travis squawked. "It just ain't ladylike!"

Ellie twisted a glance at the youth. He was wringing his wool cap and looking as though he were witnessing the end of civilization. "Neither is childbirth, Travis. But I'm sure we're both grateful that at least once in their lives, our mothers were not ladylike."

Seeing the boy's face flame to match his hair, Ellie rolled her eyes. She had no patience for codes of chivalry that made boys like Travis believe themselves to be experts on what was and wasn't ladylike yet rendered them as ignorant about women—and life—as turnips. Although she'd been much too busy remodeling the store these past months to study that species known as the "Southern Gentleman"— Mr. Bond excepted—she knew all she needed or cared to know about the breed. Observing those of the gentlemen's wives who patronized Bond's, she'd concluded that their lives were as corseted as their bodies, narrowly shaped to please their husbands.

The corset, Ellie had already forsaken, though she wouldn't like her customers to know. She could hardly recommend what she herself refused to wear. As for a husband, although she had long ago accepted that there would never be one, she could now truthfully say the choice was entirely hers. Along with his *carte blanche* to transform the store, Mr. Bond had given her a salary as progressive as his thinking. Her financial independence meant that she would never again have to tailor her dreams to fit a man's prejudices. *At long last,* she thought as she started up the second ladder, *I'm on my own and on my way.*

"Look out, Miss!" Travis's shout followed the blast of wind that whisked away Ellie's hat, and very nearly Ellie herself.

Regaining her foothold, Ellie embraced the ladder's rails. Despite her deafeningly thudding heart, she squared her shoulders and gazed perturbedly down at Travis.

"Don't just stand there issuing silly orders. Go find my hat!"

"But—"

"I'll *be* all right, Travis. Please, just do as I ask."

After the boy took off across Market Street, Ellie closed her eyes, the hand on her breast coaxing her breathing back to normal. Then, tilting her head back, she focused on the spot where she'd tack a corner of the sign to the eaves. Noting that the last portion of her climb appeared disproportionately steeper than the first had, she murmured, "Just keep looking up, Ellie." On a deep breath, she hoisted herself to the next rung. "Never stop looking up."

Kit strode up Twelfth Street toward Market, his thigh muscles counterpunching the wind. He was glad for the exercise. Many more lunches like the one he'd just taken at the club and he'd suffer the gout, as his father had. Lord knew, he'd never wanted anything his father had, not even those things the man had prized. Not his fashionable home on Broadway nor his church eldership, nor his vaunted standing in polite society. He hadn't even wanted the store.

But McCarron's, as Robert repeatedly reminded him, was his now. Still, he had no intention of letting it deny him what he did want most. Freedom. The mark of a real man, he'd always thought, was freedom from the shackles that bound men like his father and Robert—principally, marriage and the endless flow of money it required them to produce. Having to satisfy the privately voracious appetites of women who publicly ate like sparrows left a man little time to expand his horizons.

Recently returned from a photographic expedition to Alaska, Kit now saw his horizons stretch toward Arabia and an equine bloodline he hoped would one day garner him a Derby win. He had only to fulfill a pledge he'd made

Philby. His father's loyal manager had insisted that Kit's presence in the store was vital to reaffirming the faith of both employees and customers in the McCarron tradition. Kit had thought Philby overestimated his value, but, indebted to the man for relieving him of responsibility for the store's operation, he'd agreed to appear daily for a month. And on that final day, he'd no sooner bid his farewells than he'd be on an eastbound train that would take him to an Atlantic steamer.

Pausing beside a ladder to shelter a match for his cigar, Kit wondered how much the Arabian stallion would set him back. Unquestionably, his horses taxed his inheritance as much as a wife would. But until he found a woman with the spirit of a great thoroughbred, the innate passion to outpace the field, he'd reserve his name for his stables.

"Damnation!"

Unaccustomed to hearing profanity shaped by feminine tones, round and alluringly breathy feminine tones, Kit shook out the match flame. Flicking away the charred stick he looked about but saw only a scrawny matron he refused to believe was the owner of that velvety voice. Thinking he must have turned some trick of the wind into a phantom siren, he bit on his cigar, shrugged, then stepped forward.

A hammer whizzed within an inch of his nose, clanging at his feet. His gaze exploded on it, then shot up in search of the soon-to-be-thrashed workman who'd dropped it.

"Do you realize you nearly killed me, you—" Catching a glimpse of a tantalizing lower limb stockinged in black, Kit paused. Rolling his unlit cigar between his lips, over his tongue, he made detailed notes of the limb's curvaceous calf and the way it tapered to a neat, booted ankle.

"It's your own fault," Ellie called down, halting her descent with one leg stretched from beneath her skirts to the rung below. "Loitering beneath scaffolding when there's work in progress seems to me highly imprudent."

Pushing back the brim of his fedora, Kit cocked an eye

at her, then at her daringly exposed leg. He spoke around the cigar between his teeth. "That all depends on who's doing the work."

Ellie's eyes slanted down at her leg, then at Kit. She lifted her chin. "If you expect that your impudence will cause either me or my leg to retract our positions, you're in for disappointment."

Kit *had* been expecting the blushing demurrals his blatant attentions usually elicited from the fair sex. But he knew they were really flirtations and lately, he'd found them boring. He decided that a woman who refused to feign an offense against her improbable modesty was a woman he had to know better. Removing his cigar with V-ed fingers, he folded his arms across his chest. "On the contrary, madam. Something tells me you would far from disappoint any man."

Ellie inhaled sharply. He wouldn't have been so brazen had he been standing nearer, near enough to make out her features. Still, she had no reason to pretend, as she sometimes did, that she had to defend her virtue. Obviously, the man whose brassy gaze she found more challenging to meet than most such looks—even from a distance—was no common masher. For one thing, his cigar was expensive, hand-rolled. The kind whose pleasure her brother had never spared himself. More tellingly, his coat was the latest fashion and too well fitting to have been anything but hand-tailored to his measurements, though, from this height, she could accurately calculate only one of those measurements: Broad. His speech was cultivated and his wit sharp, obligating her to blunt it.

"The only man I hope I never disappoint is my employer."

"Your employer?" Kit glanced at the lettering over the door straight ahead, then gazed up at the hatless woman. Her hair was as black as a stallion he once owned and as blood-stirring to watch wilding in the wind. So stirring that until now, he'd paid little attention to her accent, which was far from the sugary drawl practiced by Louisville's gentle-born females. As far as Boston. Could she be the infamous Miss Eleanor Barlow? Reaching up, he grasped a rung. "You work for Josiah Bond?"

"At the moment, thanks to you, no." Ellie thrust her hand out. "Now, will you please give me my hammer?"

After lazily glancing at the tool still lying on the walk, Kit grinned up at her. "I meant to speak to you about that. If you'd wanted me to hang your sign for you," he said, nodding at the oilcloth streaming from a rung above her head, "all you had to do was ask."

Ellie gazed into his eyes. The only challenge in them now was one not to laugh. She met it, barely. "I am asking. For my hammer."

With a shrug and a sigh, Kit turned to retrieve the hammer. As he crouched over it, a shriek like a spooked mare's jolted him upright. Snapping his gaze skyward, he froze. Eleanor Barlow—if she was Eleanor Barlow—was hanging backwards from the side of the ladder, by one arm and two stories up. Her feet scrambled futilely for the perch she couldn't see because the banner was plastered against her face and coiling around her neck like a thick, oily serpent.

Ellie involuntarily sucked in cloth, that damned slick nuisance of a cloth that had entangled her feet, spinning her soles off the ladder. She groped for a hold, then froze as the ladder shifted downward with a sudden tug on her weight. The wind was flying her like a pennant from a mast.

"Hold on!" Flinging away his cigar, Kit grabbed the rails, then shimmied the base until the ladder was once again perpendicular to the walk. Hand over quick hand, he scaled toward the woman. Reaching her, he wrapped his arm about her waist and drew her to his side. "You're safe now. I've got you."

With her right foot once again on the ladder and the man's broad body shielding her from the wind, Ellie lowered the banner. The rush of chill air into her lungs made her head go light. Pressing her palms to his chest, she closed her eyes and nestled her head beneath his chin.

Kit tightened his hold of her, feeling her heart thud so frantically against his that he just now realized he had probably saved her from plunging to serious injury, perhaps even to her death. Instantly, he felt an unexpected kinship with her, a woman whose face he'd yet to clearly see. "Shh, it's all right now," he murmured in response to her trembling.

To her surprise, Ellie felt her body obey his gentle suasion. Needing to see him up close, to see the face of this singularly compelling man more than she had ever needed to hide her own, she gazed up at him. Her breath caught, a fisted ache near her heart. In a vast world, there was this man's face; all else was ugliness.

Kit peered down at the upturned face of the woman he'd so quickly come to feel satisfyingly alone with in the world. He took all of it in, then studied it feature by feature. He saw eyes as green as magnolia leaves, skin like the milky bloom itself, a nose refreshingly lacking perkiness, and lips that neither used nor needed a cosmetic to advertise their purpose. Lastly, he shifted his gaze to the feature it had earlier grazed, her left cheek, high and round. And bisecting it lengthwise, the deep, white remnant of some ghastly event. Kit didn't want to stare at the scar, but its contrast with her classic beauty had captured his imagination as well as his gaze, defying him to make sense of such breathtaking incongruence.

Feeling his sight trace her disfigurement, Ellie instinctively turned the marred cheek from his view. She hated that she'd done so. She'd thought she'd finally eliminated that reflex long ago, when she'd thrown away her arsenal of heavily veiled hats and practiced boldly returning the

stares she'd invited. But she'd never invited the stare of
any man quite like this man—quite so impeccable in form
and feature—nor from so near. Unable physically to escape him, she looked down. She'd never imagined she'd
find the sight of Travis, grinning and waving her hat from
below, a comfort.

"Are you okay, Miss Barlow?"

"I'm fine," she called down. "Which is more than I can
say for my hat." Seeing his grin fade, she wanted to bite
off the sharp tip of her tongue. Snapping at Travis wasn't
going to make the man still pressing her tightly to him
disappear. She forced herself to look at him. His eyes were
a lucent grey, flecked with charcoal and lined with lashes
as densely black as brush heads. His nose was like an arrow
to full lips mutely parted. His handsomeness was uncommon, but his expression was far from new to her. A mixture
of pity and revulsion. "As you said yourself, I'm safe now.
Kindly let go of me."

How can I when you won't let go of me? Unable to decide which he found more fascinating, Eleanor Barlow's
face or her facade, Kit reluctantly released the slim waist
he could have sworn was corsetless.

"Don't move," he said, as she started up. He reached
toward the left side of her face, his fingertips scuffing her
jaw.

Ellie's wrist crossed his, barring his touch. "What do you
think you're doing?"

Kit saw green lightning in her eyes and the pain it revealed. He spoke softly. "This sign you're so determined
to hang is about to hang you."

As he took the snaking banner from around her neck,
Ellie studied his flawless features, paying special attention
to his mouth. She thought it sensuous but saw no hint of
cruelty, capable of delivering a tease but not a jeer. Since
the accident, her own mouth had never been so close to
a man's. She'd forgotten how dizzying that nearness could

be. No, until now, she'd never really known. But that was all she'd ever know, the intoxicating nearness of this or any man's mouth. Never the touch, the taste.

"I'll take that now," she said when he'd removed the banner.

"What you'll do is get down from this ladder and send that boy up with the hammer."

Ellie quickly forgot both his mouth and his previous persuasiveness. "I take orders from no man but Mr. Bond."

Kit thought the reverse was more likely. "Think of it as returning a favor then," he said. "I saved you from falling and breaking your lovely limbs—I assume the other matches the one I saw—and now you can save my reputation as a gallant, if somewhat roving, Southern gentleman."

Following his gaze to the spectators gathered below, Ellie took his point, even if she thought it a ridiculous one. Still, she did owe him a debt. She began her descent, but halfway down, paused and looked up. "I want the right corner of the sign there," she said, pointing up at the eaves.

Kit looked to the spot she'd indicated. Then, cocking a grin, he saluted her. "Will there be anything else, General?"

With the arch of one brow, Ellie countered the urge to smile. "Yes. Any more of your insolence, and there'll be a court-martial." Then, unable to refrain, she saluted him back. Reaching the sidewalk, she sent Travis up with the hammer. When he returned, he was squeaky-voiced with excitement.

"Gosh, Miss B., all of Louisville's gonna be talkin' about this by julep-time tonight."

Ellie circled her gaze at the intent onlookers. "Talking about what?"

Travis gestured up at the man climbing toward the roof. " 'Bout your sworn enemy savin' you from fallin' off'n that ladder and then puttin' your Grand Sale sign up for you, what else?"

"Sworn enemy?" Ellie frowned at the boy. When had she ever declared to him that she had a— Her gaze scaled the ladder. "Kit McCarron!"

"Ye-e-e-s, ma'am. Ain't he the one?"

Ain't he though, Ellie thought, recalling that her "enemy" had heard Travis shout her name before he'd asked her to return his "favor." No doubt he'd have a good laugh along with his julep tonight, and at her expense. She could hear him now, regaling the puffed-up, condescending males of his class with the story of how he'd rescued Josiah Bond's "girl," who couldn't stay on a ladder much less run his business. Mercy, he'd even had to hang the poor creature's sign for her! But that was the least any true gentleman of the South would do. Besides, before long she'd surely bankrupt her employer, leaving the old boy's customers entirely to him.

"Damnation!" Galled to think that she'd actually saluted the man, Ellie now captured him in her sights. "You may have won this battle, Mr. McCarron. But the war is mine."

Two

The Day after Thanksgiving, 1888

"So, Kit, what do you make of the stir over at Bond's this morning?" Henry Callard wiped a splash of bourbon from his tie. "The crowd was three-deep. It's that Miss Barlow's doing, of course."

Crossing his legs as he hoisted his newspaper higher, Kit angled away from Callard. He was in no mood for Henry's gossip, particularly bulletins regarding J. Bond's or Eleanor Barlow. Especially Eleanor Barlow. One time too many this past month, he'd actually found himself regretting that his Middle East trip would take him away from the woman with the extraordinary face and even more extraordinary self-command. As a result, he'd grown irritable with Philby for holding him to the pledge that kept him in proximity to her, and with just about everybody else for every imaginable reason. With Henry, for example, for now occasioning him to defy his better judgment, and inquire, *"What* is Miss Barlow's doing?"

"The Christmas displays in J. Bond's new windows," Robert volunteered, sitting opposite his friend. He frowned into his brandy. "You really ought to see them, Kit. Scenes right out of Dickens, live carolers and all."

Behind his paper, Kit looked up from a travel story, then regained his focus. "You can take the worry out of your tone, Robert. Apparently, Miss Barlow is under the impression that the MacCauley Theater is stiffer competition than I am."

"Kit, that's the first time I heard you identify yourself with the store," Robert said, his tone indeed brighter. "Does that mean you've decided to stay and take it over?"

Laughing, Kit put his paper aside. "That would take more than Miss Barlow's shallow attempt to lure my customers with a few choruses of 'God Rest Ye Merry Gentlemen.' "

"There's more, all right," Henry said. "She's hired some old boy with whiskers to play Santa Claus for the kiddies. The little beasts tell him what they want for Christmas, then he sends them back to Mama with a 'Ho, Ho, Ho!' and a bag of goodies."

Glancing out the window, Kit covered a yawn. "I'm confident no customer of mine would allow her child to participate in bribery."

"Delia would," Robert muttered.

Kit gave him a sharp look. *"Your* Delia?"

Robert ran a hand through his wispy hair. "I'm sorry, Kit. I reminded her that McCarron's was my client and expressly forbade her to take the children to Bond's this morning. But she said that if I wanted our boys to be the only two in Louisville not to see Santa, then I could tell them so myself!"

Lurching, Henry Callard sprayed bourbon. He wiped his mouth with the back of his hand, then looked from Robert to Kit. "There, you see? She's a menace, I tell you. If we don't do something about this Miss Barlow, she'll have my Louise and every other woman in Louisville wearing trousers—"

"And buying them at Bond's!" Robert signaled a waiter for another brandy, asking Kit if he'd like a drink.

Kit consulted his watch. In only a few more hours, he would start out by train on his quest for a great thoroughbred. Time enough, though, to satisfy his curiosity about a racehorse much closer to home, as close as J. Bond's. And since the air was brisk, one bourbon to warm his blood before he started out couldn't hurt. He accepted Henry's offer.

Moments later, Robert lifted his brandy. "Whom shall we toast today, Kit? I know, that stallion you're after."

Kit stared into his glass. Suddenly, his quest of that or any horse was the furthest thing from his mind. "I think not."

"Surely not Miss Barlow?" Henry jested.

Kit hesitated, recalling the unflappable creature who had refused to demure at his blatantly appreciative assessment of her leg. The independent spirit who, with a defiant toss of her head, had informed him she took orders from no man save her employer. The scarred soul who, not realizing the greater of her wounds lay beneath her skin, had blocked the touch she'd assumed he'd meant to give her riven cheek. Then, discovering she had erred, had neither explained nor apologized. Instead, as he had freed her from the coiling banner, she'd boldly estimated the character—or lack, thereof—in his own face, disconcerting him not a little. Without knowing how, he knew she had earned the right to do so. *That* Eleanor Barlow was no common "Miss."

He raised his bourbon. "Gentlemen, to that Barlow woman."

On the second floor of Bond's, Ellie stood watching tots with smooth, apple cheeks whisper their wishes to Santa. Behind dense netting on a new hat, she smiled. One of her own fondest wishes had come true, to see such magic as she now saw reflected in the eyes of these children and to know that she had been the conjurer. She was gratified, too, of course, that her sorcery was conjuring record sales for the store. Since she'd opened the doors this morning, the aisles had been thronged, her clerks besieged. Already, some had warned of dangerously low stock. And now, it appeared a red-faced young salesgirl was hastening toward her with even more dire news.

"Miss Barlow, thank God I found you," she said, clapping a hand over her heaving chest. "We've run out of the item my customer wants, and she's raising the most awful fuss. She's telling everyone we're trying to deceive them by advertising merchandise we don't have. Miss Barlow, she's telling them to go McCarron's!"

Now, as always since meeting Kit, Ellie heard his name and felt an unwanted heat at her core, like the explosion of a tiny sun. She had tried to quell the fire by reducing him to a caricature of her "sworn enemy," the competitor who had tried to diminish her with his condescension. But she had found no means of making a cartoon of the memory of his darkly handsome face, or of denying that he had first studied her own face feature by feature before turning, inevitably, to her hideousness. For one brief moment, she had thought he was about to tell her she was beautiful. She'd almost felt beautiful, and for that, she could never forgive him. That was why she'd taken to wearing veils again. The netting before her eyes was an inescapable reminder of the truth about her repulsiveness and the tormented years she'd spent reckoning with it. She couldn't risk reversing her victory over despair, couldn't risk running into Kit McCarron unarmed with self-truth.

Nor could she afford to forget that because she worked for Bond's, McCarron's was her adversary. She put her arm around the frazzled clerk's shoulder. "Sarah, I want you to tell the lady that she's absolutely right. We have no excuse for running out of an advertised item, but we'd be happy to give her a rain check for it at the sale price. *And* a gift wrapping, compliments of J. Bond's."

A dawning light spread over the young woman's face.

"Thank you, Miss Barlow," she said, then hurried toward the stairs.

As Ellie made for her office, she paused, taking one last look at the North Pole, at the children and their doting mothers conspiring in make-believe. A smile lifted the corners of her mouth but soon faded. Touching her fingers to her rent cheek, she recalled the day she'd forever stopped making believe.

From behind a display of wind-up toys, Kit had been watching Ellie watch the children. Given the intricate netting obscuring her face, he couldn't be sure, but he thought he'd seen her smile. Actually, he'd felt her smile more than seen it, a softness pressing into him much the way her body had that day on the ladder. He resented the feeling, resented that it deepened his curiosity about this woman, especially when he was headed out of town. Not to mention that she *was* his competitor.

A damned wily one, too. Clever, that ploy to mollify irate customers with a free gift-wrapping. McCarron's didn't even offer gift-wrapping, much less Santa's village, which, he had to admit, was charming, even magical. And cunning. By locating Santa on the second floor, Eleanor Barlow drew shoppers farther into her retail web, giving them no choice but to tour her wares. Now that he thought about it, that smile of hers had probably had more to do with sales than with Santa. He'd been wrong to underestimate her. *Wrong?* He'd been a damn fool. He'd even put up her damn sign for her. *Damn!*

Kit saw Ellie slowly lift her fingers to her damaged cheek, barely touching it. He swallowed. "Damn."

Ellie wound around a display of mechanical toy soldiers and came face-to-face with her sworn enemy. Startled, she fired the first shot. "Mr. McCarron, how flattering that you should go to all the trouble to spy on me."

"If I had wanted to spy on you, Miss Barlow," Kit replied, "I would have sought you and your hammer out on the roof, erecting Santa's sleigh." Removing his hat, he gave her a sidelong smile. "Or perhaps in gift wrap, bribing disgruntled customers not to take their trade to me."

Ellie's veil multiplied the glint in his clear grey eyes, making them appear like two glittering diamonds. She took a step back and turned aside, giving him her good profile. "So, you admit you eavesdropped on my conversation with one of my clerks."

"That wasn't my intention, I assure you," Kit said. He started to close the gap between them, then drew back. "But I won't deny I'm glad I did. Two can play at your game, Miss Barlow."

Picking up one of the toy soldiers, Ellie cocked a sharp look at him. "I hope you're prepared to play for keeps, Mr. McCarron."

Kit was taken aback. There was something eerie about so dire a warning coming in so plush a voice and from behind so delicate a mask. Also something that sparked him to combat. "Your concern is touching but unnecessary. I never play unless it's for keeps."

Ellie wound up the soldier and set it marching on the floor between her and Kit. Rising, she met his gaze. "That remains to be seen, doesn't it, Mr. McCarron?" Turning, she walked away.

Kit shoved his hands in his pockets, pondering Eleanor Barlow's indirect but unmistakable challenge. Most of the women he knew were artful at acting inferior to men while believing in their coy little hearts they were quite superior. This Barlow woman was incapable of such duplicity. She merely defined the battleground—for that was truly the right term for wherever men and women met—confidently looked him in the eye, and so much as said, "May the better of us win."

Looking down, Kit saw the marching toy soldier halt toe-to-toe with him. He gave a low whistle, then went after the object of his grudging admiration.

That Barlow woman.

Seeing her whispering to Santa, he waited for her at the entrance to the North Pole. As she walked toward him, a surge of cries from tots disappointed to learn that Santa was briefly leaving to feed his reindeer, faded away. Her walk was every sound that had ever intrigued him, a lapping tide, a horizontal rain, the wind haunting a mountain pass. In that veiled hat, she did indeed appear a phantom, a mystery begging to be revealed. Why must he find her, of all women, so damned compelling?

Seeing Kit, Ellie felt her heart take a strange leap. He was looking at her in that most unusual way again, as though the least fascinating thing about her was her disfigurement. The veil made that possible, of course. Were she not wearing it, his gaze would reflect a struggle but inevitably root in her ugliness. Even if her face were whole, she couldn't allow herself to be seen conversing with him too freely, if at all. Her employer might construe it as disloyalty; her customers, as a reason to doubt her allegiance to Bond's and to withhold theirs.

"Santa must rest, Mr. McCarron, but I haven't that luxury." Without pausing, Ellie brushed past him.

"That's too bad," Kit said. Then louder, "I was hoping you'd be here when I tell Santa what I want for Christmas."

Ellie halted, wishing he'd go away, determining to make him go. People were watching them. Turning and seeing him leaning on a candy cane, one foot crossing the other, she marched up to him. "Since I can guess what that might be, I'll save you the trouble of waiting and tell him for you. Please don't be too disappointed, though, if you awake Christmas morning and find I'm still in town."

Until this moment, Kit hadn't really thought about what he wanted for Christmas. All he'd known when Eleanor Barlow walked past him a moment ago was that he had to stop her, he had to look once more into those veiled eyes of hers. He was peering at them now, seeing them gleam like jade treasures behind barbed-wire. Suddenly, he knew what he wanted for Christmas. Pictures formed in his imagination—photographs. Too fantastic a dream, he supposed, even for Santa to realize. Yet, too challenging to ignore.

Neither could he ignore the Barlow woman's challenge. She'd accused him of fearing her enough to want her out of town. The damnable woman had insulted his manhood!

"I can't imagine why you'd suppose I'd prefer Louisville without you." Kit's voice was darkly retaliatory. "You wouldn't be overestimating your abilities, would you, Miss Barlow? Or worse, underestimating my resolve?"

Despite his return of an effrontery she'd intended, Ellie looked into Kit's eyes and saw what she had often seen in her brother's eyes, too often. An addiction to the next unseen place, untried adventure, unkissed woman. With her, the most unkissable of women, his bravado would surely evaporate between here and McCarron's.

She laughed derisively. "Do you really think you possess the resolve to stay in one place long enough to best my abilities?"

Kit inhaled, drew up, took the arrow. He couldn't deny that for the past month, he'd counted the hours until he'd fulfilled his promise to Philby and won his freedom to leave this place. Still, he advanced on Ellie, pausing beside her so that they were like two trains on opposite tracks. He gazed down at her, at that defiant yet secreted face, then rose to the full advantage of his height.

"That remains to be seen, doesn't it, Miss Barlow?"

After he'd given her a polite nod, Ellie watched Kit walk away, fascinated that he appeared as physically imposing in the distance as he did when near. Like Donald, he was a head taller than the average man and in all likelihood would prove, as Donald had, that a man's size was no measure of his character. She knew all about Christopher McCarron, Jr. In the last month, Travis had talked of little but his idol, an adventurer who'd sailed the Atlantic, dug among Mexican ruins, mined for gold and photographed the wilds of the Yukon. He'd answered the calls of his sirens, caring little that the legacy he'd left behind was floundering.

Oh yes, I know all about your store, too, Mr. McCarron, she thought as she headed to her office. She wondered if he really imagined he'd been original in spying on the competition. Before she'd even reported to Mr. Bond with her plans for the store, she'd donned widows' weeds, walked to McCarron's, and, beneath a heavy, black silk veil, posed as a customer.

The store had been everything Barlow's was, and less, before Donald had dealt it the final blow: Sedate to the point of seeming funereal, sacrificing a variety of offerings to the security of the tried-and-true, anchoring clerks to tedium behind counters. Customers were forced to wait for attention rather than allowed to browse at their leisure. The only asset, as far as she had been able to tell, was a gentleman she'd heard addressed as Mr. Philby as he briefly stepped from his office overlooking the first floor. Older, with a head of beautiful white hair, a mustache to match, and an aristocratic bearing, he was wasted behind an office door. If she ran McCarron's, she'd have Mr. Philby walking the floors, greeting the customers, cajoling complainants, keeping the staff on its toes.

But she wasn't running McCarron's, she reminded herself as she sat at her oak desk, making entries in a ledger. Its founder's spoiled heir was—through his negligence—into the ground. She almost wished she weren't about to play a part in that destruction. Almost.

Laying down her pen, Ellie lifted her purse from a bottom drawer in her desk. She took out an envelope, soft
and grey with much handling, and removed the letter inside it. Long ago tears had faded the ink, but the words
were as stark as they'd been the day she'd first read them.
Though she could recite the painfully apologetic missive
by heart, she needed to read it aloud now so that she
wouldn't read anything but the awful truth in the disturbing way Kit McCarron looked at her.

"My dearest Eleanor. I hope, in time, you will find it in
your heart to forgive me for what I am about to do . . ."

When she'd finished, Ellie walked to the window that
overlooked the store's main staircase. Customers clogged
it, laden with packages wrapped in the distinctive white
paper stamped with gold fleur-de-lis she'd ordered, adopt-
ing the city's symbol for the store. When Louisvillians
thought of their city, she wanted them to think of Josiah
Bond's, the way she'd wanted Boston and Barlow's to be
synonymous. At last, she had a fighting chance to get what
she wanted.

"Forgive you, Frank?" she murmured. "You did me the
greatest of favors." Returning to her desk, she put the letter
away. Nothing would stop her now, least of all the strangely
admiring gaze she only imagined she saw in one man's
beautiful grey eyes.

"Philby!"

Kit took the stairs to James Philby's office by twos. The
men collided as Philby, his eyes popping a nervous blue,
burst onto the second-floor landing.

"Is something amiss, Kit?"

"Not a miss, Philby," Kit said. "A woman. That Barlow
woman!" He shoved past his manager into the office that
was the heart of McCarron's. For the first time in his life,

he wondered just how healthy the store's heart was. "Philby, I want to take a look at our books."

Philby stared uncomprehendingly at Kit beneath white brows, then burst into laughter. "Forgive me, Kit. For a moment, I thought you said you wanted to examine the books."

Tossing his hat on the desk beneath which he, as a thoroughly undisciplined boy, had tormented James Philby by lacing his shoes together, Kit propped his hands on his waist. "And exactly why should my wanting to look at my own business's books prompt such hilarity?"

Philby shrugged. "I suppose because you've never wanted to before."

Folding his arms, Kit lifted his chin. "A man can change, Philby."

"Yes, a *man* can," Philby replied, twisting one end of his mustache. "Well, you certainly don't need my permission to look at the books, Kit. But what about your train?"

Kit glanced at the wall clock. "I still have time."

"Not much."

"I'm not leaving without seeing the books!"

"Fine!" Philby turned to the door.

"James?"

"Yes?"

"Where *are* the books?"

Wordlessly, Philby walked to a large cabinet on the back wall, unlocked the doors, and revealed shelves filled with ledgers. "Will there be anything else?"

"No." Kit stepped to the cabinet. "Yes! Why don't we have a gift-wrapping service?"

"A gift—"

"And a Santa? Can you give me one good reason why there's no Santa Claus?"

Steepling his index fingers, Philby brought them to his lips. "I thought we'd settled that when you were still in knickers."

"You thought wrong, old friend. We both did." Kit glanced at the books behind him, then at the clock to his left. Which would he choose, his legacy or his next adventure? But then, wouldn't it be high adventure to pick up the gauntlet Eleanor Barlow had cast at his feet, to duel her for an entire city's trade?

"Philby," he said, "I want you to do something for me."

"Would this be in regards to a lady?"

Kit gave the man who'd taught him about women—little good it had done him—a mock scowl. "Not in the way you're thinking. The only regrets I want you to deliver are to the railroad." Reaching inside his coat, he handed Philby a packet. "Take this to Union Depot and request a refund. I won't be needing it."

Philby looked at Kit's ticket. "I must meet that Barlow woman."

That evening, Ellie got off the trolley ahead of her stop, walking an extra two blocks to her rooms in an unfashionable but respectable part of the city. The air was unusually crisp, she noted, its invigorating, woody scent the perfect complement to her lively step. It had been quite a day, the greatest single day in J. Bond's history. She'd actually had to turn customers away at closing time. Before she'd left, Mr. Bond had not only expressed his delight, he'd given her a raise. Now, she could do more than just support herself. She could put a little aside for—

Ellie came to an abrupt stop, as though by halting her step could also halt her train of thought. She was too young to think about growing old, much less growing old alone. And too realistic not to. As she walked on, her gait less energetic, she wondered what it would have been like to grow old with Frank. Like being half of a comfortable pair of slippers, she supposed. They'd already been that when he'd broken their engagement. After all, they'd grown up together.

As she unlocked her door and lighted a gas lamp, she wondered if that was what she had really wanted then, merely to be accustomed to a man. Removing her gloves and coat, she rubbed a tingling in her arm, the same tingle she'd felt each time Kit McCarron had stood near. She could certainly never get accustomed to him, an adventurer who paid little heed to anything but his whims. Not that she in any way desired the opportunity to try.

Still, there was something about the way he looked at her that made her question the inevitability of her future as she had come to foresee it. Not only she, but everyone who looked on her face read her lonely tomorrows in it. She suspected that even dear old Mr. Bond, as much as he treated her as an equal, assumed that the store would always be her only life and so, felt a certain satisfaction in having provided an unmarriageable woman with the opportunity to provide nicely for herself. Only Kit McCarron looked at her as though he saw a story yet to be written, the story of a beautiful woman.

Either he was mad, or she wasn't nearly as hard to look at as she'd thought.

Ellie crossed from her small kitchen/parlor to her bedroom, lighting another lamp. As she approached the cheval mirror in the corner, a favorite piece because its length reflected the whole of her, she removed the pin from her hat. Stepping close, she lifted her veil, expectantly, hopefully. She turned away.

Kit McCarron must be quite mad.

Tossing her hat on the bed, Ellie sank onto the mattress. Kit, she knew, wasn't crazy. That left just one other explanation for why he, a man who obviously had his pick of beautiful women, was going out of his way to give her, a disfigured woman, the illusion that she beguiled him. To undermine her will to best him in business. All he had to do was addict her to the one thing every woman craves and she, of all women, entirely lacked. A feeling of the power of her allure.

Jumping off the bed, Ellie stomped to the parlor. Finding the newspaper she'd carried home, she searched for the discreet notice in the classifieds that would have been forgettable had it not been her job to recall it.

"McCarron's Emporium is pleased to announce the arrival of the Stratford Shoe for Ladies," she read aloud. "Made of the best materials. New common sense toe for the practical-minded woman." She laughed. "Yes, I can see how this will have women beating down his doors, clamoring for Stratford shoes."

On the other hand, she could certainly show Christopher McCarron just how practical-minded—and powerful—one woman could be. "Starting now," she said as she crumpled the paper, "I'll give him the most powerful lesson of his life."

Three

"So, Kit, what do you make of—"

"I know, Henry. J. Bond is now Bond and Barlow. I think it's—" Glancing to his left, Kit met Robert Eldham's expectant gaze, then downed his second shot of bourbon. "Remarkable."

"Remarkable?" Henry harrumphed. "It's scandalous!"

If he'd been totally honest with Henry just now, Kit thought, he'd have chosen any of a number of words other than "remarkable" to describe his reaction to the news that Josiah Bond had made Eleanor Barlow his partner. But "scandalous" wasn't one of them.

"Alarming" was.

The first time Kit had examined McCarron's books, he'd understood Robert's concern. Business had steadily declined since Ellie's Grand Reopening Sale. The drop had steepened in the last few weeks, coinciding with the brazen advertisements she'd been running on the news pages of all the papers. Oh, he wasn't denying they were far more persuasive than Philby's dull notices in the classifieds. But to promise success, popularity, attractiveness to the opposite sex with the purchase of the advertised item? If anything was scandalous, that was. And so effective, he'd begun to run similar ads of his own. Business had picked up some, but not enough for him to avoid one plain truth: To compete with Bond and Barlow in the long run, he'd have to shut McCarron's down for renovations.

"What's scandalous," he began, lighting a cigar, "is the time and money it's costing me to remodel the store."

"Just be thankful that the Barlow woman isn't doing the job for you." Callard gave a bibulous grunt. "She might set to work on you next, just the way she did on old Bond."

Through a swirl of smoke, Kit frowned. "What are you talking about?"

Robert Eldham looked up from his *Times.* "What Henry means, Kit, is that he suspects Miss Barlow of using her feminine wiles on Bond to get her partnership."

An unintentional draw of smoke wracked Kit with a coughing spasm. Throat smarting, he looked at Robert. "Are you trying to tell me Eleanor Barlow is Bond's mistress?"

Robert shrugged. "One certainly doesn't have to jump far to come to that conclusion. Personally, though, I find the notion ridiculous. The woman may have been pretty, once. But a man would have to be blind to find her desirable now."

"The way you're blind to Delia's flaws, Robert?" Feeling a sudden strong urge to wring Robert's neck, Kit stalked to the window.

"Just this once, I'll overlook that you've insulted my wife, Kit," Robert said quietly, "because you and I go back a long way."

"And couldn't be more different!" Kit turned to Robert, sad to see the pain his words had caused. Sadder to know they had nevertheless been true. "It wasn't my intention to insult Delia," he said, his tone subdued. "I'm sorry."

Robert appeared mollified. "I'm sure you were only trying to say that beauty is in the eye of the beholder, Kit, and I agree. But—"

"But you assume that because Miss Barlow's complexion

is marred, she's defective as a woman, as well." Unable to contain his indignation, Kit marched toward Robert. "Perhaps you even think she's barred from living as a complete woman."

Robert swiveled in his chair, resting one arm on the back of it. Rather than offended, he appeared bemused. "Kit, if every woman I've ever seen you with weren't more beautiful than the one before, I'd say you had an interest in Miss Barlow."

"Now that really is ridiculous," Kit replied. He flicked ashes in the stand beside the chair, careful not to let any fall to the carpet. "The only interest I have in the woman is as my competitor."

"And all *I* said was that I find it hard to believe that Josiah Bond could have a romantic interest in her." Robert turned back. With a snap of his paper, he added, "I really don't see why you should find that so upsetting."

No, you wouldn't, Kit thought. Shoving his hands into his pockets, he returned to the window. Men like Robert married long before they took wives. They married convention. It was impossible for them to comprehend that other men, like himself, sought beauty, excitement, passion in the unconventional. Especially in the unconventional woman.

But that wasn't the reason he'd lashed out at Robert just now. The source of his near derangement had been the knowledge that of all the men he'd encountered, the one most like himself was Josiah Bond. Nothing could be easier for him to believe than that Bond saw incomparable beauty in Eleanor Barlow, not merely beneath her skin, but including it. Because of it. Beyond it.

On top of it.

What had driven Kit to temporary madness was the very idea of Eleanor Barlow in another's man's arms. Another man's bed. He hadn't been prepared to react that way, didn't want to recognize that he had. Months ago, when he'd sent Philby to redeem his train ticket, he'd only meant to postpone his trip to Arabia until after he'd gotten the store on its feet, met Ellie's threat. But now, her threat was to something infinitely more important to him than the store. His freedom. For no matter how unconventional a woman might be, once a man desired to keep her for himself alone, he had no choice but to enter into the most enduring convention of all. Marriage.

As though he were peering at the fires of hell instead of a gentle snowfall, Kit turned his back on the window. "Waiter!" He ordered another round of drinks.

Shortly after, the three men, glasses in hand, stood in a circle.

"Whom shall we toast today, Kit?" Robert flashed a mischievous grin. "That Barlow woman?"

Kit recalled his first meeting with the damnable creature. He heard her voice, plush as velvet when she thought no one was around. The rest of the time, pure imperial Yankee. 'General,' he'd addressed her with a salute.

Well, my dear General Barlow, meet Johnny Reb.

"Gentlemen." Kit raised his glass high. "To the South!"

April, 1889

On her rounds of Bond and Barlow, Ellie progressed from puzzled to worried. Even in bad weather, the store bustled by this time of morning. Beneath a blue spring sky, then, where were her customers?

"Mornin', Miss B."

From the corners of her eyes, Ellie saw a thatch of red streak past her. "Stop where you are, Travis Partee."

The youth halted with near-military precision.

Ellie half circled him, noting she had to look higher this morning to meet his gaze. "Is today a local holiday I'm unaware of?"

"I don't think so."

"Is city hall on fire?"

Travis's red brows arrowed down. "It weren't when I went by it not an hour ago."

Making an L of her arms, Ellie laid her finger alongside her mouth. Then she jolted, reaching up to take Travis by the shoulders. "We haven't gone to war?"

"Could be." He raised his arm and pointed past Ellie to the Market Street entrance.

Gathering her skirt, Ellie ran up the aisle and out the door. She narrowed curious sights on a man walking to the corner with a placard on his back that read "GIFTS FOR ALL!" When he turned around, her eyes popped at reading "COME TO McCARRON'S GRAND REOPENING!"

"You!" Ellie swarmed at the man like a disturbed beehive. "How dare you? Leave this instant, or I'll call a policeman."

The man cowered at Ellie's frantic shooing. "I'm only doing my job!"

Ellie froze, looking askance at the man. "How much is Mr. McCarron paying you?"

"Five dollars for the week."

"I'll give you five to go away and five more for the signs."

Ten minutes later, Ellie was ten dollars lighter and charging along Market toward Ninth Street, girded for battle with Kit McCarron. But reaching Eighth, she ran into a queue snaking toward his doors. Dazedly, she moved past it, noting "GIFTS!" flyers in the hands of nearly everyone in line. "I don't believe this."

"Yes, isn't it thrillin'?" a woman replied.

Ellie's mouth fell open as she recognized the woman as one of her regulars.

"What do you suppose they're givin' away?" another woman, also a regular, asked.

"The store!" Ellie shot back as she picked her way past the crowd. *My store.*

Approaching McCarron's, she heard organ music pipe

"My Old Kentucky Home" from inside. She shoved her way through the doors and looked around for Kit, vaguely aware of a woman in antebellum dress greeting her. Suddenly, she recognized the distinguished-looking gentleman she'd earlier thought should be a floorwalker. She barged toward him.

"I dem*ahn*d to see Mr. McCarron. Immediately!"

The man's smile was beatific. "I'm Mr. Philby, at your service, Miss Barlow."

Ellie's breath caught. "How did you—" She touched the fingers of her left hand to her cheek, pressing her veil to it.

"My grandmother was as Boston as baked beans, Miss," Philby replied. "I must say, your accent brings back fond memories of her. She, too, was an extraordinary woman. Now, how may I help you?"

Ellie let her breath out, though it rankled her to realize that in a small Southern city where a Northeastern accent was as rare as snow in April, she'd automatically thought of her scar as her only distinguishing feature. Apparently, though, she had one other. When Philby had said she was extraordinary, he'd undoubtedly been referring to her reputation as a businesswoman, one that had appeared to have struck fear into his employer's heart. Kit had obviously spent a small fortune to remodel the store. Too bad, considering her latest plans for Bond and Barlow, that it wouldn't be enough.

Still, she gave Kit credit for the wisdom to make the debonair Mr. Philby the face of McCarron's. The man's charm, however, was wasted on her.

"I told you, I want to see Mr. McCarron."

"I'm sure he'll be pleased to hear that, Miss Barlow." Philby gazed over Ellie's shoulder. "It appears that Mr. McCarron wants to see you."

"There she is, Officer Trimble. Do your duty!"

Hearing Kit's dark-molasses drawl, Ellie whipped around

to find him bearing down on her with a policeman on one side and the man she'd bought the signs from on the other.

"Yes, Officer, do." She pointed at Kit. "Arrest that man!"

Kit stared at her, half in amazement at her outrageous demand, the other half in thrall to the jade green of her eyes, the pink of her lips behind her white chiffon veil, the yellow balloon she held in her right hand casting her like his favorite tree in sunlight. He'd thought that because the dogwoods had bloomed two weeks earlier, spring had arrived in Louisville. He'd been wrong. It had just now blossomed before his eyes.

And it wanted him arrested. "On what grounds, may I ask?"

"On the grounds in front of Bond and Barlow." Ellie turned to the policeman, who looked baffled beneath his pot hat. "Officer, Mr. McCarron hired that man to parade in front of my store and—" She didn't suppose stealing customers was an actual crime.

"And *what*, Miss Barlow?" Kit folded his arms. "Come now, don't waste the officer's time."

"Oh, that's all right, Mr. McCarron," Trimble said. "I've got all the time in the world."

Kit frowned at the man, then glared at Ellie. "What, exactly, is your charge against me?"

Ellie looked around, as if searching for a prosecutable crime among Kit's merchandise. Before she could find one, she jumped at the sound of a small explosion. Looking in its direction, she saw that she was holding a slender stick. At the end of it were the fragments of a balloon the belle must have handed her at the door. A moment ago, when Kit had stared at her, she'd imagined his clear grey eyes were holding a vision of her no other man had ever held. Indeed, they were. A laughable vision of a harpy with a balloon in her hand. What a gift she'd made of herself to her "sworn enemy."

Gift. Ellie looked at the policeman. "Misleading the public, Officer. That's my charge against Mr. McCarron."

"Mislead—?" Unbuttoning his jacket, Kit propped his fists on his waist. "Officer Trimble, you may add libel to my charges against Miss Barlow."

Ellie's breath quickened, as much at the exposure of Kit's broad, solid chest as his diabolical accusation. "Officer, is it libelous to point out that Mr. McCarron promised gifts to lure the public into his store and then gave out nothing more than balloons?" She looked at the yellow rubber shards. "*Cheap* balloons?"

Scratching the side of his nose, Trimble turned to Kit. "Well, I guess the lady does have a point."

"Yes, at the end of her tongue," Kit japed. Snatching the stick from Ellie, he removed a ribbon from around the torn balloon's neck. It was striped in the new colors he'd chosen for McCarron's, the jade green that reminded him of Ellie's eyes, and the creamy white, of her skin. "Congratulations, Miss Barlow. This gold star on your ribbon means that you're one of the fifty lucky customers who will receive our most exclusive gift. Philby, would you do the honors?"

Philby vanished and quickly returned with two midnight blue velvet pouches drawn with gold ribbon. He handed both to Kit, who gave one first to Ellie. "A quarter ounce of a new Parisian perfume sold exclusively at McCarron's. It's called Hidden Passion."

Ellie looked at the pouch as though there might be a genie inside. Even she, who knew a sales ploy when she saw one, momentarily fell under the spell cast by the perfume's name.

Kit gave the other pouch to the policeman. "For Mrs. Trimble, with my compliments. Unless you'd prefer the gold mustache comb?"

"No-o-o, sir," Trimble replied. "Knowin' how my Gert forgets herself over a posy, I can't wait to see what she does when I take this Paris toilet water home to her."

"My congratulations on your rare good fortune in marriage," Kit said to the blushing policeman. "Seeing how you must be anxious to be on your way, you may arrest Miss Barlow."

Ellie tore her gaze from the perfume to Kit. "I was wrong. You *are* mad."

"Of course I'm mad." Kit stepped closer to Ellie, drawn by her face behind the veil, by her mystery. *Don't forget her audacity, Kit.* "You assaulted my faithful employee, Mr.—" He turned to the little man on his left and asked his name. "My faithful employee, Mr. Glimscher, and stole the signs I'd given him to carry."

Ellie stared slit-eyed at the weasly, bad-smelling little man. "Faithful employee. Hmmph! I *bought* those signs from him. But don't take my word for it. Search him. Assuming you found him before he could drink it, he should have a crisp new ten-dollar bill on his disreputable person."

With that, Mr. Glimscher ducked behind Kit and took off out the door.

Officer Trimble put the stopper back in the bottle he'd been sniffing and looked at Kit. "Do you still want to press charges against Miss Barlow?"

Sighing, Kit shoved his hands in his pockets. "Not at the moment. Please give my regards to Mrs. Trimble."

As the policeman left, Ellie stepped to Kit's side, aiming for the door. "I really must be going, too, Mr. McCarron." She looked around the store, at the balloons swaying yellow, green, and white like a Kentucky meadow, the salesgirls costumed in crinolines, the organist appropriately accompanying this Southern tableau with Stephen Foster's melodies. It wasn't her taste, but she gave Kit his due for understanding what she hadn't even considered, the heritage of the city in which he did business. Nevertheless, she gave him a sharp look. "In spite of all this, you do know that the South lost?"

Kit bent over her, his diamond gaze holding her jade one, his lips so near hers he could feel her silky veil grace them as he spoke. "Perhaps that, too, remains to be seen."

Ellie had never fainted, not even when she'd had the accident. But if she didn't escape this man's lips and quickly, she feared she would fall into his arms.

Is that really something to fear, Ellie?

She stepped back. "Only perhaps," she said, then walked away.

"Just a minute, Miss Barlow," Kit called, then strode to her. "I believe you have something that belongs to me."

Looking down, Ellie saw the velvet pouch in her hands. She held it out to Kit. "Do you intend to reclaim the 'Hidden Passion' of Mrs. Trimble and the forty-eight other lucky women, as well?"

Like a blow to his abdomen, the realization struck Kit that the only woman whose passion he wanted to claim was Eleanor Barlow's. And for the first time in his life, he might desire something that no amount of adventurous pursuit could gain him. He might best Ellie and her partner in business, but what if they were also partners in bed? He clenched his fists, feeling that same heat-forged tensile strength he'd felt that day with Robert, when he alone understood Eleanor Barlow's attraction for a man like Bond. A man like himself.

Still, he wanted one other thing at this moment that was well possible. He wanted to give something to Eleanor Barlow, not as he had before, to vindicate himself, but freely. Forgetting their differences except for the most important one, that they were man and woman. He wanted to gift her simply for being the extraordinary woman she was— smart, bold, yet irresistibly enigmatic. The only woman he hadn't been able to forget simply by willing himself to.

As Kit took the pouch from her with one hand, he circled her wrist with the fingers of the other. Turning her
palm up, he placed the pouch in it. As he held her gaze,
he was unaware that she felt as he felt, as though they were
the only two people on a spinning carousel. All around
them was a blur of fantastic color and light and sound.

"The perfume is yours, Ellie. I want you to have it. It's
new and rare, like you."

Her hand cupped in Kit's, Ellie curled her fingers
around the genie in the midnight blue pouch. Was it possible she really hadn't misunderstood the unique way he
looked at her? "Thank you."

Ellie's voice was as soft as the velvet around his gift, Kit
thought. And if he wasn't careful, it would turn him softer
still. He cleared his throat. "Think nothing of it," he said.
"Just . . . just send my signs back."

Ellie's fingers curled back from the pouch. *Think nothing
of it.* Nothing was all she would ever mean to any man. But
she didn't care about any man, just this man. *My sworn
enemy.* She pulled herself to her full height. "I'll send Travis
over with them this afternoon. With a bill for the ten dollars I gave Mr. Glimscher—" Turning to leave, she paused.
"I almost forgot. About Mr. Glimscher—"

"The walks in front of Bond and Barlow's are public
property," Kit said, his back going up. "You can't prevent
me from sending him or anyone else to advertise on
them."

"Naturally not." Ellie smiled sweetly. "But I wasn't referring to your bad manners, only your bad judgment. You
know, Kit, you really should check a job applicant's refer-
ences before you hire him. If you'd asked me, I could have
told you I had to fire Mr. Glimscher from a janitor's position two weeks ago."

Kit gathered as much sincerity as he saw in her smile—
none. "We must keep that in mind, mustn't we, Philby?
Thank you, Miss Barlow."

Locking gazes with him, Ellie let the perfume drop from her hand into her purse. "Think nothing of it, Mr. McCarron." With a nod at Philby, she turned and glided away.

Kit and Philby stood side by side, silently watching her until the tips of the plumes on her hat disappeared.

"Philby?"

"Hmm?"

"Did you notice she never said she *would* have told me about Mr. Glimscher?"

"Yes," Philby replied, twirling his mustache. "A *most* extraordinary woman."

Think nothing of it.

Walking back to Bond and Barlow, Ellie tried to think nothing of the way Kit McCarron made her feel, but she simply couldn't ignore the brew of emotions he concocted. Enmity. Desire. How could any woman look into those coal-and-diamond eyes of his and not feel the demands of her womanhood? Other women could entertain those demands, delight in them, but not she. Lest she ever forget, she'd kept the wedding gown she'd never worn. Nor ever would.

But the nearer she came to Bond and Barlow, the more she realized she'd been wrong to think she could never mean anything to any man. Josiah, dear Josiah, esteemed and, in his way, even loved her. So much so, that when he'd set up their partnership, he'd given thought to her reputation as well as to her security.

"Ellie, you're the closest thing to a daughter I've ever had," he'd said. "You've earned a share in this store, and there's no one I'd rather leave it to outright. But Louisville is still a small town and . . . What I mean to say, my dear, is that someday the right man will come along, and I wouldn't want him to doubt that you and I were nothing more than partners and friends."

"I've already thought of that," she'd replied. "Not that I might marry. Present company excepted, the man who could tolerate my dedication to my work doesn't exist." She'd believed that to be true, but more to the point, she'd also known that the man who could look at her, kiss her, without first having to steel himself didn't exist. "I don't care a whit what people say about me," she'd continued. "But I wouldn't want your good name tarnished."

And so, they'd agreed that Ellie would immediately receive a minority interest in the store as just compensation for its growth under her management. After Josiah's passing, she would draw on a prearranged bank loan to purchase his majority stake. The proceeds of his estate would then be used to establish a business college for young women.

Crossing Market Street, Ellie smiled, recalling how Josiah had blushed at the mere thought of gossip linking them romantically. His innocence about such things was just one of his many endearing qualities. Another was the eagerness with which he always greeted her at their weekly meetings. Often, they didn't discuss business at all, but his many travels and interests. She suspected he was merely lonely and used their conferences as a means of meeting her under "respectable" auspices. Hurrying toward the entrance, she hoped she wasn't late for this week's session, especially because she'd owe any tardiness to Kit McCarron.

Dashing inside, instead of Josiah's expectant face, Ellie met with a grey pall perforated by the sobs of red-eyed salesgirls. They stood in huddles, whispering to one another, unavailable to customers, had there been any.

"What's going on here?" she asked, eliciting only mute stares in response.

"He was lyin' on the floor in his office when I found him, Miss, already near-gone. He said to give this to you and to tell you—"

Travis's choked voice struck terror in Ellie. She turned toward him. His eyes pooled with tears, his nose was swollen. Lowering her gaze, she recognized the key he was holding out to her, Josiah's own key to the store. Slowly, she reached for it, then, squeezing it tightly, closed her eyes and pressed it to her heart.

As Ellie opened her eyes, they spilled tears. "Tell me what?"

Travis's chin puckered beneath his words. "He said to tell you to hold the dream."

Ellie lowered her forehead to her fingertips. "Josiah," she murmured. After a moment, she understood that her grief would have to wait. She, alone, was now at the helm of Bond and Barlow and had a store full of employees depending on her. Handing Travis her own keys, she told him to lock the doors, then gather everyone around the main staircase.

"I almost forgot, Miss," Travis said.

Ellie turned to him.

"Mr. Josiah said one other thing, though I guess maybe he wasn't in his right mind at the end."

"What did he say?"

The youth ran the back of his hand under his nose. "He said to tell you that somewhere, there's a younger version of himself waiting for you."

Beneath her veil, Ellie grazed the backs of her fingers along her damaged cheek. A single tear ran between them and touched a smile to her lips.

"If you ask me, she looks the part of the grieving widow, all right." Henry Callard inclined toward Kit as they stood listening to prayers at Josiah Bond's gravesite.

"No one asked you, Henry," Kit retorted loudly enough to attract disapproving looks.

Moving away, he wound around the gathering toward

the casket, where Ellie stood. In his present mood, he would be better advised to keep his distance, but he wanted to see her face. He wanted to see for himself evidence that the rumors he'd heard from sources far more reliable than Henry were true.

Listening to the preacher, Ellie could barely hear him over the low, steady sound of her grief. For the first time since Josiah's death, she realized that from now on, she would not only be alone in running the store but alone in the world. She supposed that after her father's death and her brother's disappearance, she'd been as much, but neither of those losses had left her as bereft as that of Josiah. He'd truly been father, brother, mentor, and friend to her. At the moment, she almost hated him for giving her what she'd never had and never would have missed but for him.

"Josiah," she whispered as she laid flowers on the casket, touching her gloved fingertips to it and preparing to say her final good-bye "To whom will I t—" Suddenly, Ellie's vision went as black as the veil before it. "Turn," she murmured, then ceased to feel her legs.

As she sank, she felt strong arms lift her, whose she neither knew nor cared. She felt safe in these arms, though she was still blind. Closing her eyes, she rested her head on the man's shoulder as he carried her, realizing she would probably never know such rest again. Nor such gallantry. Soon, she heard a horse nicker and then the sound of a carriage door opening, releasing the embracing scent of leather. The cushion did indeed receive her, and, as she laid her head back, she opened her eyes, seeing the roof of the carriage. Her vision restored, she turned gratefully to her Galahad. "Thank—"

Kit stood peering down at her. "How are you feeling?"

Ellie sat up. "Much better, thank you," she replied, not quite truthfully. Her faintness had passed, but she no longer felt safe. She slid right, preparing to exit the phaeton, only to have Kit climb in beside her, take the reins, and drive off. "What are you doing?"

"A ride in the country will do you good."

"I told you I'm quite all right. Stop. Now!"

Kit drove faster, forcing Ellie against the back of the seat.

"Do you realize the scene you've created?" she demanded, holding her hat from the breeze. "People will talk."

"Isn't it a little late to worry about that?"

Ellie grabbed his arm, feeling the hard muscle beneath his jacket. "What exactly do you mean?" She yanked but felt no give. "Tell me!"

Kit pulled hard on the reins, bringing the phaeton to a stop beneath a spreading dogwood. "You tell me," he said, turning on her with a gaze that made shreds of her black veil. "How many women nearly faint at the funerals of men who were supposedly no more than their business partners?"

Ellie's jaw dropped. "There's no supposedly about it. Josiah Bond was just that, a partner and a friend. I'm sorry if in your sordid mind that doesn't qualify me to suffer the consequences of a very real grief." Without waiting for a reply, she climbed out of the carriage and started for the road back to the cemetery.

Kit came quickly to her side. "Ellie, wait. Please."

"There's nothing to wait for," she said, picking up her pace. "Whatever my relationship with Mr. Bond was, it's none of your concern, and, furthermore, I couldn't care less what you think of it. I only set the record straight because I won't allow spoiled, idle-minded ne'er-do-wells like you to sully his reputation." Suddenly, she ground to a halt and slowly turned toward Kit. "Or perhaps that's how you intend to compete against me, by spreading the vicious lie that I gave Mr. Bond my bed in exchange for the store."

Kit took her by the shoulders. "Why must everything in your life come down to that store?"

"Because that store *is* my life," Ellie shot back, trying hard not to feel his hands on her sleeved arms, not to want to feel them on her bare flesh. "It's the only life I want!" *Or will ever have.*

Kit locked his gaze on her eyes—large, green, defiant, and veiled. "You're a fool, Eleanor Barlow. You think that veil hides you from the world, but it only hides the world from you. You've made a prisoner of yourself, Ellie." He gave her a shake. "It's wrong!"

"Let go of me," she cried, struggling for release. "You have no right to say these things!"

Suddenly, Kit tore her hat from her head.

Ellie froze, then gazed up at him with barefaced hatred. Kit knew then he would gladly suffer her contempt as long as he could see it openly, see her perfectly imperfect beauty, be haunted by it. Photograph it. Cupping her face in his hands, not tenderly, he brought his mouth down on hers. Her lips were as sweet as they were pink, then they turned to a consuming flame. But he wouldn't die in this conflagration alone. He would take her with him so that neither of them would ever die but burn forever. One fire. One light. He crushed her to him, deepening his kiss; and when she moaned, mercilessly claimed her tongue.

Ellie's whole life was in her throat, a cry, a scream, a moan of desire, a sigh of ecstasy. His lips were fire, forging her disparate urges into a command to surrender, to take what she could find in his arms, if only for this one moment. And oh, what arms, what strength wanting her, possessing her as no other man's arms ever had, ever would.

But Ellie had always possessed herself. If she'd shut the world out, it was because the world was neither ready nor willing to accept a woman who defied every feminine ideal. She had dared to compete in a man's world without membership in the female cult of beauty to mitigate her flouting the rules. But Kit was smarter than most, too smart to ignore her threat to his interests. Smart enough to recognize that she *was* above all, a woman. He meant to divide her woman's heart between its two great passions, her work and her need to love and be loved by one man, and then deny her fulfillment of both.

She pushed away from him, raised her hand as if to slap his cheek, then crossed her palm over her own. "My hat. Pick it up."

Kit stared at her. Though her hat lay in the road, he nevertheless saw a veil descend over her expression, one only she could lift. He retrieved the hat. Ellie reached for it, but he held it back from her. Then he stepped close and gently placed the hat on her head. Gazing into her eyes, he lowered the black chiffon veil over them. "One day, Eleanor Barlow, you'll remove this for me, of your own will and forever." Then he cupped her elbow. "For now, I'll take you home. I'll take you to Bond and Barlow."

Four

Ellie sat at her desk, going over the estimate for the construction of additions to the store. Tearoom, ladies' lounge, nursery, reading room—she dreamed of such amenities as the big-city department stores offered and more. But they would require her to go farther into debt. Still, if she was to maintain her dominance over McCarron's, she had to expand. Kit had revitalized the once-dying concern and was encroaching on her trade.

She rubbed her eyes then, reaching for a stack of invoices, uncovered the blue-velvet pouch Kit had given her. She remembered showing it to Travis the day after Josiah's funeral, when she'd reopened the store.

"This is what McCarron's is offering women," she'd said. "Hidden Passion."

His eyes wide, Travis reached for the pouch. "Jehoshaphat."

"Please don't use that expression. It isn't dignified," Ellie had replied, tossing the pouch on the desk. Without knowing why, she hadn't wanted the youth to handle it. "Now that you're my special assistant, one of your new responsibilities will be to help me think of a similar promotion for our store." She'd known full well that Travis was likely to suggest free fish-bait. But she'd also known that with Josiah gone, she needed a male presence in the store, one to compete with McCarron's charming Mr.

Philby. Travis, surprisingly, was maturing into an attractive young man, one she could still mold to her standards. One who would appeal to the daughters of the women who went to McCarron's for Hidden Passion.

Now, Ellie reached for the pouch, then withdrew her hand, ashamed of herself. She, of all, people, should be immune to subtle promises of ecstasy. Whatever Kit McCarron hadn't previously known about retailing he was certainly learning quickly.

There were some things, of course, at which he was already far more expert than she. Recalling his mouth on hers, his tongue coaxing and claiming hers, his arms crushing her to him, Ellie closed her eyes at a coursing shiver that ended in an arrow of desire at her core. Though her office was suffocatingly warm, his words raised chilblains on her flesh.

One day, you'll remove this veil for me, of your own will and forever.

She no more knew what to make of those words now than she had when he'd spoken them. She knew only that they intrigued her, terrified her, infuriated her. Thrilled her.

Once again, she stretched her hand toward the velvet pouch, paused, then snatched it up, setting it in the palm of her hand. She realized she'd never opened it, never looked at the genie's bottle, freed its scent. Widening the pouch's drawn neck, she removed the bottle, her eyes flashing at the relief of a woman's head and bare shoulders, and the cascade of tresses that hid one side of her face. The visible half of her mouth quirked in an invitation to feminine mystery. Ellie removed the stopper and waved the bottle beneath her nose. The exotic fragrance drew a shade over all her other senses and, with her eyes closed, she lingeringly stroked it over her throat, behind her ears.

A knock came at her door. Ellie quickly hid the perfume,

then put on her hat, arranging the netting over her face. "Come in."

Officer Trimble peeked inside. "Sorry to bother you, Miss Barlow, but Judge Kincaid wanted me to give you this." Handing her an envelope, he tipped his pot hat and quickly retreated.

"I don't know any Judge Kincaid," she muttered as she removed the envelope's contents A moment later, she dashed out her door. "Tra-a-a-a-vis! Tra—"

"Jehoshaphat, Miss B!" Travis looked up at her as he collected the boxes he'd dropped when she bumped into him. "You seen a mouse?"

"How many times have I told you not to say 'Jehoshaphat'? And what I have here is a rat." Ellie rattled the legal notice at him. "Kit McCarron is taking me to court over those damned signs. Between Josiah's death and running the store, I forgot to send them back. Do you know where they are?"

Travis's jaw dropped. "Je*ho*shaphat."

In Lester Kincaid's city courtroom, sunlight cut a swath of dust motes up the center aisle, obscuring Ellie's view of the opposite side. But as she waited for the clerk to call their case, she didn't have to see across the aisle and a row behind to know that Kit was there, to feel his gaze slant across her face, hotter than the sun. She stared straight ahead, unwilling to give him the satisfaction of knowing he'd made her disturbingly aware of his presence.

"McCarron versus Barlow."

As Ellie reached the aisle, a figure emerged from the blinding light, solid, commanding—

"Good morning, Ellie."

And odious. Ellie angled toward Kit, his eyes smoky, his slight grin shadowy against the brightness behind him. For the first time, she sensed that the veil she was peering through was more his than hers, a shroud concealing his motives in bringing this ridiculous action against her. "You'll regret this," she said.

Ellie's low, faceless warning felt like a velvet-gloved stroke down Kit's cheek. He sought the jade gaze behind her veil, but she appeared like a figure in an overexposed photograph, featureless, ghostly. A shard of jealousy sliced through him at the thought that Josiah's death might have robbed her of all carnal existence. No, not jealousy. Envy that Josiah might have known her as he longed to know her, if only through the lens of his camera.

And yet, with his camera, he could give her what Josiah never could. A record of her haunting beauty, an incarnation that would survive a man's admiring gaze, worshipful touch. But, considering that she'd rebuffed his every attempt to see her since the funeral, he'd first had to find a way to reach her.

Earlier, he'd suggested to Robert Eldham that he buy Ellie out, concealing that his motives had more to do with gazing at her across the bargaining table than in actually acquiring her store. But Robert had advised against his taking on more debt.

Then, recalling that Philby's brother-in-law was a city-court judge, Kit had struck upon the cheapest and surest way of getting Ellie in the same room with him. And now that he had, she was telling him he was going to regret it. The only thing he was going to regret was not seeing the flash he knew he was about to spark in her eyes.

"I've always believed that unless something's worth regretting, it's not worth doing. After you, Miss Barlow."

Infuriated by his grin, Ellie nevertheless held her tongue as the clerk ordered them to the bench. She charged up the aisle. "Your Honor," she began, fixing her gaze on the man whose bald head protruded turtlelike from his black robe. "I'm innocent!"

Ellie jumped at the bang of Judge Kincaid's gavel. "You

can't be anythin' until the clerk reads the charges," he said. When the clerk had done so, the judge looked at Kit.

"Stole signs advertisin' your sale, you say?"

Sighing, Kit clasped his hands behind his back. "I'm afraid so, Your Honor. Though perhaps, this sort of thing is common in Boston."

"Oh, she's a Yankee. I thought so." The judge squinted ominously at Ellie. "Do you still want to plead innocent, Missy?"

"Of course I do!" Ellie wired Kit a scathing look. "And also gullible, for not anticipating that Mr. McCarron's line of argument would be as crooked as his advertising."

"I believe Miss Barlow is referring to my Hidden Passion, Your Honor," Kit said, stepping to her side. He sniffed her neck. "With which, I might add, she's most familiar." He bent close to her ear. "It's lovely on you, Ellie."

"You're despicable," she whispered back with what little breath he'd left her.

Judge Kincaid turned to his clerk. "You didn't tell me this was a domestic dispute. The state ought to be hearin' this case."

Aghast, Ellie picked up the judge's gavel and pounded it three times. "Your Honor! I wouldn't share a domicile with Mr. McCarron if it were the only shelter from a storm. And I did not steal his signs!"

The judge rose, looking pop-eyed from one empty hand to the other, then at Ellie, then at the gavel she held as if uncertain which of the four of them to find in contempt. At last, he reached for the gavel.

"You'd better let me, Your Honor," Kit said, slipping it from Ellie's grasp and handing it to the judge. "Miss Barlow once attacked me with a hammer."

"Oh!" Ellie stomped her foot. "This is outrageous."

"This is also *my* courtroom," Judge Kincaid shouted above his own hammerblows. "Now, Missy, if you didn't steal Mr. McCarron's signs, why is he askin' you to return them?"

Ellie's words came through clamped jaws. "Because I bought them from Mr. McCarron's employee for ten dollars."

"That does it," Judge Kincaid said, hammering. "You're in contempt, Missy. A five-dollar fine will teach you no Nawthener can make a mockery of this court."

"But Your Honor—"

"Stealin' a competitah's signs I can undahstand. But you must take me for a fool if you think I'd believe you'd buy them."

Kit stepped forward. "In Miss Barlow's defense, even a Northerner could plainly see that you, Your Honor, are no fool." Kit grinned at Ellie. "And as such, would ask for a receipt."

The judge cleared his throat. "You read my mind, young man," he said, then looked at Ellie. "Well, Missy? Do you have a receipt?"

Glaring at Kit, Ellie pressed clenched fists to her sides. "I didn't think I'd need one, Your Honor. But if you'll give me a little time to locate Mr. Glimscher, the man I bought the signs from—"

"Glimscher?" Giving her a description, the judge asked Ellie if it could be of the man who'd sold her the signs.

"Why, yes," she replied, beaming at the prospect of publicly proving Kit McCarron a scoundrel.

"Then you won't need time to look for him," Judge Kincaid said. "Mr. Glimscher's in jail, where I just put him for disturbin' the peace. Now, you got any *reliable* witnesses?"

Digging her fingers into her upper arms, Ellie looked murderously at Kit. "No, sir."

Kit broadened his smile at her, then sobering, turned to the judge. "Your Honor, I'd be willing to drop my charge if Miss Barlow would simply return my property as she promised to do."

Judge Kincaid folded his hands. "How 'bout it, Missy?"

"I'd be only too glad to return the signs, Your Honor. Only, I haven't got them." Ellie focused on Kit. "My assistant correctly identified them as trash and threw them out weeks ago."

"Oh, that's too bad," the judge replied. "You'll have to pay for them. How much would you say they cost, Mr. McCarron?"

Kit looked up, as if calculating, moving his finger to borrow and carry. "A dollar sixty-five should do it, Your Honor."

Judge Kincaid added a thirty-five cent fine and ordered Ellie to pay the clerk an even two dollars plus the five-dollar contempt charge. Then he banged his gavel and called for the next case.

When Ellie emerged from city hall, she saw that the sky had tarnished, the breeze grown acrid with approaching rain. If she hurried, she could make it back to the store before the storm broke. Before Kit, collecting his spoils inside, could catch up with her to gloat. Her mood was as dark as the clouds gathering ammunition over the river, and she just might give him real cause to haul her back into that Yankee-hating judge's courtroom. Lifting her skirt, she headed toward Market.

"Ellie, wait!"

As she turned to see Kit running toward her, the half block between them went blue-white. Her heart picked up current, speeding her away from him and the storm. But not quickly enough. As he turned her toward him opposite a small shop, she saw the same infuriating bemusement in his expression she'd seen in court. "I'd always suspected you were self-indulgent and undisciplined, but I never guessed you could be so petty."

Kit glimpsed her gaze flickering behind her windblown

veil. No fusillade of lightning could excite him the way one of Eleanor Barlow's charged glances could. Yet, he found himself wishing he were seeing less fire in her eyes now and more warmth. "As hard as you play, Ellie, you don't have a right to be a sore loser."

Her head reared back. "I've lost nothing to you today but a little time."

Taking her hand, Kit filled her palm with seven gold dollars. *"Now* you've lost nothing but time. Unless you count the loss of trust in your defenses."

Ellie made a fist around the coins. "What are you talking about?"

"What happened today wasn't about the signs, Ellie. Or even about our rivalry. But I think you know that." Kit stepped closer, forcing her gaze—and her mouth—to tilt up toward his. "Why have you refused to see me, refused even to answer my notes?"

Standing this close to him, Ellie felt exactly as she'd felt when she'd held those notes. Like kindling for a bonfire. She'd discarded them unopened as she must now leave his curiosity unsatisfied or risk his torching her ordered life, her dreams. "As you said, we're rivals, and, for the sake of my business, I intend to keep it that way."

"And for the sake of that military self-discipline you maintain," Kit shot back. "But it's a sham, Ellie, because you're really very afraid."

Ellie inhaled. "Of what?"

"Yourself." Kit cupped her right cheek, the unscarred one. "You're afraid that one day, you might willingly let me look at the other cheek, touch it the way I'm touching this one now."

Ellie shivered. "Why should I fear anything I might willingly do? Besides, according to you, I allowed Josiah such intimacies."

Kit brushed his thumb across her veiled cheek—like her, a study in softness and underlying, bone-hard resistance.

"Josiah was an old man who was content to behold the beauty he saw in you. He never demanded, as I would, that you see it, too. He never asked you to chance, as I do now, that the reflection you see in my eyes at this very moment might be a lie."

The wind gusted, bringing rain pellets from the river armory to the north. Ellie raised the back of her right hand across her left cheek, sending the coins clattering to the walk. She jolted at the sound, angry at it for awakening the fear she had tamed but had never fully conquered. Angrier at Kit for awakening something far more painful than fear. Truth. But Kit, too, had a dose of truth coming.

"When you've lost everything that mattered to you to outright lies and the self-deceptions of others," she said, thinking of Donald, who deceived her out of her inheritance, and Frank, who tried to deceive himself he could make love to her, "then I'll gladly suffer your pieties about learning to trust." She blinked Kit into focus through raindrops splattering diagonally across her veil. "Until then, I suggest you return to your business while you still have it. I told you you'd regret today, and one thing I never fear is making a threat I can't deliver on."

Kit sidled a smile. "That remains to be seen, doesn't it? Miss Barlow."

"Have no fear, Mr. McCarron."

Still smiling, Kit watched Ellie walk confidently away. But as she reached the shop two doors up, the sky at last split open with battering wind, rain, and hail. The shop's thin windowpanes rattled under the assault and with the next of the storm's blows, would surely explode. Fearing for Ellie's safety, Kit started toward her.

But when she released a scream that sliced through him like flying glass, and—shielding her face—dropped to her knees in a snail-like curl, he feared more for her sanity. Grabbing her by the shoulders, he pulled her to her feet and hauled her under cover of the doorway.

"It's all right, Ellie." Turning her toward him, he grasped her wrists. But she resisted his lowering her hands from her eyes despite a quaking that would have fractured an ordinary woman's will. Circling his arms about her, he leaned against the doorway and drew her tightly against him. She released a whole body sigh, then, clutching his lapels, pressed her cheek to his shoulder.

"That's what scarred you, isn't it, Ellie?" Kit asked softly. "Shattering glass."

Ellie squeezed her eyes shut, but she couldn't keep from seeing the curtains blowing in the window of her upper-story bedroom in her family's Cape Cod cottage. She saw herself walk from her writing table, where she'd been addressing her and Frank's wedding invitations, to shut the window. She was returning to the invitations when she heard a crash—a tree limb through the window, she later learned. *Don't turn around,* she pleaded with herself as she always did when she relived the scene. But as always, she did, and met the shard of glass that cleaved her life into before and never again. Never again to be regarded—no, to be disregarded—as anything but pitiable.

Though still trembling, she steadied her gaze up at Kit. "I don't need your pity."

Slipping his hand beneath her veil, Kit cupped her left cheek, feeling the fineness of her skin and the badge of her courage to make a life for herself when most women would have thought theirs ended. Her only failing was not seeing that she could have a complete life. His failing was not seeing until this moment, that to share in her completeness was his greatest quest, and though she was in his arms, his most distant.

"Ah, but I need yours, Eleanor Barlow. And I'm going to have it, and more." Lifting her chin, he brought his lips down on hers, the veil between their flesh only further arousing his hunger for her. "Much more," he whispered.

Then commanding her to wait for him, he turned up his collar and dived into the storm to find a hansom.

Watching him, Ellie now trembled with desire. And confusion. What pity could he, a man renowned for captaining his own fate, require of her? And what had she, beyond pity, to give him? She raised her fingers to her lips, curious to feel what he had felt when he'd kissed her. She discovered the silkiness of her veil, the fullness and warmth of her flesh. Then, sliding her fingers beneath the silk, she explored her left cheek and found its smoothness, and the mar that rendered it, surprisingly, like fine, broken china. Still, she couldn't know what he'd thought when he'd touched her, only that he meant to continue this encounter.

And yet, if a gaze could lie, as Kit himself had cautioned, then how much more deceiving a touch?

Seeing a hansom stop at Kit's hail, Ellie ran to it. As Kit helped her inside, she paused. "Bond and Barlow, Driver."

"Not this time, General," Kit said, hoisting her into the cab. Then he handed the driver several coins. "Take us to Sixteenth and Broadway."

"Why there?" she demanded as he settled in beside her.

"I'm taking you home again," he replied, tipping water from the brim of his hat. "To my home."

Ellie sat curled in one corner of the gold-velvet settee farthest from the windows in Kit's parlor, sipping the hot tea he'd prepared himself. She must have been mad to allow him to bring her here, to the mansion in the neighborhood where so much of the carriage trade that patronized Bond and Barlow lived. Her personal reputation aside, she shuddered to think what the rumors would cost the store if she were seen "consorting with the enemy."

Why had she come then? Because of his gaze, his touch, his kiss? Persuasive as all three had been, she could have resisted them. She'd done so before. What she couldn't resist was the lure of a very ungentlemanly Southerner, a man who refused to make allowances for her, as all men did, because as both a woman and disfigured, she was doubly afflicted.

All men save one, that is. Josiah. Like Josiah, Kit saw past her "afflictions" to her formidability. Josiah had wanted it on his side; Kit knew he must match it. He was, in fact, so decidedly un-sorry for her that he'd not only sued her, he'd expected her to lose to him in sportsmanlike fashion! The beast. The dear. The younger version of Josiah.

Setting down her cup, Ellie walked to the vestibule and gathered the wet jacket Kit had insisted she remove. That she should find such a man in her competitor was unthinkable; certainly Josiah could never have imagined it. Suddenly, just being in Kit's house, she felt disloyal. Clutching the key Josiah had bequeathed her, now hanging from a chain around her neck, she reminded herself to hold their shared dream.

As she opened the door, she glimpsed herself in the pier mirror. When she'd told Kit that she didn't need his pity, she might have told him that though she was disfigured, she was far less so than women who allow men to make perpetual children of them and that no man would make a child of her. When he'd withheld his pity, he might have answered that he had no such intentions. He wanted a complete woman, one who would love him and fight beside him for their right to live in a world as much of their own making as was humanly possible.

Was that the "pity" he wanted of her, that she consent to be that woman?

"And how much of your pity would it take," she said to her reflection as she removed her hat and veil, "when you know you want to be that woman?"

* * *

In his upstairs bedroom, Kit, attired in dry clothing, paused at the door. For as long as he could remember, he'd sought the freedom to live life on his own terms, to live a life as different from the ordinary man's as possible. He never dreamed his terms would turn so conventional, nor his freedom beckon him from the veiled heart of a most unconventional woman. He never dreamed of Eleanor Barlow.

And now, she waited for him below. But between here and there were two thriving department stores rivaling for each other's trade. Ellie would never be happy until there was just one, and he would never be happy without Ellie. There was only one solution, a drastic one, perhaps, but dammit, he was in love with the woman!

Halfway down the stairs, Kit came to an abrupt halt. Ellie stood at the bottom, unveiled. Her green eyes met his like beacons lighting a path to his freedom, the freedom to behold and touch and adore her. The freedom to love her so completely he would never have to roam again except in the country of her heart, her mind and soul. An adventure for all time.

Meeting Ellie, Kit cupped her face in his hands. Slowly, his gaze traveled her hair, radiant and black and wilding about her head. It roved her face—feature by feature—wide, eager, rightly more awed than it had been at seeing so many lesser wonders of the world.

"Thank you," he said, his voice hushed. "Thank you for daring to believe me when I tell you you are the most beautiful woman I've ever seen." Tenderly, he kissed her, first on the left cheek, then the right, then on her lips. "Or ever will see."

Ellie slid her hands up his warm, solid chest. "Once in every woman's life, with one man, she *is* the most beautiful woman in the world." She circled her lips under his, then kissed him. "I want my once-in-a-lifetime to be with you."

Frowning, Kit clasped her hands between his. "Maybe

you didn't understand me before, Ellie. I want more from
you than a moment of—how shall I put it?—hidden passion."

"You know that can't be," she said, her heart echoing
the pounding of his. "Believe me, Kit, other than Josiah,
no man has met me on my own terms. And I do love you
for that. But I still mean to own this city's premier department store. That rules out my becoming involved with
you."

Kit gave her a shake. "You are involved with me whether
or not you, or your employees or your customers, or this
whole damn town likes it! You're involved with me because
I do meet you on your own terms and because when you're
with me, you find your terms include being a woman. A
complete woman. And that," he said, tracing the fragrance
he'd given her down her throat, "you like very much."

The shiver that had started with his touch to her throat
washed over her like a hot-cold tide. "You know better
than to expect me to give up the store, even for the pleasure of what I feel when I'm with you."

"You won't have to," Kit replied, taking her hand and
starting to the top of the stairs.

Withdrawing, Ellie twined her arms. "Are you saying
you'll give up *your* store? Because I wouldn't want a man
who would do something so foolish."

Throwing back his head, Kit burst into laughter that
resonated throughout the great hall. "I'd already surmised
as much. But I have no intention of giving up McCarron's." His grey gaze suddenly sobering, he held out his
hand. "Marry me, Ellie. Now." He glanced upstairs. "No,
after. I'll get Judge Kincaid to perform the ceremony."

"Judge—?"

Kit quirked a smile. "He's married to Philby's sister. The
woman's been crazy about me since I was in diapers."

As a smile spread across her lips, Ellie closed her eyes,
shook her head, and leaned against the wall. How could

she not love a man who pitied her so little he fixed his case against her? But could she marry him and merge their enterprises? And how was she to know that such a merger wasn't really the aim of his proposal? After all, he'd said nothing about love. Of course, there was one way to find out.

"I'm in debt for Josiah's holding in the store," she said.

"You know, Ellie, one of the things I most admire about you is the way you keep your business sense about you, even when being proposed to." Kit gave her a wry smile. "Would you like me to summon Robert Eldham, my accountant? He can be here with my financial statement within the hour."

"That won't be necessary." Ellie smiled back, all doubt about his motives now vanished.

"You know what *is* necessary?" Bending toward her, he swept a tress away from her left cheek, then looked into her eyes. "That I tell you I'm in love with you, Eleanor Barlow."

Ellie pressed her hand to her heart. *In love.* Foolish to put so much store in words, but no man had ever spoken them to her before, not even Frank, not even before the accident. She looked to the top of the stairs, then gave Kit her hand.

"Show me, my beloved sworn enemy. Show me a man in love."

Five

"No, Ellie, don't dress. Not yet." Sitting up in bed, Kit pulled her against him as she reached for her camisole, pressing her beautiful, bare back to his naked chest.

With both hands, Ellie clasped the strong arm that crossed above her breasts and kissed it. "Getting cold feet?" She smiled softly. "I could sue you for breach of promise, you know."

So abruptly he stole her breath, Kit shot forward and turned her beneath him, pinning her with one leg. "I'd only fix it so you'd lose," he said, stroking flat fingers down her left cheek. "But it just so happens I have no intention of letting you out of my sight until we're married."

Ellie palmed the back of his beautiful, dark head. "Does that mean you liked my hidden passion?"

Kit trailed his caress from her cheek, down her throat, around her shoulder to her breast. He let it linger there and do as it pleased, becoming a graze now, a tease later, an abrading of her nipple to a hard peak, a full-handed capture of the large, luscious globe. "Forgive me, Miss Barlow," he said, traveling his sight down the length of her and back, "but there's no longer anything hidden about your passion." His grey gaze went to her cheek, then poured itself into the green depths of her eyes. "And if you really love me, you'll never hide anything from me again."

Ellie ran her splayed, straining fingers down his back. "I love you, Kit. Oh God," she cried, reaching for the bed post above her head and spreading her legs beneath him. "How I love you."

Kit responded to her invitation, once more plunging his hardness inside her, once more finding himself inside her.

Tears trickled from the corners of Ellie's eyes as she wrapped her legs around him, taking him deeper inside, deep to the place where she'd buried her pain only to feel Kit resurrect new life there the first time he'd made love to her. Even now, she felt like new soil, rich and moist, and his thrusts were like an unearthing of all that had lain dormant in her, a planting of all that had lain rootless in him.

"Children," she whispered, raking her fingers through his hair after he'd found release. "What about children, Kit?"

With his cheek on her breast, Kit pressed the mound between her legs, entrance to treasures more precious than the gold he'd once sought, a sacred place. With his fingers, he began to worship. "Of course, children," he said. Then, with a grin, "We're going to have branch stores all around the state."

Ellie laughed, then closing her eyes and quickening to the pleasure Kit was giving her, heard him whisper, "Yes, we'll have babies, Ellie. And they'll all be as beautiful as their mother." Ellie surrendered to her new dream, the dream she shared with her lover, the man she was going to marry.

Later, as they lay sated in one another's arms, Kit said, "Ellie, do you remember when I told you that I would demand something of you Josiah never did, that you see with your own eyes the beauty I see in you?"

"You make me feel beautiful, Kit." She kissed his neck. "That's enough for me."

"But not for me." He looked at her. "I want to photograph you, Ellie."

Feeling a chill, Ellie sat up and reached for her clothing.

Kit grasped her wrist. "You promised you'd never hide anything from me again."

"I'm not hiding," she replied, her eyes flashing at him. "But I won't be photographed, ever."

As she slid out of bed, Kit followed her, turning her toward him. "Why not?" Holding her by the shoulders, he gazed down her body. "Look at you. You're standing in front of me, gloriously naked. Refusing to let me make a portrait of you makes no sense."

"A camera isn't a portrait artist, Kit. It won't lie to its subject."

"That's why I want you to see yourself as the camera will. As my camera will."

Ellie broke from his hold. "Why must you create the one thing that will destroy my illusions?"

Kit stepped toward her, trapping her between his will and the wall behind her. He took her face in his hands. "That's no way to start a marriage, Ellie. With illusions."

Ellie closed her eyes, but she could still see the look in his, reasoning, honest, loving. Did she dare risk, as he'd once challenged her to do, that that look was a lie? Yet, how could she even think of marrying him if she didn't dare trust him?

With a sigh, she opened her eyes and gazed directly into his. "I'm ready," she said, then melted in the warmth of his embrace.

The storm had long since passed when Kit walked with Ellie to the front door. "Are you sure you won't change your mind and marry me today?"

Smiling, Ellie tenderly touched his cheek. "As far as I'm

concerned, I did. But if you insist on making an honest woman of me, I need time to prepare."

Kit kissed the palm of her hand. "If you're not in Judge Kincaid's chambers at exactly two tomorrow afternoon, I'm going to spread the word that you had your way with me then left me cold."

"Who had whose way?" Ellie chided. Pinning her hat, she turned to the mirror. "You got your photograph."

Stepping behind her, Kit caressed her shoulders as he met her gaze in the mirror. "Are you sorry? Because if you are, I'll destroy the plate right now."

Ellie leaned against him, drawing his arms around her. "I am sorry, a little." She removed the veil from her hat and let it flutter to the console beneath the mirror. Laughing, she turned to him. "I have so many hats to alter. Moreover, my darling, you won't destroy my portrait. You believe in it, and so must I."

Overwhelmed with gratitude for the gift of her trust, Kit brushed his lips across her forehead, down her cheek, and across her mouth, mingling their breaths. Then he kissed her, hard and long, and felt that only God himself could possibly tear him away from this incredible woman. He pressed his aching hardness against her and when she responded, dangerously grinding away his resistance, he forced her away.

"If you want time to prepare for your wedding, General," he said between labored breaths, "order me to take my hands off you while I still can."

Ellie grinned woozily, drunk with a new kind of power. For the first time in her life, she held a man at her mercy, a man she adored. She held Kit back, then ordered him to hail a cab for her.

Kit stroked his finger behind her ear and down her neck. "Let me take you home."

Ellie breathed in and instantly wished she hadn't. She only inhaled his touch, sending its powers of arousal throughout her body. "No," she said, moving toward the door.

Kit caged her there, molding his palm to the curve of the side of her breast, his black-lashed gaze shamelessly molesting her. "Why not?"

Ellie turned her shoulder to him, marshaling the little that was left of her defenses. "Because you'll want to come in and you won't take no for an answer and I won't have time to get ready for tomorrow and we'll have to put off the wedding."

Kit straightened. "You, General, are entirely too logical." He smiled. "And quite right." He walked Ellie to the street, where he soon found a cab to take her away, much sooner than he would have liked. He didn't know how he was going to last without seeing her for twenty-four hours.

"Until tomorrow," he murmured, as she looked at him from behind the cab's window. Placing a kiss on the first two fingers of his right hand, he touched it to the glass that shielded the beautiful mouth he'd bruised with his kisses. Though his hunger would grow more ravenous, he'd take more care with that mouth tomorrow. And for the rest of his life, he thought as he waved her off.

"Kit? Did I just see you put that Barlow woman into a cab?"

Dammit. Of all people. "Henry," Kit said, turning to Callard. Casually, he lit a cigar, stalling for time to decide whether or not to lie to the man. But denying the woman was Ellie would only put the worst possible connotation on the gossip Henry would inevitably spread. "Yes, you did, Henry," he said through a swirl of smoke. "But she'll be that Barlow woman only until this time tomorrow afternoon. After that, she'll be—" *What will she be?* Kit wondered. *My wife, yes, but more.*

"She'll be that McCarron woman."

* * *

"Jehoshaphat, Miss B."

Standing hatless before the mirror in Bond and Barlow's ladies' department, Ellie shot an amused glance at Travis. "What are you Jehoshaphatting about now?" Placing her hands on her hips, she suddenly turned to him with a scolding look. "You haven't forgotten your tie again? Travis, how often must I tell you that it's part of your job as my assistant to project a proper image of the store?"

Fixed on Ellie's image, Travis set down a stack of boxes, showing her he was wearing the striped tie she'd picked out for him.

"Why, then," Ellie demanded, "are you looking at me as though you were seeing a ghost?"

"Not a ghost, Miss," Travis replied. He smiled at her. "An angel."

"Jehoshaphat!" Turning back to the mirror, Ellie again saw herself in the ivory batiste and lace dress she'd decided on for her wedding. It *was* heavenly, and she did feel as though she were walking on air. Last night, she'd freed herself of the past, discarding the dress and veil she was to have worn for her and Frank's wedding along with Frank's letter. They had served to remind her of what she'd once thought could never be and now was, with Kit. She slanted a look at Travis. "Do you really like the dress? Because it's for a very special occasion."

Travis straightened to his full height. "If you don't mind my saying so, Miss Barlow, you never looked so beautiful."

And he isn't even blushing, Ellie thought, suddenly fond of the young man who only a year ago, when she'd come to Louisville, had been a boy. He was going to make a wonderful assistant floorwalker and, eventually, when Philby retired, head floorwalker of her and Kit's new store. "Travis, I'm sure I can trust you to keep a secret."

"You can rely on me, Miss Barlow," he said, his voice deep and steady.

Stepping closer, Ellie laid her hand on his sleeve. "Not

Miss Barlow, Travis. At least not after two o'clock this afternoon."

Travis's eyes narrowed. "What happens then?"

Ellie looked at her full reflection in the mirror and smiled. "A miracle."

Ellie returned to the fitting room to change back into her navy blue skirt and white shirtwaist. She still had so many things to do—order flowers and select a gift for Kit. And though she really preferred to keep the wedding a secret from all but Travis, she supposed she would have to ask one of her female clerks to be her bridesmaid. Suddenly, her eyes misted over. She wished Josiah were here to give her away.

"And Delia Eldham, did Ah tell you that Henry said her mouth was red and swollen—and you know what from— when Kit put her in the cab?"

Buttoning her shirtwaist, Ellie froze at the question that came from behind the curtain two fitting rooms away.

"Louise, you can't mean it. My Robert claims you couldn't pay him to kiss that Barlow woman."

At the women's laughter, Ellie's hand instinctively went to her left cheek. Who were they and where had she heard the name Robert Eldham?

"But Delia," the woman called Louise said, "Ah suspicion Kit might really love her."

"You suspicion there's a man in the moon, too, Louise Callard," Delia replied. "You know full well Kit McCarron could have his pick of beautiful women."

" 'Course he can, Delia. That's why Ah'm thinkin' he must really love the poor creature."

"Love her store, you mean." Delia Eldham's voice was like a julep, syrup masking a mean streak. "Robert says Kit once asked him about buying her out, but when Robert told him he wouldn't advise it on account of the debt Kit took on just to keep up with her, he decided to eliminate the competition by marryin' it.''

Louise Callard gasped. "Did Kit come right out and tell Robert that's what he was plannin' to do?"

"Ah'm sure he would if Robert could find him," Delia Eldham replied. "Since your Henry brought us the news of the weddin', Robert's been lookin' all over for Kit, wantin' to congratulate him on his grand strategy to preserve the South or some fool cause the three of them drank to. But Robert knows Kit like the back of his own hand, on account of their growin' up together, and if he says that's what Kit's plannin' to do, you can just bet on it.''

Against the backdrop of the rustling of fabric, Delia Eldham's words drove a blade into Ellie's infant happiness. Mrs. Eldham was the wife of Kit's accountant, Ellie realized, the man Kit had offered to summon to attest to his financial health before they made love—was it only yesterday?

She stood very still as the two women passed by her dressing room on their way out. Then, slowly circling her fingers over her temples, she gazed around the tiny room as if trying to remember what she'd been doing there. Seeing the ivory dress hanging on the wall, she walked to it with small, uncertain steps. She ran her hand lovingly down the bodice. How heavenly the lace was. Yes, now she remembered. She'd been going to wear the dress to a miracle. Even Travis had said she looked like an angel in it.

Now pressing her fingertips hard against her temples, she turned away. "I really must put chairs in these rooms, she murmured, then lurching, clutched the curtains for support.

Angels sometimes fall.

Pacing outside city hall in cutaway and top hat, Kit paused to consult his pocket watch.

"Kit, that's the fifth time you've looked at your watch in the last ten minutes," Philby said. "Now put it away. And straighten your tie. Miss Barlow will arrive in due time."

Smiling, Kit adjusted the knot at his collar. "You're surprisingly calm, Philby. Frankly, I thought that by now you'd be pleading with me not to rush into this marriage, reminding me that I hardly know the Barlow woman."

"I—"

"Too late now," Kit said, rubbing his gloved hands as he resumed pacing. "I can assure you I already know all a man needs to know about the woman he's about to marry."

"Yes, but—"

"I know that she's beautiful in so many ways, and clever and brave." *And that she makes love like a she-devil.* "Oh, I know she's got a definite mind of her own and a will that could bend iron, but I much prefer that in a wife. She'll be a true partner, and I'll certainly never be bored."

"But—"

"There's no use arguing with me, Philby," Kit said, halting before his best man. "The truth is, I'm hopelessly, desperately in love with her."

"I know you are, Kit," Philby said, clamping Kit's shoulder. He smiled. "If I could have picked a wife for you, I would have picked Miss Barlow."

Kit released a sigh. "Thank you, James," he said, then once more, checked his watch. Shaking it, he held it to his ear. "What time do you have?"

James Philby checked his own watch. "Three minutes of two," he said, snapping the watch shut and returning it to his pocket.

"That's what I have, too," Kit said, frowning. "Perhaps she's taken ill . . . or had an accident!"

"You'd have received word, Kit," Philby replied. "Now

take a deep breath and get hold of yourself before I'm forced to render you unconscious."

Kit laughed uneasily. "You're right. I'm sure she's busy fussing over whatever it is brides fuss over."

But when Kit looked at his watch for the last time, it was three-thirty. Taking the carnation from his buttonhole, he threw it to the pavement. "Philby, I'd appreciate it very much if you'd join me at my club, where I intend to render myself thoroughly unconscious."

Six

March 27, 1890

"Would you like me to go to court with you today, Ellie?" Travis peered in on her as she sat at her desk, hunched over stacks of paperwork.

"No, but thank you," she replied without looking up. "As many times as I've appeared before Judge Kincaid, I could find my way to his courtroom with my eyes closed."

"Who's bringing the complaint this time, you or Kit?"

Ellie retrieved a thick file from the corner of her desk and looked inside. "I am," she said, setting the file aside and returning to her paperwork. "Since Mr. McCarron hired that hedge trimmer to answer my ad for a hair stylist, *he* can pay for Mrs. Sanderson's wig."

"Well, don't worry about things here, Ellie. I'll mind the store."

Rising, Ellie walked toward her trusted assistant. "I know you will, the same as you have been all these months I've spent fighting Kit McCarron in court." She clasped his arm. "I'm grateful, Travis."

Taking her hand, he squeezed it supportively then walked to the door. "Ellie?"

"Yes?"

"This war between you and Kit, I hope it ends soon."

Ellie frowned. "Have I relied on you, too much?"

"No. I just miss you, the way you were before it started, I mean."

With a snort of astonishment, Ellie put her hands on her hips. "And how was that?"

Travis skewed a smile at her. "Bossy, but always so full of hopes and dreams. You could see farther than anybody I ever knew." He glanced down. "Now it seems you can't see any farther than Ninth and Market."

"Ninth and— But that's where McCarron's is."

"Yes, ma'am." Giving her a salute, Travis left Ellie agape and trying to decipher his meaning.

"What nonsense," she said a moment later, deciding she had no time for riddles. She returned to her paperwork, but, before long, her gaze traveled to the thick file that held the record of every charge she'd leveled at Kit since the day they were to have married. Was this what Travis had been alluding to when he said she couldn't see farther than McCarron's? And what was it, really, but the record of her revenge against Kit for his cruel deception? A revenge that so obsessed her she'd lost her vision, not just for Bond and Barlow, but for her life.

Yes, it was that, she thought, looking away from the file. But it was also a record of Kit's countercharges, of a revenge of his own. He hadn't been able to afford to buy her out of her business, and he'd failed to marry her out of it, so he'd determined to make her wish she'd never laid eyes on it. But he'd failed at that, too. *He* was all she'd wished she'd never laid eyes on. Still, she'd go on seeing him—in court—until the day he would make a wish of his own. That he'd never been born.

As Kit worked at his desk, James Philby leaned over him, depositing the day's mail. "You haven't forgotten you're due in court in fifteen minutes, have you, Kit?"

Glancing up, Kit nearly bumped noses with Philby. "No,

I haven't. And there's no need for you to smell my breath.
I'm completely sober."

Philby straightened. "Forgive me, but that hasn't always
been the case in recent months."

"From now on, you may rely on it!" Rising sharply, Kit
began pacing. "I've made a decision, Philby. After today,
I'm through avenging my wounded pride in court. I've
paid for my little vendetta, with my soul. Perhaps I can get
it back, somewhere." He came to a halt. "I leave for New
York at eight-fifteen this evening."

Though appearing neither surprised nor disapproving,
Philby asked, "And the store?"

Kit returned to his desk, closed the file he'd been working on, and handed it to Philby. "I've left detailed instructions for you, and my itinerary. You'll always know where
to cable me."

Tucking the folder under his arm, Philby clasped his
hands in front of him. "Do you really think leaving Louisville will make you forget her?"

Kit's jaw flinched. "I'll never forget her, Philby. Nor forgive her. But I'm no longer willing to devote my life to
punishing her. Besides"—he walked to the coat rack, removed his hat, then opened the door—"I have faith that
before too long, Miss Barlow will be called to account for
her many deceits."

"Kit, before you go, I'm going to give you one last piece
of fatherly advice." Philby approached, placing his hand
on Kit's shoulder. "Give in and talk to her. Ask her once
and for all why she jilt—failed to appear that day."

"It's all right, Philby, you can say it now without fear I'll
disappear for days only to return broke, foul-smelling, and
with no memory of where I'd been or with whom. Miss
Barlow jilted me." Kit patted Philby's arm. "But we've been
over it all before, old friend."

"Not to my satisfaction," Philby replied. "Eleanor Barlow is a woman to reckon with, to be sure, but I can't

believe she seized on your proposal as an opportunity to return the humiliation you'd handed her in court. If there's one thing she knows, it's the pain of public scrutiny."

All the more reason to inflict it on her "sworn enemy." Beloved sworn enemy, she'd called him, beguiling him then. Still. "I'm sorry to disillusion you about Miss Barlow, Philby, but she swore I'd regret that day in court. But take heart. If I can survive disillusionment—"

"Is that what they call running away these days, surviving?"

Kit settled his hat on his head. "Let's just say I'm making up for lost time."

Outside his door, he slipped his hands into his pockets. Inside the right one, he fingered the scrap of chiffon veil Ellie had removed from her hat that long ago day, the day he'd felt as though he'd unearthed the secrets of the pyramids, climbed Everest, and discovered Atlantis without ever leaving his home, his bed, and the woman in his arms.

He'd lied to Philby. He wasn't setting out to make up for lost time, but to spend the rest of his life searching for that lost adventure, the adventure of traveling to the center of the universe through the love of just one woman.

Searching, but never finding.

Inside Judge Lester Kincaid's small courtroom, Ellie pleated the bill for Mrs. Sanderson's wig and fanned her flushed cheeks with it. Walking here from the store, she'd felt as though she were wading though a bog—the air was that sultry. Not that after two years of living in the Ohio Valley she hadn't learned that the price of its lush beauty was constant humidity and frequent—frequently violent— rainstorms. Still, the atmosphere today was unseasonably warm, almost suffocating, and in this small room, more unpleasant than usual. And Kit hadn't even arrived yet.

When he did, she'd know. She'd feel his stare—icily
calm, chillingly vengeful. There were times she actually
took satisfaction from it. It meant she'd wounded him
enough to make him hate her. Then she would remind
herself that no matter how long or hard she tried, she
could never teach him to hate as she'd been taught when
a chance encounter with the truth had stripped her of all
but the sinews of her existence.

Still, she might have hated him even more. She might
never have overheard that conversation between Delia Eldham and Louise Callard, and married him. Oh, she would
have guessed the truth eventually, as he repeatedly excused
himself from lovemaking. But by then, she'd have lost not
only her pride but her beloved store.

So beloved, she thought, chiding herself, that for nearly
a year she'd neglected it to carry on a vendetta against a
man who simply wasn't worth the sacrifice. Travis had been
right, after all, she decided. It was time to pick up her life,
her hopes, and her dreams where Kit had left them,
dashed on the shoals of his greed. It was time to forget
she ever knew him, ever shared his bed. Ever loved him.

But she couldn't, not as long as one link remained between them. One she was powerless to destroy. Her photograph.

Though she'd never seen it, the knowledge of its existence tormented her. Why, she ceaselessly asked, had he
insisted on taking it? Had he planned to keep it as insur-
ance in the event that her inevitable discovery of how her
husband had defrauded her out of her store didn't drive
her mad? Mad enough, at least, for some judge he'd bribe
to grant him sole ownership and control of the single new
store resulting from their marriage.

Or perhaps there was a simpler, even more chilling explanation. Perhaps he was just so senselessly cruel that he'd
enjoyed making her believe she was beautiful for the pleasure of inwardly scorning her.

And yet, she wondered now, did it really matter? Because he *had* made her feel beautiful, made her *believe* she was, enough so that she had made Travis believe it, too. *See* it, too. Other men saw it now, she'd noted, men who came into the store and flirted with her. And whether or not her beauty owed more to her new belief in it than conformity to some standard, she had at last learned to trust in the power of her womanhood. A womanhood that despite Kit's intentions, was nearer to completion because of him. Since the day they'd made love, she'd never again worn a veil.

"Barlow versus McCarron."

Rising at the clerk's calling of her case, Ellie stepped into the aisle and bumped into something tall and unyielding—

"Miss Barlow."

And surprising. Ellie gazed up at Kit. Strange that she hadn't sensed his malevolent presence in the courtroom. Then again, perhaps not. She'd never seen such a faraway look in his eyes, and, for a moment, she was sure that after today, she would never see him again.

Pondering the prospect, she found it surprisingly disturbing. She wasn't proud of having thrived on her revenge. Still, the abrupt departure of its object would take some getting used to. Without reply, she preceded Kit up the aisle to the bench.

Sitting behind it, Judge Kincaid passed a stern look from one to the other of them. "I can understand why you two don't feel the need to engage attorneys. You can litigate with the best of them." Shifting his weight, he folded his hands. "What seems to be the trouble this time?"

Ellie presented her case. Then, unpleating the bill for Mrs. Sanderson's wig, she laid it out for the judge. "As you can plainly see, Your Honor, Mr. McCarron owes me four dollars and thirty-five cents for the wig I had to buy for my customer to wear while her hair grows in."

"Miss Barlow," the judge began, reaching into his trousers pocket. "If I give you the four dollars and thirty-five cents, will you promise not to come back here for at least a month?"

"But Your Honor, I'm also asking the court for $2,500 in damages for malicious intent."

"Young woman, I admit to imagining all sorts of mishaps befallin' you every time your name shows up on my docket," the judge said. "But all you'll get out of me is four dollars and thirty-five cents!"

"Your Honor!" Ellie heaved a frustrated sigh. Despite his connection to Kit, on most days Judge Kincaid had proved fairly impartial. Today, unfortunately, wasn't one of them. "I meant Mr. McCarron's malicious intent to ruin the reputation of my store, of course."

"Oh." Lester Kincaid turtled his bald head in Kit's direction. "Did you do that, set out to ruin her reputation?"

Ellie and Kit exchanged glances. *What are you waiting for, Kit?* her gaze asked. *You know you're dying to tell the judge and the whole town that my reputation is beyond ruin.*

Believe me, I'm tempted, Kit's gaze replied. But not even when he'd been his drunkest had he revealed that he and Ellie had been lovers. Not even to Philby. And not just because when all was said and done, he really was a Southern gentleman. Because to turn his memory of her lying in his arms, sweet-scented and ripe, into grist for scandal would be to admit it had all been a lie. An illusion. And there was a part of him, even now, that didn't want to surrender that illusion.

He turned to the judge. "Your Honor, Miss Barlow's personal reputation is sterling and deserves to remain so."

Ellie's jaw dropped. Gallantry was the last thing she expected from Kit.

"But as for the reputation of her store," he continued, "I confess to wishing to tarnish it just a bit."

A confession? From Kit? That, Ellie couldn't begin to

believe. He's up to something, she thought, planning some counterattack. "What do you mean, 'tarnish'?"

Judge Kincaid banged his gavel. "I'll ask the questions, if you don't mind." Looking at Kit, he cleared his throat. "What exactly are you confessin' to, young fella?"

Kit spread his hands apart. "Your Honor, I'm merely admitting that I hired someone to sabotage Bond and Barlow's ladies' salon. I'm perfectly willing to pay for Mrs. Sanderson's wig and any damages the store's reputation may have suffered."

"What do you say, Miss Barlow?" the judge asked, propping his chin on his fist. "Does Mr. McCarron's offer meet with your approval?"

Ellie didn't know what to say. Somewhere in Kit's offer, there had to be a Trojan horse. She fixed a gaze on him, trying to read his eyes, but once again, saw only that strange, distant look in them.

"I know you think this courtroom is at your beck and call, Missy," the judge said, "but believe it or not, a nice man comes round here at four o'clock every day and locks it up."

"Your Honor, I think no such thing," Ellie shot back. Then, making fists, "Oh, all right. I approve Mr. McCarron's offer."

"Oh, that is a shame." Lester Kincaid shook his head. "Because I don't!"

Ellie and Kit gaped at the judge, then at one another.

"Perhaps Your Honor didn't understand me," Kit said, scratching one corner of his mouth. "You see, I'm willing to give Miss Barlow everything she asked for."

"Are you impugnin' the court's intelligence or its hearin', Mr. McCarron?"

"Neither, Your Honor, but—" Kit broke off at the bang of the gavel.

Kincaid swabbed his neck with a handkerchief. "I could have gone fishin' today but for the two of you. And the last time y'all came before me, I ended up bein' late for my grandson's birthday party. Let me see, that would have been when you, Mr. McCarron, brought a complaint against Miss Barlow, accusin' her of arrangin' for the circulars advertisin' your sale to go missing from the newspapers."

"Actually, Your Honor," Kit said, stepping closer, "I brought that case against Miss Barlow last June."

"That's right," Ellie said, joining Kit. "Then, in July, I accused Mr. McCarron of hiring a driver to overturn an egg wagon in front of my store, causing me to delay my Independence Day parade. And the next time we came to court was when Mr. McCarron complained that I paid a railroad worker to send one of his shipments on to Cincinnati—"

"As usual, Miss Barlow is mistaken," Kit said, taking hold of the bench. "Before I brought that charge, she charged me with paying a city clerk to lose her application for a license to operate her tearoom."

The judge brought his gavel down resoundingly, and this time, all three parties jumped. "If you all will excuse me a moment." From a brown bottle, he poured a tablespoon of a liquid, swallowed it, grimaced, then set the bottle and spoon aside. "I never had to take nerve tonic until I met you two. And I don't intend to have to go on takin' it." He meshed his fingers. "It is the opinion of this court that you, Miss Barlow and you, Mr. McCarron are hell-bent on aggravatin' one another, and that no amount of fines, which you've both paid handsomely, will deter you from doin' so. Therefore, the court has determined that a more severe penalty is in order, one that will make y'all think twice before wastin' the court's time and the taxpayers' dollars." He picked up his gavel. "Thirty days in the city jail, each! Take them away, bailiff."

"You can't do this!" Kit's eyes were wide with the imagined sight of a New York-bound train pulling out of Union

Depot that night. For the second time, he wouldn't be on it.

"That's funny," the judge replied, " 'cause I just did."

Ellie decided to try reason. "Your Honor, imagine having to leave your lovely courtroom here—"

The judge smiled. "I am. Oh, how I am."

"I mean, leave it in the hands of some apprentice judge," Ellie quickly amended, prompting snickers from the handful of observers in the courtroom. Infuriated, she stamped her foot. "Your Honor, I simply cannot leave running Bond and Barlow to my young assistant for more than a few hours!"

"You should have thought of that sooner, Missy," the judge replied, motioning the bailiff away.

"Your Honor, may I approach the bench?"

Kit, Ellie, and the bailiff stopped and looked at the woman who spoke from the back of the courtroom. She was tall, tastefully dressed. The suggestion of a full head of beautifully coiffed white hair was visible beneath her large, plumed hat.

The judge sighed. "What's one more?"

"Thank you, Your Honor," the woman responded, then started up the aisle.

As she passed by them, Kit gave Ellie a smug grin. "I, at least, won't have to live on bread and water for the next month. That's Mrs. Kincaid. Philby's sister."

Ellie gaped at the woman who was now whispering in her husband's ear, the woman who, according to Kit, had adored him since he was a child and had probably had a hand in spoiling any chance of his becoming anything but selfish, manipulative and cruel. Surely, she was sparing him the consequences of his reprehensible behavior even now. As she spoke, her husband's brows shot up and beneath them, he fixed a scathing gaze on Ellie.

Case closed, Ellie thought. The only unknown was whether she was going to get the rack or be drawn and quartered. Watching Kit gloat, she couldn't imagine loathing him more than she did at this moment.

Abruptly, Judge Kincaid gave a big nod. As his wife returned to her seat, he instructed the bailiff to return Kit and Ellie to the bench. He fixed them with an implacable gaze. "It has been brought to the court's attention that incarceratin' the two of you would only put the city to more trouble and expense. Therefore, I rescind your jail sentences."

Kit and Ellie heaved twin sighs of relief.

"Thank you, Your Honor," Kit said. Smiling, he turned to leave.

"Yes, thank you," Ellie echoed. Sweeping her skirt aside, she started for the exit.

The judge's gavel brought them both to lurching halts.

"Did I say y'all could go?" Judge Kincaid looked at his clerk. "Did I tell them they could go? I didn't think so. Come back here you two before I have you thrown in the pokey for contempt."

Scowling at one another, Kit and Ellie returned to the bench.

"As I was about to say," the judge continued, "this court is determined that you two keep your squabbles to yourselves, or at least, out of this courtroom. That's why I'm fixin' matters so that from now on, you can give some other judge"—he pressed the pommel of his fist to his sternum—"heartburn."

Ellie leaned toward Kit. "Some clout you have. I think he's going to send us up to Circuit Court. That means we'll be breaking rocks for the county."

"That shouldn't worry you," Kit whispered back. "After all, you're so good at breaking things. Like promises."

Ellie gaped at him. "How dare you criticize—" Seeing Judge Kincaid rise, looking like black-robed doom, she straightened.

"Eleanor Barlow and Christopher McCarron, this court

hereby sentences you to—" After erupting with a string of sneezes, Lester Kincaid loudly blew his nose. "Where was I?" He leaned toward his whispering clerk. "Oh, yes, this court hereby sentences you to marriage. Now take off your gloves and join hands."

Laughter bounced off the small room's walls.

Kit and Ellie bounded to the bench.

"You can't—"

"I won't—"

"Take your pick," the judge ordered, glaring first at one, then the other. "Marriage or the hoosegow."

"Is there any difference, Your Honor?" Kit asked, eliciting more laughter.

Ellie hammered her fist on the bench. "This is blackmail!"

"Maybe so, Missy," Judge Kincaid said, shouting her down. "But by the time you get a hearin', I'll have enjoyed a whole lot of peace and quiet. So, what'll it be?"

"Your Honor," Kit said, "may Miss Barlow and I have a moment to discuss the matter?"

"Go ahead, but make it quick. I'd like to get out on the river before it rains."

Kit shagged Ellie to one side. "It doesn't appear as though we have much choice."

"You needn't pretend to look so glum," she said, tearing her arm from his hold, unable to bear his touch. Realizing that every time she thought she couldn't possibly despise him more than she did at that moment, he proved her wrong. "I knew you were up to no good the minute you agreed to all my terms. But I have to admit, I never dreamed you'd go this far to get Bond and Barlow."

Kit gave his head a shake, not sure he'd heard correctly. "You think I arranged this?"

Ellie cast a glance at Philby's sister. "Women just can't seem to deny you your heart's desires, can they?"

I wish that were true, Kit thought, though only when it

came to just one woman. "Ellie, I don't expect you to believe me, but I had nothing to do with this." *I have a good idea who did, though. Philby, you meddlesome old fool.*

"You're right, I don't believe you."

"What if I were to tell you that I'm perfectly willing, when the time comes, for you to file for an annulment on the usual grounds, that your groom left you unkissed, as the expression goes?"

Giving a snort of derision, Ellie folded her arms. "You can't really expect me to believe you'd consent to that."

"Why not?" Kit gazed into her eyes, jade as ever. And jade was cold and hard. "Even you can emasculate a man only once."

Ellie's head jerked back. If she'd injured his precious manhood when she'd jilted him, he'd had it coming. "That remains to be seen, doesn't it, Mr. McCarron?"

The judge hammered. "Time's up, folks. Name your poison."

The sneer that slackened one side of Kit's mouth when he looked at Ellie was for himself. "Miss Barlow, will you marry me . . . this time?"

The gall of the man, Ellie thought. How dare he show indignation that she'd once been fortunate to escape a marriage he'd never intended to be anything but a vehicle for his greed? "This time I will," she said, removing her gloves. "But only because the store needs me."

"Ah yes, the store." Pulling off his own gloves, Kit laughed scornfully. "Are you sure that by marrying me you wouldn't be committing bigamy?"

"You sound jealous, Mr. McCarron," Ellie said, returning his scorn. "And to think Bond and Barlow might have been yours if not for the fact that your friends' wives prefer *it* to *your* establishment."

Kit stepped closer to Ellie, so close her breathing accelerated to match the pace of his. "What the devil are you talking about?"

"Bailiff," Judge Kincaid said, preempting Ellie's response. "Lock Mr. McCarron and Miss Barlow up. That'll help them decide."

"That won't be necessary, Your Honor." Kit approached the bench, dragging Ellie with him. "Though we do ask for the court's mercy," he added, sending her a look that contained none. He took her hand and when she chafed at his grasp, he clamped a tighter hold on it. "Marry us as quickly and painlessly as possible."

Quickly, perhaps, Ellie thought, but not painlessly. Throughout her life, she'd tried hard never to indulge in self-pity for the losses she'd suffered, of family, friendship, a pleasing face, and most of all, faith. One couldn't live without loss. But now that she was about to gain something, a husband, she felt inconsolably sorry for herself.

Not a year ago, she'd counted the moments until she would stand beside this man and promise to love him until the day she died. And now that she was doing just that, her promise would be a mockery of the love she once held sacred.

As Judge Kincaid began the ceremony, Ellie tried to shut out the words. But what her ears refused to hear, her heart recognized. And mourned. This wasn't a wedding, it was a funeral, the burial of her every ideal of love and marriage.

Kit kept a firm hold of Ellie's hand, the hand she was to have given him in marriage nearly a year ago. He was tempted to pretend that the last year hadn't happened, that he hadn't spent it in a bourbon-induced numbness to the pain she'd inflicted when she'd failed to publicly make the vows she'd already pledged in the privacy of his bedroom. In his arms. But her hand was cold, as cold as her heart, reminding him that she'd already extracted as much of his life's blood as he was willing to surrender. He'd fought mightily to get sober and sober he was going to stay.

"Eleanor Barlow, do you take this man—"

"No!"

The judge pointed his gavel at her. "You can't change your mind unless Mr. McCarron does, too!"

"I haven't changed my mind, Your Honor, though I wish I could." Ellie heaved a sigh. "But, we don't have witnesses."

Grinning broadly, Kit dropped Ellie's hand. "I guess you'll have to release us to find some, Your Honor," he said, thinking New York might be a good place to begin looking.

"Well, you guess wrong, Mr. McCarron." Judge Kincaid ordered his wife and the bailiff to serve as witnesses. "Now you two join up hands again and for the sake of Mrs. Kincaid, who you can plainly see is bawlin' her eyes out, try not to look as though you each wish the other was swingin' from the nearest tree." He ran his finger down the page of the book he held open. "Do you Eleanor Barlow take this man to be your lawfully wedded husband, etc. etc.?"

Muttering, Ellie removed her gloves and placing her hand in Kit's, gazed up at him. Suddenly, she saw him as he appeared that day on the ladder outside Bond and Barlow, the day they'd met. She recalled thinking at the time that in a vast world, there was this man. All else was ugliness. He was handsome still, but there was a weariness in his eyes that spoke of struggle, not so much of their petty struggles, but of one deep inside him and more virulent. For a brief moment, she forgot the past that stretched between them like a battlefield, littered with the corpses of her illusions. She nearly asked him what inner fight had left him so battle-fatigued, then, realizing that would have been like Grant inviting Lee to confide in him, she stopped herself. Still, she couldn't stop her eyes from querying his, prying into the recesses of his soul to discover the cause of his conflict.

That some small part of her own soul could still care about this man startled her.

That she was now being forced to marry him enraged her. He was, after all, what he'd always been and always would be. Her sworn enemy. She took a breath, then clenching her teeth, looked away, and said, "I do."

"Oh, that's fine. I can see the fish jumpin' already," the judge replied. "Now, do you Christopher McCarron take this woman to be your lawfully wedded wife and so on and so forth?"

Gazing down at Ellie, Kit saw her as she'd appeared on the ladder the day they'd met outside what was then only J. Bond's. Her eyes were as green as magnolia leaves, her skin milky white as the blossoms themselves, her mouth made for kissing. Only then, he hadn't known the taste of it, sweet and wild and never to be forgotten. Unforgettable, as well, was the contrast he'd seen then between her classic beauty and the wound he would always think of as her badge of courage—regardless of the heartache her memory would always cause him. Then, her expression had been the stage for the drama inside her: Apology, the pulling back from the brink of complete womanhood, and the calling on reserves of strength that was her trademark bossy independence.

Later, there was Bond and Barlow and Ellie looking up at him from the foot of his staircase. She'd unveiled for him as he always knew she would, she must. She was ripe and ready to risk. Or so he'd thought at the time. The risk, as it turned out, had been all his. But if that were true, why had she let him photograph her? To this day, he'd been unable to satisfactorily answer that question. However cunning Ellie had been in plotting her revenge that day, her fear of being photographed had been real. All he could think was that she'd steeled herself to pose for his camera only to draw him farther into her scheme of deceit.

And yet, the camera truly had not lied. Even he had seen things in her portrait he could never have imagined capturing, things like— But what was the use of going over it one more time when a thousand times had failed to change the fact that she had jilted him for vengeance?

Kit looked away from her. "I do."

"Dandy," the judge replied. "By the power vested in me by the Commonwealth of Kentucky, I pronounce you man and wife. Mother, where'd I leave my tackle box?"

"Lester!" Mrs. Kincaid stopped crying long enough to send her husband a scolding look. "You forgot the ring." Rummaging in her reticule, she pulled out a gold band and handed it to Kit.

Taking it between his thumb and forefinger, he stared at the ring he'd chosen for Ellie nearly a year ago. From what little he recalled of what would have been their wedding night, other than that he'd drunk the city dry of bourbon, he'd hurled the ring at Bond and Barlow's doors, hoping never to see it again. Philby must have retrieved it. As Kit slid the band over Ellie's finger, his heart wrenched. This should be the beginning of his greatest journey. Instead, it was a dead end.

Judge Kincaid clapped his hands. "Okay, now you're hitched. Sign here."

After Kit and Ellie had signed their marriage certificate, Mrs. Kincaid kissed them both then followed her husband out of the courtroom.

The newlyweds stood in stunned silence.

"I guess that's it," Kit said, more to himself than to Ellie after the last onlooker had left the room.

"I guess so." She began pulling on her left glove.

"You know," Kit said, capturing her hand, "I bought this ring for you almost a year ago."

Jerking her hand away, she resumed putting on her gloves. "If you bought it at McCarron's, you paid too much."

Kit smiled sardonically. "You're right. I paid far too dearly for it. But at least you won't have to wear it any longer than is necessary."

"Necessary for what? For you to lay claim to Bond and Barlow?"

Kit gave a laugh. "Good-bye, Mrs. McCarron," he said, stepping toward the exit. "Should you need anything, anything at all, just ask Philby. He'll know where to reach me."

Ellie stayed his arm. "Reach you? Where are you going?"

"I am going, madam, to find what I'd been searching for when I met you." He fingered the brim of his hat. "What I thought I'd found in you."

"Oh yes," Ellie said sarcastically. "I know all about what you thought you'd found in me." *The easiest way out of financial trouble. Still the easiest way out.* "And you're asking me to believe you're really leaving?"

"I'm finished asking you to believe in me, Ellie, for good. See for yourself." He reached inside his jacket, removed his train ticket, and handed it to her.

As she read it, Ellie understood the reason for the faraway look she'd seen in his eyes. He really *was* leaving. She really might never see him again. Beset by a conflict of emotions, she handed the ticket back to him. "When will you return?"

"I'm not sure. How many countries are there in the world?" Giving her a wistful smile, Kit bent down and placed a kiss on her left cheek. "You're still the most beautiful woman I've ever known," he said, then, placing his hat on his head, he walked away.

Ellie watched him, puzzling. No matter how much she considered that he might be the most arrogant of men, manipulating her to the end, or that she might be the most foolish of women, she could not hear in his parting words the tin sound of a lie.

Seven

After returning to Bond and Barlow, Ellie announced that all employees were to remain after closing to take inventory. She'd rationalized that she'd been meaning to count stock for some time, but the truth was, she didn't want to be alone at quarter past eight tonight. When Kit left town—and her life—forever.

As she entered her office, she removed her gloves, and for the first time, noticed how striking the design of her wedding band was, a classic interplay of strength and grace. She would love to believe that Kit *had* chosen it for her nearly a year ago, and with great care. She would love to believe Delia Eldham, and not he, had told the lie. But how could she? His every word and action this past year proved he'd never loved her.

But hadn't *her* every word and action indicated she'd never loved him when she'd loved him so much his betrayal had nearly killed her? When a part of her still loved him?

Stop it, Ellie. If he had any feeling for her at all, why had he spoken of annulment? Why was he leaving Louisville tonight?

Why was she letting him go?

Closing her eyes, Ellie pressed her knuckles to her forehead. *Let him go,* she thought. *Let him take the truth with him. At least this and every other war you and he have fought will end.* Slowly slipping the ring off her finger, Ellie placed it inside the top drawer of her desk.

Much later, taking a break at last from the inventory figures Travis had been dispatching to her, she was surprised to see how dark her office had grown. Lighting the lamps, she checked the watch pinned to her blouse. In less than half an hour Kit would ride a train out of her life. Suddenly, she felt as bereft as she had at Josiah's passing, when she'd lost the only other man she'd ever really loved.

As she gazed out the window, the oddest shade of dusk she'd ever seen eclipsed thoughts of both men. Perhaps, she reasoned, it owed its grey-green cast to nothing more than intermittent lightning to the southwest. Still, she felt chilblains erupt.

Stepping outside her office, she quickly navigated the aisles on the second floor and, leaning over the banister, spotted Travis with Sarah, who'd been commanding so much of his attention lately. "You'd better send everyone home," she called down to him. "It may be nothing, but I don't like the way the sky looks."

Dashing back to her office, she quickly tidied her desk, then slipped into her jacket. Her sense of urgency was undoubtedly due more to her emotional turmoil than to anything the sky might portend. Nevertheless, she felt an imperative duty to clear everyone from the store.

"Ellie?"

"Travis, I thought I told you to go home."

"I wouldn't leave you here alone."

"I'm almost ready," she said, hastily pulling on her right glove.

Walking past her, Travis retrieved a large, thin envelope that was lodged between her desk and a file cabinet. "I guess you missed seeing this," he said, handing the sealed envelope to her. "It came for you earlier, when you were checking stock in the basement. It must have slipped off your desk."

Ellie took the envelope—plain, brown, and with no indication of who'd sent it. She turned to toss it on her desk, but something made her change her mind. "You go ahead," she instructed Travis as she opened the envelope. "This won't take long, and I don't mind seeing myself home."

Travis took a wide stance. "I *do* mind."

Ellie's brows went up. "Is that some kind of an order?"

"Begging your pardon, Miss Barlow." Sarah, pretty but white-faced, appeared in the doorway. "Travis, it's gettin' awful dark and scary outside."

Ellie smiled to herself. "Go," she said, giving Travis instruction on how to issue orders and turning him toward the door.

Reluctantly, he left, but not before warning her to follow quickly with her own departure.

Smiling, Ellie watched the young couple as she removed the contents of the envelope. When they disappeared from view, she looked down at the single, thick sheet of paper in her hand.

And reeled at an unexpected cut to her heart. She was holding her own image. Kit had sent her photograph.

Legs trembling, she walked to the wall and beneath a sconce, turned the portrait to capture its light. After a moment, she took the photograph to the window and the strange dusk, to be certain the gaslight hadn't falsely portrayed her. But no, all that she had seen before she saw now, as the camera had seen her, then. Beautiful.

She might have thought the camera had lied except for the long white line clearly visible down the center of her left cheek. Most remarkable of all was not that her other features compensated for her wound, but that, seeing herself now—no, seeing herself as Kit had seen her, then—she could not imagine her face without it. The woman who gazed back at her had more than an ephemeral kind of beauty. She had strength and grace and confidence.

She had the love of an extraordinary man.

Hastily, Ellie set the photograph down and took her wedding ring from the top drawer of her desk. Holding it to the lamp, she found what she'd hoped for, an inscription. "Beloved General. I surrender," she read, noting the date she and Kit were to have married nearly a year ago.

Cupping her hands over her mouth, Ellie fought back tears. Kit had asked her to believe him, but she'd chosen to believe gossip, instead. To exchange a year of the happiness they could have known for a lifetime of bitterness over a lie. She didn't know how Delia Eldham had come to tell that lie, but she knew now that the sound she'd heard from the woman's lips had been as hollow as tin.

Shaking, Ellie once again checked the time. Kit was leaving in fifteen minutes. Union Depot was at Seventh and River Road, eight blocks from the store. But she could make it. She had to.

Slipping the photograph back inside the envelope, then into a slender case, Ellie grabbed her umbrella and hurried out her door. As she made her way downstairs to the store's entrance, she turned out the lights Travis had left burning to guide her way. She couldn't believe how dearly she'd come to love that young man. She only hoped Sarah loved him half as much as she herself loved Kit at this moment, which God willing, was only the start of a lifetime of loving him.

After she locked the doors, she began running up Market toward Seventh, feeling the hair on the back of her neck bristle. The lightning was now constant, but the air ominously still. Picking up her pace, she searched ahead and behind for a trolley or a cab, but the street was all but deserted. Anyone with a lick of sense had already sought shelter or would do so now, before it was too late.

But for the first time in her life, Ellie hadn't any sense.

None, at least, that would keep her from the depot. Yes, a gale force wind had suddenly swooped down on the city. Yes, she was keenly aware that at any moment, she could be caught in a crossfire of shattering glass. But she also knew that if she stopped to shelter herself from this storm, she'd face every future storm alone.

As she crossed Main at Seventh, a gust drove her back, pelting her with rain. Tucking the slender case containing her photograph under her arm, she opened her umbrella only to have it torn from her hands by a chill blast piercing the dankness. As she stepped forward, her hat blew away. She pressed on. She could see the depot ahead.

Entering it, she brushed back the wet, straggling debris of her chignon and saw she had just three minutes to find Kit's train. Heart pounding, she scanned the departures board, then asked a porter for directions to the right track. She ran toward it, praying.

In vain. "No!"

Seeing the train pull away, Ellie chased after it, desperately searching for Kit in the windows streaming by, calling his name. Finally, reaching the end of the platform, she gave up the chase, and hope. Tears coursing down her already damp cheeks, she let the slender case containing her photograph slip from her fingers.

"Ellie?"

Ellie gazed across the track, at the platform engulfed by steam from the train behind it. When it cleared, she saw him gazing back at her, tall, broad, elegant, and infinitely to be loved. "Kit!"

Running up the platform where, at the last moment, he'd jumped from the train, Kit watched Ellie hurry up the parallel platform toward him. He wanted to believe his eyes but was afraid to, afraid that the fire he saw burning in hers wasn't at all the love he'd decided to stay and fight for. Yet, by the looks of her, she'd braved the storm to find him. She, who was understandably terrified of storms. He ran faster and saw that the fire burned brighter the nearer he came to it. As he reached her on the platform beside the empty track, she stretched her arms out to him and the fire consumed him. Dropping his bag, he swept her up, holding her tightly as she encircled his neck, pressing her left cheek to his.

"Ellie, my love," he murmured, rocking her in his arms as he buried his face in the sweet, wet scent of her neck. "I couldn't do it. I couldn't run away. I still love you."

Oh, the power of those words, Ellie thought. *I should have trusted them.* "Kit, can you ever forgive me?" As he set her on her feet, she gazed up at him, taking his face in her hands. "I chose to believe a lie instead of you, in your love." She told him about the conversation she'd heard between Delia Eldham and Louise Callard.

As she did so, Kit pieced together the puzzle that no amount of bourbon had been able to help him solve. "Can *you* forgive me?" He told her he'd believed she'd jilted him to return the humiliation he'd handed her the first time he'd taken her to court. "Until a moment ago, I was too proud to come to you and ask for the truth."

"Kit?" Ellie pressed her palms to his chest. "Kiss me."

Lifting her chin, Kit smiled down at her. "My beautiful, beloved general," he murmured. Crushing her against him, he claimed her mouth, her love, his lost soul.

As Kit turned her in his arms, deepening his kiss, Ellie heard not only the sound of truth, but of undying love. It *was* a kind of music, a perfect harmony. And yet, as she savored the taste of his tongue, she heard a distant, dissonant chord. It grew louder, obliterating the whooshing sound her hands made as she ran them over his strong back.

Straightening, Kit righted her. "Do you hear that?"

Ellie listened to the approaching roar. "It sounds like a train pulling in."

Kit gazed up the track, but there was no sign of a train

and a glance at the arrivals board told him none was due in. The roar was now deafening and, strangely, overhead.

"That's no train!" Clamping a hold on Ellie's wrist, Kit dragged her to the edge of the platform, jumped down onto the track, then reached up for her. "Hurry!"

Ellie stretched her arms toward him. "Wait!" She took off down the platform.

"Ellie!"

Scooping up the precious portrait of his love, Ellie started back to Kit. But she was still far from the safety of his outstretched arms when the rafters above her groaned like the waking dead. Stopping at the edge of the platform, she looked up and saw them become toothpicks as the entire roof exploded.

Kit ran to her, grabbed her ankles and tipped her off the platform into his arms. Forcing her below the wood planks, he pushed her down, facefirst into the dirt, then threw his body atop hers.

It didn't last long, the sound of destruction. When the tornado's roar had passed, Kit scrambled from beneath the platform that, somehow, had held together above them. He pulled Ellie up beside him. They stood on the track, clinging to one another in the sudden darkness.

"Are you all right, Ellie?"

"Yes. You?"

"Yes." Kit struck a match. Together, he and Ellie surveyed the horror the flame revealed.

The train on the next track was demolished, crushed beneath the debris of the collapsed roof and fallen rafters. Cries of pain and terror emanated from its buried compartments.

Shaking out the match, Kit jumped up on the platform, then hauled Ellie up beside him. "Stay here," he said and started toward the wreckage.

"No!" She caught the crook of his arm, forcing him to look at her.

"It's too dangerous, Ellie."

"I can help in a way you can't, darling," she said. "I know what those people are feeling. All they have to do is look at me to know I know."

Clasping her hand, Kit kissed her fingertips. "Remind me to show you later how much I love you, Mrs. McCarron."

"That's General McCarron to you," Ellie said with a grin. Tucking her photograph inside her jacket for safekeeping, she squeezed her husband's hand. Together, they ran to assist the passengers trapped inside the train.

They worked for hours, alone at first, then alongside police and fire crews, and ordinary citizens who'd volunteered to help with the rescue.

Ellie now knelt on the platform, comforting a terrified child. Kit had gone back inside the wreckage to search for the little girl's mother. If he didn't emerge soon, she was going to need comforting herself. She couldn't lose him now. They'd come too far. They had too far yet to go.

"Mommy!"

Ellie gasped as the child tore from her lap and ran to her mother. Then, seeing Kit beside the woman, holding a lantern, his clothes in shreds and his expression both weary and gratified, she ran to him. He beamed the moment he saw her, and when she reached him, he wrapped one arm about her, hugging her tightly. "At least we'll never forget our wedding night."

Walking up the platform beside him, her arm around his waist, she gave him a provocative grin. "And it's not over yet."

Kit buried a laugh and a kiss in her hair. "In that case, let me waste no time in getting you home."

Outside the ruins of the depot, they picked their way through the rubble beneath the light from Kit's lantern. As they reached River Road, they heard a man call Kit's name.

"Philby, what are you—"

"Thank God, Kit, you're safe," Philby said, catching his breath. "And you, also, Miss Bar—Mrs. McCarron." Then, he fell strangely silent, shifting a tense gaze between them.

"What is it, Mr. Philby?" Ellie asked.

As he released a pent-up breath, James Philby's shoulders sagged. "The tornado cut a path from Thirty-second Street to the river. Just about everything between Eighteenth and Maple, and here is damaged or destroyed. I believe the block you live on was spared, Ellie. But Kit's house is gone, and McCarron's. And, I'm afraid, Bond and Barlow." Philby touched Ellie's arm consolingly. "I saw young Travis Partee, there. He was looking for you."

Squeezing back the tears, Ellie pressed her forehead to Kit's shoulder and released a sob.

"It's all right, Ellie," Kit said, brushing back her hair and cupping her cheek. "We can start over. We'll build our own home and a new store. We'll make them both everything you've ever dreamed of."

"We've ever dreamed of," she said. She gazed up at him. "Oh, Kit. I'm not crying because of the stores. And I don't care where we live as long as we have room to grow. I'm crying because I'm so blessed. I have Travis and you, James—" She clasped Philby's hand. Then she turned to Kit, wrapping her arms around his neck. "Most of all, I have you, my beloved sworn enemy." Raising her lips to his, she kissed him. "And a place where we can make our peace."

Kit and Ellie walked off, their arms about each other, leaving all ruin behind.

Folding his arms, James Philby smiled. "Yes, indeed. A most extraordinary woman."

AUTHOR'S NOTE

On March 27, 1890, a tornado did destroy large sections of Louisville, Kentucky. The roof of Union Depot collapsed on an outbound train, killing one passenger. In all, nearly one hundred people died, and hundreds more were injured. Proud of their self-reliance as a community, Louisvillians graciously but firmly refused offers of outside assistance. The author salutes them and their descendants who, in response to the devastating flood of March 1997, so generously aided those of their neighbors in need.

The Bride and the Brute

Laurel O'Donnell

One

England, 1392

The stone statues in the chapel towered high above Jayce Cullen's head, their cold, chiseled arms outstretched in welcome, their sculptured eyes empty of emotion as they stared at her. But even though the ghostly white men and women were hewn from lifeless rock, Jayce felt more warmth emanating from them than from her future husband. She cast a quick, sideways glance at Lord Reese Harrington. He was tall, taller than her father by six inches. His broad shoulders were four of her hand's breadth wide, tapering to a slim waist. His thighs were hidden by his black tunic, and his legs were concealed by black hose. Standing near the white statues, his black clothing made him appear like some dark angel. He was dressed more as if he were in mourning than celebrating marriage to his wife.

Wife. The term rocked her body with anxiety. Lord Reese Harrington's wife. Jayce studied his strong profile, the downward turn of his brooding lips, the slight flaring of his nostrils, his narrowed blue eyes. It should have warmed Jayce's heart that he had chosen her. But it did not. Something was wrong. He had shown her no more than polite disdain when they had met moments before. As a matter of fact, he had only inclined his head slightly at her in a mockery of a greeting before whirling and pre-

ceding her through the chapel doors. Not quite the greeting Jayce had hoped for. But what was it she had hoped
for? Did she want him to kiss her hand? To smile, perhaps?

Yes! She had wanted to know the man she was marrying
was more than the wealthy, powerful, womanizing lord she
had heard about. She wanted reassurance that once he
came to her bed, there would be no others. She wanted
reassurance that her life with him would be a happy one.
She dropped her gaze to her clasped hands. But that had
not happened.

Wealthy. Powerful. Womanizing. That wasn't all she had
heard about Lord Reese. The final piece of gossip that
had reached her ears was the most troubling. She had
heard he had sworn off marriage, vowing never to be troubled with a wife. She wondered what had changed his
mind. When her father had joyously come to her with Lord
Reese's acceptance of his marriage proposal and told her
he was giving his blessing to the union, well, she couldn't
say much. And now, standing before the eyes of God, she
could say even less.

Why had he chosen her?

"Get on with it!" Reese rumbled at the chaplain, his
voice thundering through the chapel like an angry curse.

Startled, it was all Jayce could do not to jump and flee
down the aisle. She turned and cast her father a wary gaze.
He sat in the first pew, the only man other than the chaplain and Reese in the chapel. She saw her father's clenched
jaw relax, then he gave her his most reassuring smile.

"Yes, yes," the chaplain stuttered. He dabbed the top
of his head with a cloth he held clutched in a trembling
hand. "Well, then, I pronounce you man and wife."

Jayce started to turn a cheerful smile on Reese, but he
seized her wrist, storming down the aisle. She had to run
to keep up with him. He flung the doors of the chapel
open with an angry shove and moved into the inner ward.

Jayce barely had time to notice as the peasants halted

their work to glance at them. A man just outside the black-smith's shop stopped his hammering to raise his eyes, his tool frozen in mid-strike. He shook his head and continued with his work. An alewife glanced out the window of the brewery, ignoring the amber liquid that had just splashed all over her arm. A small child scampered out of Reese's path, her large brown eyes wide with fear. For a fleeting instant, Jayce wondered why anyone was working at all; wasn't it a holiday when the lord married? But embarrassment welled up inside her, forcing the thought aside.

Reese pulled her into the great hall and up a set of spiraling stairs. "Where are we going?" she managed to choke out.

Reese didn't reply. He kicked open a door, and it banged loudly as it slapped against the wall. He all but hurled her into the dark room. The little bit of sunshine that shone into the room through its only window illuminated only a corner of it. Jayce gasped at the sight of a four-poster bed with an enormous mattress filling its wide frame. Rich, blood-red velvet curtains hung from the top, draping down the sides, cloaking the bed's heart in deeply shadowed mystery. It was a magnificent bed, the biggest she had ever seen.

She whirled to Reese to find him undoing the belt around his waist. Horrified, she looked around nervously, searching the room's dark shadows as if they could somehow hide her. She knew it was his right to take her . . . but she had hoped they could get to know each other. She had hoped he would give her time. Now, she knew he would give her nothing.

"Lord Reese . . ." she ventured, her voice sounding strangely hoarse in her own throat. "Perhaps we could—" Her voice died completely, strangled into silence, as he lifted his eyes to her.

The belt dropped from his fingers to fall to the floor.

Jayce's heart hammered her chest; she couldn't get

enough air. A flash of light caught her eye and her gaze locked on his right hand. She saw what she hadn't seen before. A small dagger glimmered in the shaft of sunlight. Reese approached her and she backed away quickly. What was he doing? Was he going to kill her? She held her hands out before her as if to ward him off but she knew the thought of fighting him was absurd. If he wanted her dead, who was there to offer any kind of resistance? She was no match against his strength.

The backs of her knees slammed into the bed frame, and she fell over onto the mattress. She quickly propped herself on her elbows, waiting for him to come forward and take what was now rightfully his. For a moment, she saw nothing but a wall of dark shadows before her. Her mouth felt dry, her hands moist and slick. Then, he emerged from the darkness like a ghost, stepping into the sunlight, the black shadows sliding from his shoulders as if he were shedding a dark cloak. For a moment, she thought she saw satisfaction in his blue eyes, but then grim resolve filled his face. He stretched his left arm out over her, his hand tight in a fist, and Jayce cringed back, pushing herself into the mattress. Was he going to strike her?

He held the dagger out over her.

Or was he really going to kill her? A scream welled up in her throat.

Reese pushed the sleeve of his tunic up over his elbow, baring his strong forearm. Then, he pressed the tip of the blade to his skin, slicing a small line down his arm.

Jayce half rose, crying out, "Don't!" But the blood trickled over his arm and dripped down onto the sheets beside her face. She lifted her astonished gaze from the dark red blood to meet his steely blue eyes. For a long moment, they locked gazes, hers filled with questions, his resolve.

He set the dagger down on a table beside the bed.

Jayce rose off the bed, grabbing a towel from the same table, and turned, reaching out to his arm. Reese snatched

the towel free from her grip as if her touch would be un-
bearable. He hurled the towel into the dark shadows of
the far corner.

Shocked and confused, Jayce watched Reese roll his
sleeve down to cover his cut. He stepped past her to the
bed and ripped the sheets from the mattress. He was angry
with her for something. But what had she done! They
hadn't exchanged two words! Without a second look at
her, he marched to the door, yanking it open.

Her father stood in the open doorway, turning surprised
eyes to Reese. Reese shoved the stained sheets into her
father's arms.

Jayce felt the heat suffuse her cheeks and for a moment
had to look away. Her father was making sure the marriage
had been consummated. She should say something. She
should tell her father the truth. She lifted her eyes in time
to see the look of surprise fade from her father's blue eyes
to be replaced by suspicion. His jaw tightened, and he
snapped his eyes to lock with his daughter's. "Jayce?" her
father queried.

She should tell him that Reese chose to shed his own
blood instead of her virgin's. She should tell her father
the truth. But then, she felt Reese's hot stare on her. The
impact of his gaze sent shivers down the length of her
body. He was her husband. Her loyalty was to him now.
"Yes, Father," she lied.

Her father's fist seemed to relax in the sheet, and he
whirled, taking it with him. "It is done," he proclaimed,
and marched down the hall.

Jayce watched him go, sadness creeping into her spirit,
putting a cloud of melancholy over what should have been
the most joyous day of her life. Her father had left her in
a strange castle. He had abandoned her to a man she
didn't know. And he hadn't even said good-bye.

Jayce tried to lift her chin as she turned her back on
her father, but her head felt heavy and it was a struggle

just to get her chin away from her neck. She knew she had to be strong to face her future. She wasn't a child anymore. She had been raised to be lady of a castle, to marry a man of her father's choosing. She was prepared for this.

As she turned from her previous life to face her new life, she locked eyes with a set of angry blue ones. What she wasn't prepared for was her husband.

He seized her wrist, hauling her back into the bedroom, and slammed the door shut.

Two

Reese faced Jayce's startled expression with a heart of stone. His anger was fierce, lashing him like a storm. It wasn't that she was ugly. He had seen far, far less pleasant faces to gaze upon. It wasn't her tiny body. Her shape was quite curvy, could make the stoutest of men desire to protect and shelter her.

It was that she was a liar. He shook her slender wrist. "Why did you lie to your father?" he demanded. He squeezed her wrist tightly as he gazed into her innocent blue eyes. Innocent. He scowled at the thought. She was anything but. No innocent could lie that easily, could make her false expressions so believable.

He could see confusion and apprehension in those large sapphire eyes. But no fear. Reese scowled. *No fear?* he thought. *Men greater than she have trembled before my wrath.*

She parted her lips and they moved. It was a moment before he realized she was speaking. "You are my husband," she said simply.

Husband. The word sent tremors of horror and anger up his spine. He tossed her arm aside and whirled, moving for the door.

"Wait!" Her voice sounded desperate.

He halted, straightening his shoulders.

"I—Have I done something to displease you?" she asked.

Reese whirled on her, his fists clenched tight, his eyes wide in absolute disbelief. "Displease me?" he echoed, hotly. "Yes! You married me!" With that, he stormed from the room, leaving her completely alone.

He didn't care if she fled the castle. He didn't care if he never saw her again! This entire marriage was a farce. He didn't care for the woman. He didn't love her. And he had vowed long ago that he would not marry unless he loved the girl.

His father had married his mother for her lands; not an uncommon union, but one empty of affection or devotion . . . or love. His father had married for fields of wheat, rolling hills, and cattle pastures. There had been no love between his parents. And Reese had seen the terrible consequences of that.

All his life he had heard pieces of the servants' gossip, whisperings of his mother's infidelity. He hadn't believed it. Didn't want to believe it. Any of it.

But when he was eight years old he witnessed something that forever left a scar on his heart. He had been walking through the castle's halls when he saw his mother in a dark alcove, laughing quietly. He heard the whispering of a man's low voice coming from the darkness and assumed it was his father. He started to run toward them, to tell them about the grand adventure he had just had exploring the guards' barracks, but then stopped abruptly as he saw his mother step from the alcove. She adjusted her dress, her hand resting casually on the chest of a man . . .

Reese pulled back into shadows of his own.

. . . a man who was not his father.

Reese's jaw and fists clenched at the bitter memory. The pain had long since receded, but the anger was still fresh in his mind. After that, stories circulated throughout the castle of her liaison with a baron. Rumor had it that there had been a wandering gypsy amongst her numerous lovers as well.

He had been too ashamed to mention any of this to his father. But his father eventually discovered his mother's treachery. Reese had been eleven years old when he had awoken to shouts and screams. He had raced from his room to find his mother, half-dressed, standing in the middle of the hallway. His father faced another man, a man clad only in leggings, their laces untied. Reese shook his head, remembering the disgust in his father's eyes as he turned to look at his wife. Then, his father turned his back on her and challenged the man to a duel. Reese remembered feeling a surge of pride for his father as he confronted the bastard who had bedded his wife under his very nose.

But his pride was very short-lived. His father died the next day on the field of honor. An honorless man.

Their mother had tried to raise Reese and his sister, Nicole, but she was not very good at it. Reese wanted nothing to do with her anyway, and he and Nicole ended up looking after each other. Their mother died in childbirth eight months after their father's death, leaving them a brother to raise as well as themselves.

At the age of twelve, Reese had become lord of the castle.

He had planned to take his time and find a woman he could love, a woman who could love him, a woman he was destined to marry. Not this.

As he stormed down the hallway, servants paused in their tasks to glance in his direction and shake their heads. Reese greeted their sympathetic looks with a guttural growl. He paused only long enough to snarl at one of the servants, "Have James sent to me."

He entered his den, slamming the door shut on prying eyes. He prowled the room for a moment, thinking of his sister. He slapped his palms on the ledge of the window, looking out over the darkening skies toward Lord Cullen's lands. So help Cullen if Nicole was not returned safely. He would storm Cullen's castle himself and find his sister.

Reese shook his head in disgust. Forced into marriage.

A loveless marriage. The thought made him sick. But he would not risk the life of his sister. Not for all the threats on the earth. Cullen had repeatedly petitioned him to marry his daughter, Jayce. After three refusals, Reese had put the matter out of his mind. A mistake he realized only too late.

Nicole vanished from the castle grounds a few days after his final refusal.

A missive arrived shortly after Nicole's disappearance, announcing that Lord Cullen would have Reese marry his daughter, or the health of Nicole would be at stake.

Why would a father do that to his daughter? Reese didn't know, and he didn't care. The deed was done. Nicole was his primary worry.

Suddenly, a knock sounded at the door. Reese granted entrance, and a slim, elderly man entered the room. His haughty demeanor gave him the aura of nobility instead of the head castle servant that he was. He wore a stylish sleeveless doublet of grayish purple and a white shirt beneath that. His leggings were black, and his leather shoes curled at the toes.

"James," Reese ordered the man, "have Rogue saddled. I'm riding out to the borders to see if I can see my sister coming."

"I suppose you'll sleep out there, too?" James wondered in a disdainful, sarcastic voice.

Reese would take that arrogance only from James. The man had been with him since he was a child. He respected James. And liked him immensely. "If I knew the road they were taking."

"If you don't mind my saying, sir," James said.

"That never stopped you before, why should it now?"

James's eyebrow rose slightly. "Your wife awaits you in your chambers."

Reese's eyes narrowed. "I don't have a wife."

James bowed contemptuously. "As you wish, m'lord," he answered stiffly, and departed the room.

As soon as Nicole is home safely, I will right this entire fiasco, Reese vowed silently. He picked up the note he had begun earlier and scanned the words, nodding in satisfaction.

Jayce changed into a simple gown of blue velvet and sat on the bed for a long time, wondering if Lord Reese would return. She tried to put her rebellious hair into a horned headdress, but without help she couldn't get the dark strands beneath the metal. So, she settled for a braid wrapped about her head. She wondered if she was supposed to wait for Reese in the room.

So much for a happy marriage, she thought. He hated her. It was apparent that her husband didn't wish to have anything to do with her. But why had he chosen her then? Why had he picked her to marry? She glanced around the room. It was dark; if it weren't for the candle burning on a table, she would not be able to see a thing. She picked the candle up and moved through the unfamiliar chambers.

Servants had arrived earlier to tidy up the room, making the bed, changing the water in the basin.

Jayce stared at the immaculate bed piled with warm furs and blankets. Thick red velvet curtains hung from the ceiling over it. She touched one of the curtains reverently, as if it would reveal the many secrets of her new husband if she coaxed it gently enough.

Lightning shot through the sky, making her jump. She dropped the candle and it hit the floor, rolling across its wooden surface. Ever since she was a child, storms had terrified her. Jayce's mother had died amidst a horrendous thunderstorm. She remembered kneeling at her mother's bedside, holding her cold, clammy hand while deafening claps of thunder attacked her ears and white-hot flashes of lightning assaulted her eyes. She remembered crying out for her mother and for the first time in her life not hearing her answer.

The large crack of thunder boomed in her ears, echoing in the room. Jayce glanced around the blackness, her eyes wide, her hands clutching at her elbows. Her father had stayed with her through storms such as these, but now he was gone.

Wind swirled in from the open window, billowing the red curtains around her like fingers stretching, reaching to grab her. She stepped away from the curtain and smacked her head on one of the bedposts.

The searching wind found the candlelight and extinguished it, plummeting the room into a terrifying darkness. For a moment, Jayce couldn't move, could barely get her breath. The blackness clawed at her heart, threatened to drag her down into its bottomless abyss.

The wind continued to whip through the room. The curtains of velvet, now gloved fingers of doom, encircled Jayce's flailing arms, her ankles. She fought her invisible foe, the feeling of entrapment embroiling her senses. She jerked free of its hold, pulling so hard she banged into the table, knocking it over. Glass shattered and she stepped away, blindly, until her back hit the cold stone wall.

Two bolts of lightning ripped jagged holes in the sky, bringing with them twin blasts of thunder.

Fear gripped her heart in a taloned fist, and Jayce slowly sank to the floor. She encircled her knees, rocking slightly back and forth. She whispered soothing words to herself, words her father had murmured to her.

She was terrified. Confused. She buried her face in the dress at her knees.

Abandoned.

Three

When Reese returned from the border patrols, he was soaked through to his skin and his mood was darker than when he had left. He had found no sign of Nicole, no indication that her return was imminent.

He returned to his chambers, a candelabra in his hand. Outside, a distant grumble of thunder faded quickly into silence. The damn storm was finally abating after raging for hours.

As he moved into the room, his foot skidded on a candle lying in the middle of the floor, throwing Reese backward. He almost fell, but caught his balance with a flail of his arm. He cursed. He'd have to speak to his servants about being so sloppy. He moved to the bed, but before he could partake of its luxurious comfort, his booted foot sloshed in a pool of water. His gaze slid to the window. A soft breeze rippled the now soggy curtains of his bed. He moved to the window and pulled the shutters closed, cursing the servants again. Then, he turned to the bed, this time managing to set his bottom on it. He sighed and reached out to place the candelabra on the table . . .

. . . and nearly dropped it when its base did not encounter the nightstand that should have been there.

"God's blood!" he murmured. "What now?" He rose to his feet and took a step toward the empty space where the table had once stood. His foot crunched on something, and he paused, realizing that it was broken glass beneath his boot sole. His foggy, tired mind instantly came alive. His hand moved for the hilt of his sword.

The image of the woman he had left alone in his bed-chamber rose in his mind. Jayce. Even if she was only a Harrington in name, she was still a Harrington. Had some-one dared to attack her? It would be an unforgivable insult if something had happened to her.

The bed was unslept in, the covers unmoved. He shifted his gaze to the closed window, then the broken glass. Had there been a struggle? His eyes frantically searched the darkness. Had she left the room? Forcibly?

"Jayce?" he called.

Silence answered him.

He took a step deeper into the darkness and the can-dlelight washed over the hem of a blue dress tucked away in a far corner of his room. Reese lurched forward, his fist clenched tight around the base of the candelabra, until the candlelight encircled Jayce in its glow. She sat slumped at the bottom of the wall, her head slouched over on her shoulder, her arms limp at her sides.

Rage engulfed him. *Has someone dared to harm her?* he wondered incredulously as he knelt at her side. Without taking his eyes from her, he set the candelabra down on the floor. A stray strand of brown hair fell over her cheek, its darkness contrasting sharply against her pale skin.

Then, something tickled the inside of his stomach. Something he had never felt before and refused to ac-knowledge. He reached out and touched her hand. It was like ice. He engulfed her small fingers with his large hand, trying to warm them. Her fingers twitched, then curved around his, and he knew she was alive.

He scooped her into his arms, and she stirred, tossing her head, calling, "Father?" Reese gently placed her in his bed, noticing how the large bed made her appear tinier than she was. He pulled away from her, but her arms reached out, encircling his neck. Reese froze, unsure of what to do. He could pry her arms from his neck. He could settle next to this stranger and hold her. Or he could search her body for wounds.

"The storm," she whimpered.

Reese felt her body tremble. A flash of lightning lit the night sky as if summoned by her words. He leaned close to her to duck beneath her arms. When his cheek brushed hers, he was startled to find the moisture there.

Guilt twisted his gut. Had he caused her this anguish? He ripped free of her hold, telling himself it didn't matter. She was not his concern.

Her head fell back against the pillows, her cold hands leaving a path of ice along his cheek and neck. Instinctively, his hands skimmed her body, searching for wounds. But it wasn't wounds he found. It was a shapely, strong figure. His hands fluttered over her slender neck, down her curvy sides, across her flat stomach and down her slender legs. Searching for blood, he told himself. In the dark, he could not see if she was hurt. His fingers moved back up over her legs. They were so smooth and sleek. He wondered what they looked like.

Reese had to jerk himself from her, pulling his hands away from her body as if she had suddenly burst into flames. His own body had responded instantly to touching her. Disgusted at his primeval response, he told himself it was nothing but the wanting of a woman. He could sate his desires on a willing servant wench later. Reese pulled the cover up over her body, concealing it beneath the fur, hiding it from his hungry gaze.

Jayce groaned and tossed her head, and he shifted his eyes to her face. He could see the moisture on her cheeks as her tears glistened in the candlelight. He stepped closer and pressed a palm against her skin, fearing she was feverish. Her skin was cool against his hand. At his touch, she seemed to quiet and settle into the bed. Reese couldn't help cupping her gentle chin and stroking her cheek with his thumb.

Her eyes fluttered and opened slightly, revealing a teasing glimpse of her deep blue orbs. In the candlelight, he was amazed at how startlingly blue they were, deeper than the richest sapphire he had ever seen. He thought he heard her sigh before she closed them again. The flickering light from the candelabra gave her cheeks a healthy glow, the vibrancy of life. Where before her skin had been so cold and pale, it seemed that his touch had roused the vigor inside her. He was startled at the transformation, startled and somewhat delighted. A spark lit in his chest, warming his entire being.

I must be so tired I am hallucinating, he thought. *No woman could possibly be that beautiful. In the light of day, her beauty, her vibrancy, will fade, and she will be just like the rest of the women. A small, weak thing that needs protection. My protection.*

Exhaustion finally claimed him, and he stumbled back into a chair near the wall. He fell asleep quickly, a twisted resolve settling over his dark features.

A warmth touched her cheeks, and Jayce instinctively turned her face toward it. But when a painfully bright light lit her closed lids, she groaned and turned away, drawing the blanket over her head.

A clucking noise greeted her movement. "You can't lounge around in bed all day, m'lady," a male voice said.

At first she thought it was her father, but she knew that this couldn't be. Her father would let her sleep. Then, she remembered where she was.

And who she was.

Instantly, Jayce jerked the sheets from her head and sat up, prepared to meet her husband's disapproving gaze.

Instead, her eyes came to rest on a thin man bent over near the fallen table, carefully collecting the broken glass.

She flung the blankets from her and swung her legs out of the bed. What would Reese think of her if she slept all day? She was lady of the castle now, and needed to rise with the sun. She sighed slightly. She was used to staying up late and sleeping late. She would have to remedy that.

She froze as her feet touched the floor. How had she gotten into bed? She remembered the storm and trembled slightly. She also recalled a gentle touch, someone tucking her into bed.

The man cleared his throat and she turned to him. "My name is James, m'lady," he introduced. "I was instructed to aid you."

"By Lord Reese?"

"No," James answered standing before her. "By Lady Nicole."

Four

"I can't believe you left her there. Alone!"

Reese watched Nicole pace the room. Her blond hair shimmered hotly in the sun's rays with each angry turn. Her brows angled down over sparkling blue eyes, her tiny fists clenched with rage. His sister had finally been returned safely, as Cullen had promised, and Reese felt relief despite her fury at his treatment of the girl he had wed.

"No one to help her. No one to tend her needs!" Nicole whirled, pinning Reese with an angry glare. "Do you want her to think her husband is a brute?!"

Reese's eyes narrowed slightly. "I don't care what she thinks of me."

Nicole waved a small, impatient hand at him, as if she were waving away an annoying gnat. "You are a brute. How can you treat her like that?"

"How can you ask me that?" Reese roared, straightening to his intimidating height. "You were the one kidnapped! You were the reason I was forced to wed the girl! If it wasn't for you—!"

"Don't even start with me, Reese Harrington," Nicole retorted in a motherly tone, marching up to him. She was a full head shorter than he was, but managed to match him glare for glare. "I'm sure it pricked your manly pride when I was spirited away from beneath your nose."

Reese ground his teeth. "And now I have another help-less female to watch and to protect!"

"Not just another female, Reese. Your wife!" Nicole jabbed her finger into Reese's chest.

"I didn't ask her to be my wife! I don't want her to be my wife! For all I know she planned your kidnapping with her father and—"

The sound of someone clearing his throat loudly made them turn to the arched entranceway to the room. James stood slightly behind Jayce, his disinterested gaze focused somewhere in the middle of the room.

Nicole dropped her mouth slightly, her cheeks flaming.

Reese stood with his fists clenched, staring at Jayce's large blue eyes. He saw the hurt flash in those eyes for a moment and thought that surely she was going to burst into tears, forcing him to comfort her.

But for a long moment, Jayce didn't move, meeting his gaze with a pained resolve. Then, with all the dignity of a queen, she slowly turned and left the room.

Reese and Nicole stood silently in the room, staring after the woman. Reese knew he should go after . . . and took a step to do just that, then stopped suddenly. What would he do when he caught up to her? Tell her his words were the truth?

Nicole whirled on her brother, her blue eyes full of dis-gust and anger. "I pity her for being married to you," she said, and raced out the door after Jayce.

Reese cursed silently and ran a hand through his thick locks. He lifted his gaze to find James standing in the door-way, staring at him. "What are you looking at?" Reese snapped.

James's eyebrow rose slightly before Reese hurried past him, out of the room.

* * *

Nicole knocked at the door. When there was no answer,

she swept into the room like a rainbow on a stormy day. Jayce was sitting at the window, staring out over the pastures. She barely looked up, and Nicole noticed the way her shoulders sagged slightly. Her heart ached for the woman. "I'm Reese's sister, Nicole," she said. "I am terribly sorry about the way my brother has been treating you." Unnerved by Jayce's silence, Nicole walked to stand beside her, peering out the window, following her gaze. A black horse, as black as the darkest night, ran wildly within a fenced-off area, snorting like some possessed demon. Nicole returned her gaze to Jayce. "I do so hope you like your stay here," Nicole said earnestly. "I'd like to be friends."

Jayce turned to her, and Nicole was pleased to see that she was a beautiful woman. Her eyes were startlingly blue and reminded Nicole of the richest sapphires she had ever seen. She knew they would help sway her brother to take her as his rightful wife. He had a fondness for blue eyes.

"Is it true that my father kidnapped you?" Jayce wondered.

Surprised, it was all Nicole could do to keep her mouth from falling open. "Well, yes," she finally answered, looking away from her probing gaze. "But he treated me civilly."

Jayce turned to stare out the window. Nicole raised her eyes in time to notice a troubled furrow on Jayce's once-smooth brow. "Do you know why he did it?" Jayce asked.

"His demand was for Reese to marry you," Nicole answered.

Jayce dropped her gaze to her lap. "It makes no sense," she murmured.

"What doesn't?" Nicole wondered.

Jayce turned confused eyes to Nicole. "Why he lied to me. Father told me Reese wanted to marry me."

Nicole patted her shoulder, comfortingly. "It doesn't matter. What's done is done."

"How can I blame Reese for despising me?"

"He doesn't despise you," Nicole said. When Jayce turned disbelieving eyes to her, she smiled glumly and shrugged. "He just doesn't know you."

"And if he has his way, he never will."

Suddenly, two female servants entered the room. They began racing about, collecting the sparse items that belonged to Jayce. A feeling of dread began to prickle the back of Nicole's neck.

Jayce slowly rose from her seat at the window, confusion etched in her furrowed brow.

"What's going on?" Nicole demanded of the servants. "What are you doing?"

One of the women stopped before her. "Lord Reese has instructed us to gather the lady's belongings."

Jayce cast Nicole a look of dread.

Reese was tossing his new wife out, returning her to her father. Nicole grabbed Jayce's hand, squeezing it tightly, reassuringly. "Reese is not that cold. There must be some misunderstanding."

"There is no misunderstanding," a voice thundered from the doorway.

Both women turned to find Reese standing there. He filled the doorway, his dark, hulking body blocking out the torchlight from the hallway behind him.

Jayce stepped forward, turning Reese's cold, hard gaze from his sister to focus on her. "You have every right to turn me out," she murmured. Then she raised her chin and added, "I would expect that from a coward."

His teeth clenched, and he pushed himself from the wall, approaching her like a raging storm cloud. "I have been called many things, lady, but never coward."

Jayce stood her ground. "Then, perhaps it's time someone told you the truth. If you were brave, you would have faced me to tell me you were throwing me out instead of having servants tell me."

A muscle in his cheek twitched and his eyes burned with

outrage. Nicole could feel the anger emanating from his body like the heat from a hearth. She watched Jayce match his rage and was proud of her new friend.

"You are not the only one who has been duped," Jayce proclaimed, her voice gaining strength. "I could have had my choice of husbands who would have been willing, nay, even eager to claim me as wife. And yet, I am saddled with a boorish, unchivalrous lout capable of no feelings for any-one but himself. Well, Reese Harrington, I wouldn't want you as my husband if you were the last man in all En-gland!" With that, Jayce pushed past him, out into the hall.

Nicole cast a surprised glance at Reese, which trans-formed into a victorious grin. She whirled and raced into the hallway after her brother's new wife. "Jayce!"

Jayce didn't stop at Nicole's cry. She stormed down the hallway, her fists clenched.

Nicole caught up to her and seized her wrist, bringing her to a halt. "Jayce!" She smiled. "You were wonderful! I couldn't have done better—" Her words died on her lips as her gentle eyes focused on Jayce's face. "Oh, my dear," she murmured, pulling her into an embrace.

Only then did Jayce realize that her cheeks were wet with tears, and her trembling wasn't from anger, but from misery.

Five

The great hall was silent that night. Where there was once raucous laughter and loud music, there was now only muted conversation and the plucking of a few harp strings. Many of the peasants and servants cast Reese tentative looks as he sat in his chair on the raised platform that filled the west end of the room.

Reese met the stares with a harsh glare. He refused to feel guilty about returning Jayce to her father. He did not love her.

Still, he had to admire her courage and conviction. No woman had ever stood up to him, spoken to him in such a manner. He was angry, and he knew he should have been insulted. But he wasn't. Instead, he found himself admiring Jayce. Most other women would have slunk away sobbing to their fathers without saying two words to him. But not Jayce. Her eyes had sparked like the hottest part of a flame.

She was right. And that thought angered him the most. He had only thought of himself; not once had he considered how she felt. He hadn't even attempted to speak to her. And because of these damnable guilty feelings, he had allowed Nicole to invite Jayce to dine in the great hall before she left in the morning. Jayce sat on the opposite side of Nicole, only two seats away from him. He could feel her presence there; tingles tickled the nape of his neck.

A movement at the far end of the great hall caught Reese's attention, and he swiveled his head to see Dylan McNaught approaching with the usual spring to his step. Dylan was an eager, innocent, naive young man who had been recently knighted. Reese had hired him instantly, seeing in him the excitement and youth he had missed. Dylan had worked for Reese for a year now and they had become friends. His blond hair and large, boyish, brown eyes promised that in time he would break many women's hearts. He marched up the center aisle, heading directly for the head table.

Reese watched as he greeted Nicole with a bright smile. "It's good to see you safe, m'lady," Dylan said with a slight bow.

Nicole returned the smile. "Thank you, Dylan," she answered.

Reese started to rise, but froze as Dylan turned his eyes to Jayce.

"You must be Lady Jayce," he said, reaching across the table to take her hand. He bent and pressed a kiss to her knuckles. "I am honored to have you as my lady."

"Dylan," Reese called, trying to correct him.

But Dylan's eyes alighted on Jayce's face, and dread pierced Reese's stomach. He opened his mouth to stop Dylan's words, but knew he wouldn't be quick enough.

"I vow with all my heart to protect you and serve you as I do Lord Reese," Dylan promised Jayce, a smile crossing his lips.

Reese groaned and sank back into his chair, shaking his head. Dylan's grandiose sense of honor was going to cause him untold trouble. Dylan was not a man to break his vow easily. But this was one vow that would have to be broken.

Dylan turned to him. "Lord Reese!" He moved to stand before him. "The border lands are secure. I've—"

"Dylan," Reese said, lowering his voice, "we can discuss business after the meal."

"Of course," Dylan replied, rounding the table.

In the face of Dylan's youthful vibrancy, Reese suddenly felt old and tired.

It was late when Reese finally meandered up to his room. He paused before the door to his chambers. Jayce was in there. He couldn't bring himself to kick her out of his room, too. He returned to the great hall, moving toward the hearth. It was quiet; all the servants had finished their tasks and were preparing for bed. He stopped in the middle of the room, finally noticing the room's sole occupant.

Jayce stood before the hearth, her hands folded before her, staring into the fire. Reese walked toward her. He stopped two strides behind her as a waft of roses met his nostrils. He knew he should leave, but then he suddenly found himself speaking. "I'm sorry about all this," he said quietly.

He watched as she drew herself up. "So am I," she finally answered in a curt voice.

The firelight shimmered in her luxurious brown hair. "You're a lovely woman. I'm sure your father will have no trouble finding you another husband," Reese said, trying to be reassuring.

She turned to him then, and her blue eyes sparkled like liquid crystal. "Apparently not lovely enough," she answered, and moved by him.

Reese cringed slightly at her words. She was more lovely than he had imagined. He reached out and clasped her arm, halting her movement. A shock scorched through him at the touch. "You could have been Helen of Troy. It wouldn't matter. I will not be forced into marriage." He held her arm a moment longer before releasing her.

Jayce didn't say a word. Reese only heard the soft padding of her slippered feet as she walked out the door, out of his life.

* * *

Reese could not sleep that night, and the next day came all too soon. As the sun climbed into the morning sky, he stood at the window, looking down into the courtyard. He blinked away the sun's glare and watched as Dylan helped Jayce mount her horse. She would be escorted back to her father by the young knight and another of Reese's most trusted men. Dylan swung himself up onto his horse, reining the prancing animal in to cast an angry glare up toward Reese.

Reese watched Jayce's dark hair wave in the breeze as if bidding him a farewell.

Dylan was not talking to him.

Something inside Reese tugged at his heart. He would never know what it felt like to touch her hair.

Nicole was not speaking to him now, either.

He would never know what kind of passion her spirit hid.

Reese pounded the window frame with a clenched fist. If things had only been different. He might have courted Jayce. He might have actually fallen in love with her. But with the anger and resentment that burned in his heart, the poor girl had no chance. *This is the best way,* he told himself. *The only way. I will find the woman I am fated to marry. I will find the woman I am destined to love.*

The three horses started forward, moving beneath the portcullis. Reese watched them go until Jayce was just a speck on the horizon. He sighed slightly as if a weight had been removed from his shoulders. Then how come he felt as if he had lost something?

"M'lord."

Reese turned to see James standing in the doorway. He held out a piece of rolled parchment, sealed with a stamp of wax.

"This just arrived," James told him.

Reese snatched the missive from James's hand, inspecting the seal. It was the seal of a physician. Reese ripped it open, his eyes scanning the words. A scowl crept over his face. He clenched his jaw, dragging his gaze from the parchment to lock eyes with James.

"Stop her," Reese ordered. "Don't let her leave."

"I'm afraid she's already gone, sir," James replied.

"Then saddle me a horse. I'm going after her."

Six

Jayce stared down at the pommel she gripped so tightly that it made her knuckles turn white. She should have been worrying about how she was going to explain to her father that she had lied to him, that she was still a virgin, that her marriage had not been consummated. Instead, all she could think about was the feeling of betrayal that stabbed her heart. Why had Reese turned her out without giving her a chance to prove herself? He had almost been repentant at the hearth the previous night, almost civil. Almost a man she could call husband. She had begun to hope that maybe he wouldn't return her to her father, that they could try for a life together. But this was not to be.

There was no reason she should feel hurt at his cold dismissal. Reese had never chosen her. He had been tricked, forced into marrying her. Yet, even knowing this, the pain of his rejection would not fade.

She knew she should forget him. She would never see him again. But he haunted her thoughts like a vengeful apparition.

Suddenly, her horse began to slow. She turned her gaze to the two guards before her. They were straining in their saddles, their stares focused on something behind her. She turned her head to see a horse riding toward her down the road, a small cloud of dust trailing behind the animal.

As the rider approached, Jayce saw his dark hair rippling

behind him like a banner, announcing his arrival. He was bent low over the pommel, driving the animal hard to overtake them.

She knew instinctively who it was. Unwillingly, her heart beat faster, pounding in her chest with hope.

Reese reined in his horse beside Dylan, announcing with an explosive pant, "She's returning to the castle."

Jayce saw the satisfied grin that curled Dylan's lips, but when she turned gladdened eyes to Reese, he would not meet her gaze. Slowly, her happiness faded and apprehension rose inside her. "Why?" she demanded, finally drawing his gaze. "Have you decided to call me wife?"

"No," he replied, and offered no further explanation.

Jayce's scowl deepened. "Then why the sudden change of mind?" she inquired, refusing to budge her animal until he gave her a reason.

Reese's eyes narrowed slightly before he turned his face toward the breeze.

Anger flared in Jayce. He was toying with her, playing some sort of game. "Are you convinced I'm not a part of my father's plot to gain a husband?"

The soft ripples of air weaved their way through his dark hair like fingers. His stubborn jaw was set.

"Or have you suddenly developed an unselfish streak?" she asked spitefully.

He slowly turned his ice-blue eyes to her. "Your father is dead," he answered. "Wanted or not, you are my responsibility."

Dead? For a moment she thought he was lying to her. Then, Reese held out a piece of crumpled parchment to her. With numb fingers she took the paper, her dazed eyes drawn to the scroll. It was a missive from her father's doctor. Her fingers trembled as she read its contents. Her father had been sick for months, and he had finally succumbed to death.

Jayce read the note three times. Why hadn't she known?

Her father had kept his distance from her during the past months, but she had no idea he was harboring a deadly illness. Distantly, she heard Reese instructing the guards to head back to Castle Harrington.

Father is dead.

A numbness slowly crept through her body. *Father is dead,* her groggy mind repeated. *How can this be?* She heard her name called and numbly turned her head toward the voice. Reese was staring at her, but she could read nothing in his expression.

"Are you all right?" Reese was asking.

Jayce felt herself trembling and fought to keep her composure. *Alone.* The word exploded in her mind. "Yes," she whispered, and didn't know if she succeeded in controlling her weak voice.

She watched Reese turn his back on her. The shaking in her body grew until she could barely hold the reins.

Father is dead, her mind repeated. She found that she still held the parchment in her hands. The words blurred together, and Jayce swiped at her eyes. *I can't let Reese see my weakness,* she told herself firmly. And even as she said this to herself, a lump rose in her throat.

An overwhelming urge to get away filled her. But where could she go? Who would take her in? She lifted her gaze to search the landscape, as if someone would materialize there and offer her refuge. Instead, her gaze was drawn to Reese, who wavered before her tearing eyes. He sat stoically in his saddle, staring at her.

I can't let him see my pain, she thought. *I don't want to see his scorn.* She spurred the horse forward, past him, desperately blinking back her tears. If she could just ride in front of him, she was sure she could keep a straight back. She was sure that when the tears came she could keep her shoulders from shaking.

The horse walked forward, jarring loose a tear. It slid over her cheek and down her chin. With any luck, he had missed it. Jayce's horse moved past his, and she knew she had made it.

But then Reese's hand shot forward to capture the reins of her horse, halting her animal's progress. Jayce didn't turn her gaze to him; she didn't move, willing her tears to stop, willing him to release her.

"Jayce," he said, and his voice was full of compassion.

It was agony. She bowed her head, squeezing her eyes closed on the tears that now flowed freely over her cheeks. She couldn't turn to him. She couldn't be fooled by his gentle tone when she knew so well that he wanted nothing to do with her.

Then, his arm was beneath her shoulders, drawing her from her horse, pulling her onto his lap. She resisted at first, fighting the comfort his arms offered. Reese pulled her tight against his chest, her weak struggles no match for his strong arms.

"It's all right," he whispered, his words spoken into the hair at the top of her head.

Jayce buried her face in his strong chest, sobbing. His arms around her were warm and soothing. She sobbed most of the way back to his castle, and when there was nothing left but exhaustion, she succumbed to a deep sleep.

Her head pounded and Jayce eased her eyes open from the dark comfort of sleep. Her gaze swept her surroundings and she recognized where she was immediately. Reese's room. Slowly, she sat up. She was in his bed, tucked beneath luxuriously warm blankets.

She was alone. She swung her feet from the bed and had no sooner set them on the cold floor when the door opened and Nicole entered the room, a basin of water in her hands.

Nicole's eyes alighted on Jayce, and a smile lit her face. "Welcome back," she greeted.

Jayce winced and rubbed her head.

Nicole sat on the bed beside Jayce. "I'm sorry about your father," she said earnestly. "Truly I am."

Jayce shook her head, scowling. "He didn't seem sick," she mused. "I don't know what happened."

Nicole patted her hand. "He probably didn't want you to become alarmed." Nicole rose and paced to the basin which rested on a table. "So he hid whatever illness he had." She dipped a rag into the water, returned to the bed, and wiped off Jayce's face.

"Please," Jayce said, gently removing the rag from her hands. She stared down at it for a long moment. "Did Reese bring me back here?"

"Yes," Nicole answered. "He carried you into the castle and tucked you in by himself."

Jayce turned surprised eyes to Nicole. "Really?" Nicole nodded her head, her beautiful blond hair bouncing. "Where is he now?"

"In the great hall, breaking his fast."

Jayce remembered Reese's gentle touch and his comforting warmth. She could almost feel his arms around her, holding her tight. "Do you think Reese would mind if I joined him?" Jayce wondered.

Nicole appeared troubled for a moment, then said, "No. I don't think he'd mind at all."

Seven

Jayce entered the great hall with Nicole beside her. Reese was sitting in the middle of the raised table, engaged in animated conversation. Her heart faltered, as did her steps, when he turned his gaze to her. His penetrating blue eyes seared her to the spot. She barely noticed the man with whom he had been speaking lift his dark eyes to her.

Reese stood and moved down the center aisle as she approached. He was coming to meet her! Had something changed inside him? Was he truly going to see her differently? A grin tugged at Jayce's lips; anticipation burned through her veins.

But Jayce noticed with dismay that his large steps and agitated gait were not those of a happy man. With each step that brought him nearer, Jayce felt an uneasiness spread through her. Her hopes fell as he stopped just before her. His jaw was clenched, his blue eyes hard with anger. His gaze swept past her to Nicole. "Is this your idea?" he demanded.

"Your wife wished to dine with you," Nicole answered.

Jayce placed a gentle hand on Nicole's arm and stepped forward to face Reese. "It was *my* idea. I thought . . ." Her voice faded as Reese's blue eyes snapped back to meet her gaze. They were cold and dark, emotionless. She felt tears of disappointment sting her eyes. Surely she had not imagined his arms around her last night, his tender words in her ear.

"I will have your meal brought to you in my room," he told her. "Now return there at once." With that, Reese whirled, presenting her with his back, and moved toward the head table.

Jayce stared slack-jawed at his retreating back. The peasants near her murmured at his curt dismissal of her. The disappointment and crushed feelings were suddenly buried beneath a whirlwind of fierce anger. What right did he have to treat her like . . . like a common slave?

Jayce's fists clenched tight, and she marched forward after his retreating form. She would not obey him like some humble lapdog!

He stopped just before the head table and Jayce almost ran into his back. She stepped around him, forcing a false smile to her lips. But she couldn't quite unclench her teeth as she said, "Thank you for inviting me to dine at your table, m'lord." She added a mock curtsy for insult and took a seat beside the dark man who sat beside Reese.

She felt Reese's eyes at her back like daggers, but didn't turn. Finally, Reese too, took his seat.

A healthy serving of venison was placed on a trencher before her.

The young man seated to Jayce's left eyed her with curiosity. Jayce beamed him a smile, then took in his wild dark hair and beard, his savage brown eyes. His perusal of her unnerved Jayce, and she pulled away from him.

"Is this the wife you've kept hidden from me?" the dark man asked.

Reese grunted, taking a large bite of venison.

"No," she answered, still stinging from Reese's curt dismissal. "I am not a wife. No husband would treat his wife the way Lord Reese has."

The dark man scowled. "But were you not married in

the chapel? Was it not your virginal blood that stained the sheets?"

Jayce opened her mouth to reply, to deny it all. She cast a quick glance at Reese, looking at his arm, thinking of the cut that lay beneath his tunic. Who would believe that Reese had cut himself to avoid bedding her? She dropped her gaze to her clasped hands.

"Tell us, why did you force yourself on Reese?" he challenged. "How dare you so disgrace the Harrington family name?"

Jayce felt embarrassment rise into her cheeks. "I had no part in Nicole's kidnapping."

"Are we to believe that?" he wondered.

"Morse, don't bully her," Nicole reprimanded, taking a seat beside Jayce.

Morse threw back his head and chortles of glee issued from his mouth. "The victimized Lady Nicole is the only one to come to your rescue!" He laughed again.

Jayce didn't dare cast a glance at Reese. She knew his glowering visage and stern disapproval would shatter her already shaky resolve.

"Why throw yourself at a man? Desperate? Hungry for sex?"

"I didn't know," Jayce repeated, bowing her head, taking the comments one by one, outwardly showing no sign of distress, but inwardly dying with each lash of his tongue. Was this what Reese thought of her? Could she blame him if he did?

Reese wasn't going to defend her. No one was. It was what they all believed. It was what Reese believed.

"And now, why stay? Unloved. *Unwanted.*"

"Morse," Reese growled a warning.

But Jayce barely heard him. Her hands were shaking, and she clenched them so tight that her fingers turned purple.

Alone. Abandoned.

"Take back every single rude remark, sir. You have offended the lady."

Jayce looked up to find Sir Dylan standing before the
table, his hand at his sword. Relief, gratitude, and something akin to pride swept through her.

Morse leaned back in his chair, his dark eyes summing
Dylan up in a sweeping glance. "But everything I've said is
true."

Dylan's jaw clenched. "She is lady of this castle and Lord
Reese's rightful wife."

"Then why doesn't he defend her?"

Dylan cast Reese an angry glance, then turned his hot,
youthful eyes onto the dark man. "Take back your words."

One side of Morse's mouth curved into a grin. "I don't
think so," he said.

Anxiety tightened Jayce's stomach.

"Then, I challenge you to a joust for Lady Jayce's
honor," Dylan said.

Reese had come half out of his chair, but froze when
the fighting words came from Dylan's mouth.

The great hall reverberated with the challenge as the
announcement was repeated throughout the room.

Suddenly, Morse erupted in laughter, a rich rolling guf-
faw that trilled from his throat like a trumpet. As abruptly
as it started, it ended. He leaned forward, his hands
splayed over the table. "It would be my pleasure," he said.

Jayce knew that Morse would defeat Dylan. Dylan's hot-
headedness would be his downfall. She wanted to tell Dylan he didn't have to defend her, but she didn't want to
embarrass the young knight.

Reese was the one who should be challenging the man.

Jayce swung her gaze to Reese. He stood, staring at Dylan
with hard, unflinching eyes. But he didn't say a word. Finally, he whirled and left the great hall.

Morse's laughter echoed through the room, following
Reese's footsteps.

Jayce glanced at Nicole, who didn't move. The color had drained from her face as she stared at Dylan. Then, Jayce stood and raced after Reese. She turned a corner in the hallway. "Reese!" she called.

He halted, his back as straight as a board. He didn't turn to her, and Jayce clenched her fists, refusing to budge from her spot.

"You can't let Dylan fight him," she announced to his back.

Reese turned slowly, his blue eyes flashing with anger.

"You're lord of this castle," she snapped. "It's your duty to protect those beneath you. Dylan—"

"Is young and foolish. You've won him over with your charm, and now it will cost him his honor and his dignity."

"Then stop him," Jayce ordered. "Order him not to fight."

"I can't," Reese replied, moving toward her. "He would be humiliated and disgraced. You're the one that has to do it. Tell him your honor is not worth fighting for."

Jayce would do it in an instant, if she wasn't so afraid of hurting the young knight's pride. But was his pride worth his life? Many knights had been wounded in such challenges and some even killed.

Dylan was hotheaded and brash, and she admired him very much for coming to her defense, but she also knew she could not watch him face Morse.

"She will do no such thing," a voice announced from behind her.

Jayce whirled to see Dylan storming from the great hall, his eyes blazing with anger. He marched past her toward Reese. He had to look up to stare Reese in the eye, but Dylan did so unflinchingly.

"Lady Jayce's honor is worth all the gold in the land. It is worth all the stars in the sky. And it is most certainly worth my honor and my life," Dylan told him.

Jayce's pride rose to soaring heights, but was deflated

by her conscience. She opened her mouth to speak, but Dylan continued.

"But I have no intention of dying. I will defeat Lord Morse in battle and uphold Lady Jayce's virtue."

And the way he said it, with vibrancy and conviction, almost made Jayce believe it. His confidence was contagious and warmed Jayce's heart. After all, he had been the only one to come to her defense. Not even Reese had challenged Morse. She turned her stare to her husband.

His jaw was clenched tight, his blue eyes narrowed. His gaze slid from Dylan's to meet Jayce's. For a long, heart-stopping moment, there was cold resolve in his eyes. He would say nothing, could not say anything to persuade the devoted knight to call off the joust.

"Sir Dylan," Jayce called, knowing that if she couldn't convince him to stop the joust, no one could. When he turned his brown eyes to her, his gaze softened and a smile brimmed on his lips. "I appreciate all you've done for me."

"I would do so much more," he vowed. "I would walk to the ends of the earth. I would brave—"

Jayce grinned. "I'm flattered. But this joust is . . ." She sought the right words, the proper way to tell Dylan he had no chance. But when she saw the smile fade from the young knight's lips, she faltered. ". . . it is simply that I . . ." Jayce floundered, watching a crestfallen look darken Dylan's face. "It's not you. It's the joust. It is . . ." She glanced at Reese helplessly, imploringly.

"It's the blood," Reese supplied. "Her fair senses could not tolerate a drop of your blood being shed."

"Yes!" Jayce exclaimed. "I find blood repulsive. Especially when it comes from one of my favored knights."

The smile returned in full force to Dylan's lips. "My lady flatters me now. I promise that not a drop of my blood shall I spill to the earth to upset you." Dylan reached for Jayce's hand and pressed a kiss to her knuckles.

Jayce glanced at Reese over Dylan's head to find him

rolling his eyes. Jayce swallowed, and desperately blurted, "No, Sir Dylan. I want you to call off the joust."

Dylan froze over her knuckles for a long moment.

Jayce's insides trembled. If a direct order did not work, she knew there would be no way to stop the joust. He straightened stiffly to face her. "My honor is not worth your life," Jayce said, and saw the disappointment cloud his eyes.

"I'm sorry, m'lady," Dylan finally replied. "I will not call off the joust." He cast an accusing glance at Reese. "Since there is no one man enough to defend you, then I will face Lord Morse, even if I do not have your favor." He turned and walked rigidly away.

Jayce lifted her hand to stop him, opened her mouth to call to him, to explain that he had her favor, her gratitude, but Reese grabbed her outstretched hand, halting her.

"Give him time to think," he said. "He may yet call off the joust."

Jayce savagely pulled her hand free of his hold and turned furious eyes to him. "This was your idea! Now I have insulted the only man who was brave enough to come to my defense, brave enough to defend my honor. Even braver than my own husband."

Reese drew himself up to his full height, his eyes flashing like lightning. "I am not your husband."

"Because we did not consummate the marriage? You made a vow before God!"

"I was protecting my sister."

"And now Dylan is protecting me," Jayce retorted, tears stinging her eyes. "And he might die because you're too cowardly to defend me."

Reese grabbed her shoulders, his fingers curved like claws, his lips drawn back in a feral snarl. "I'm not a coward."

"Then why won't you face Morse? Why won't you protect me?"

"I will not fight my brother."

Eight

Reese watched the dance of emotions play across Jayce's face. The shock, then understanding, and finally acceptance. But with the acceptance came something else . . . hurt and resignation. He watched those deep blue eyes shimmer like the sea before she turned her head away. "I don't know what else to do," she whispered in an agonized voice that called to Reese's heart for help, for guidance, for protection.

Reese dropped his hands stiffly to his sides, releasing her shoulders. "This is your problem," he proclaimed, suddenly angry that she had somehow drawn him into this situation, furious that she had made him feel guilty when he was nothing of the sort. He turned his back on her and marched down the hallway. He didn't know how to help her! He didn't know how to stop the joust, even if it could be stopped, without humiliating Dylan and infuriating his brother.

He cursed silently as he kicked open the door to his temporary room. He swept into his chamber and began pacing from one end of the room to the other, his mutterings sounding like the grumblings of a caged lion. He didn't have the solution! He didn't have all the answers.

Why did Morse have to return now? His brother had been gone for three years, traveling through England, working as a mercenary. Reese had been angry enough when he had left, positive that he would never see Morse again. After all, what did the boy know of warfare?

Before Morse left, Reese had tried everything to draw him into the close circle that he and Nicole had formed, but somehow it had never worked. He had even offered Morse a parcel of Harrington land to rule as his own. But somehow that offer had insulted Morse greatly. He left Castle Harrington only days later. Morse had even refused Reese's generous gift of coin to help him start off.

There had not been a more inopportune time for Morse's return than now, before he had settled this situation with Jayce.

Reese raked his hands through his hair and whirled to face the setting sun, his thoughts turning to Jayce. She didn't want Dylan to fight any more than he did. *Then why couldn't she have listened to me?* Reese wondered. *Why couldn't she have stayed in her room?*

"Women," he growled.

Whatever the case, Reese knew he could not interfere in the battle. He had no desire to face his brother in a joust.

There came a tentative knock at the door. "Reese."

Reese lifted his head to find Morse entering. His brother had been but a boy when he left the castle three years ago. But now he was a man. A surge of pride filled Reese. His brother would make a fine lord. Then, his eyes met the dark orbs of his brother, so different from his and Nicole's blue ones. They were narrowed in fierce fury, his jaw clenched with anger.

They stared at each other for a long moment. The unease spread through Reese as if the three years had never happened, as if all the old discomfort had suddenly awoke from a deep slumber, still as ugly and awkward as ever. He cursed silently, wishing that they could get along as well as he and Nicole did. "Where were we?" Reese finally said. "I think you were just about to tell me of your travels. I trust they were exciting."

"Apparently not as exciting as what's happened to you," came the rejoinder. Morse drew himself up to his full height, but still was not as tall as Reese. Morse had to look up at his brother. "How can you permit her in your castle?"

"Her?"

"She has humiliated and insulted our family, kidnapping Nicole, forcing you into marriage," Morse condemned. "You should have had her beheaded the first chance you got as retribution for our family's honor."

"Beheaded?" Reese almost smiled. "That's a little harsh, isn't it?"

"You make light of the situation while the tart drags our name through the mud. She has insulted us. I, for one, will not tolerate it."

Reese's jaw clenched. He felt an odd surge of resentment course through him. "She is no tart," he retorted. "And as for dragging our name through the mud . . ." He locked eyes with his brother meaningfully. "It has survived far worse."

Morse gritted his teeth, the insult not lost on him. "People are saying you are weak to have allowed Cullen to force you into marriage."

Reese straightened. "I would have done anything to save Nicole."

"You should have stormed the castle."

"And by the time I had found where they were keeping her, Cullen would have slit her throat. Nothing was worth that."

Morse glared at him. "So, you wed and bedded the wench?"

Reese shook his head. "The marriage was not consummated."

"But the sheets—"

"The only blood shed that day was mine," Reese admitted. "I've started a letter of annulment. I will not be forced into marriage. But I will not behead a defenseless woman, either."

Morse frowned.

"I'm not a fool." Reese turned his back to Morse to gaze out the window. "So, you see, there is no reason for this joust to proceed."

"Dylan challenged me."

"Dylan is as impetuous as you," Reese said. "Still, he will not call off the joust. I would appreciate it if you did."

"Is that an order, m'lord?"

Reese heard the bitterness in his tone, the resentment. "No," Reese sighed. "It is a request."

"Then I will regretfully have to decline."

Reese turned to Morse. "Dylan is no match for you. You'll kill him."

Morse smiled. "He never should have challenged me. Besides, I fight for the honor of the Harringtons."

Reese felt anguish wash over him. He couldn't help but feel that this was his fault somehow. And there was nothing he could do to stop it.

Jayce stood beside Nicole the following day at noon, trembling. It wasn't the slight wind that made her cold. Even though the sun hid behind clouds, it was a very warm day. Yet, she still felt a chill. The wooden platform that she and Nicole stood upon creaked each time they shifted their weight.

Jayce's gaze scanned the field and the fenced area surrounding the arena for Reese, but he had not come. *He doesn't care,* she thought. She bowed her head in disappointment.

Nicole squeezed her hand. "Don't worry," she promised. "It will turn out fine."

"He's your brother, too," Jayce murmured. "Don't you care about Morse?"

"Of course I do," Nicole answered sadly. "You don't think anyone will get hurt, do you?"

Jayce turned her gaze to the field, a feeling of dread settling about her shoulders. "I hope not," Jayce murmured.

Two horses suddenly appeared from the opposite side of the field of honor. One broke away from the other and galloped to the platform the two women were standing on.

The chain-mailed knight who rode the steed flipped up the visor on his helmet. Dylan stared at Jayce with sad but determined eyes. She stepped toward him, clenching a veil of light blue in her fists. He dropped his lance to the platform so she could tie her favor on.

Jayce's gaze fell to the lance. She unfurled the material from her hands and reached out to tie it around the lance, but suddenly stopped as she heard the pounding of another horse's hooves. She looked up to see another mounted knight coming toward her. The clouds parted, and the sun shone down upon the approaching knight. The bright rays reflected off his armor up into her eyes, and Jayce held up her hand to block them. The shining armor still blinded her, and she had to look away from it, blinking. Finally, she heard the hoofbeats halt.

Jayce heard Nicole sigh.

She lifted her gaze to see that the knight had stopped before them. The elevated platform put her on an equal level with the knight. He stared down at her from the slit in the helmet's visor. The cold blue eyes that gazed at her sent a mixed form of relief and dread searing through her body.

Finally, the knight lifted his gauntleted hand and pushed the visor from his face. Reese.

A smile lit Jayce's face, and she lifted her favor toward Reese, waiting for him to lower his lance.

Reese's gaze settled on Dylan. "Your services are no

longer required. I will fight for the lady's honor." Dylan opened his mouth to protest, but Reese quickly silenced his unspoken objection. "It is my right," he told the young knight.

Dylan hesitated for a moment, then bowed respectfully and steered his horse off the field.

A thrill of joy swept through Jayce and she straightened her spine proudly . . .

. . . until Reese turned his gaze on her. There was a frostiness to his look, a frigid anger that chilled her pride and melted her confidence.

With a sharp jerk on the reins, Reese turned his horse from Jayce to meet his opponent.

It wasn't until Nicole reached out and pushed her hands down that Jayce realized he had coldly dismissed her favor. Jayce stared down at the sheer blue material in her hands for a long moment. Then she lifted her gaze to the combatants.

A silence spread through the crowd of onlookers as Morse faced Reese across the field. "M'lord!" Morse called. "My fight is not with you."

"Lady Jayce is under my protection," Reese answered in a low timbre that reverberated through the field. "As such she is my responsibility. Since you will not take back your unsavory remarks, I have no choice but to fight for her honor."

A lump rose in Jayce's throat. 'My responsibility.' 'I have no choice.' He didn't want to fight for her, anyone could hear that in his speech. "Why even bother?" she mumbled.

"Hush," Nicole whispered harshly.

Reese leveled the long jousting pole at Morse's mount.

"As you wish, my brother," Morse replied, and pulled his visor down over his eyes. He took his lance from his squire and spurred his horse on.

The two horses thundered down the field toward each other, their riders' lances pointing skyward, large clumps of dirt spraying out behind them in their wake. The two combatants lowered their weapons, aiming for each other, pushing their steeds on with sharp kicks to their flanks.

Jayce leaned forward, her fingers gripping the palisade with such force that it made her knuckles ache.

There was a loud crash and Reese jerked back as Morse's lance struck his shoulder.

Jayce gasped and pressed her fingers to her lips. Reese wavered on his horse as it continued to gallop to the other side of the field. Her heart froze in her chest.

Reese clutched the reins of the horse, righting himself. Jayce wasn't aware she had stopped breathing until she had to draw a large breath. Reese's steed circled, and the squire handed Reese another lance.

Again, the two horses raced toward each other, jousting poles leveled.

Jayce held her breath again as the horses closed on each other. Reese jerked away and just missed being hit in the same shoulder. He turned his lance at the last moment and struck Morse's stomach. The blow glanced off Morse's armor as the horses galloped past the viewing platform, but Morse stayed tall in the saddle.

Reese rode straight to his squire, grabbed the offered lance and whirled, spurring his steed on toward Morse. Morse matched his older brother's speed, driving his horse on. Reese leveled his lance, again aiming for Morse's midsection.

Jayce's heart pounded as the Harrington brothers collided in a large cloud of dust and a thunderous roar.

Reese tumbled backward over his horse and fell heavily to the ground.

Nine

Jayce ducked beneath the rail to race to Reese's aid, but something caught her wrist and held her back. She fought against it, tugging at her arm to free it. A frantic second later she realized that it was Nicole.

"Morse fell, too," she told Jayce breathlessly.

Jayce scanned the field to find Morse laboriously climbing to his feet. Jayce straightened, leaning toward Reese, silently begging him to get to his feet. The crowd's roar rang in her ears. Finally, Reese pushed himself to a sitting position. He swayed for a moment before reaching up to pull his helmet from his head and toss it aside.

"Sword!" Morse shouted to his squire.

Jayce saw Reese clutch his side. His face contorted in a grimace of pain.

A boy ran up with a large sword, its handle outstretched to Morse.

Panic welled inside Jayce. *No*, her mind screamed. *He's hurt.* She heard Nicole gasp. Jayce ducked beneath the railing and jumped from the platform to race onto the field, her heart thundering in her chest.

"Jayce!" Nicole cried.

Jayce knelt before Reese, scanning his face, her hands splayed before her in helplessness. Agony dulled Reese's deep blue eyes; his jaw was clenched hard. As he stared at her, Jayce thought she saw a wavering of resolve in his eyes.

She thought for a moment that he was beseeching her. But for what she didn't know. She glanced over her shoulder and saw Morse approaching, sword in his hand.

She stood to meet him, "Let him be," she commanded. "Everything you said was true. He cares nothing for me. I forced myself on him. I knew all about the plan to kidnap Nicole." As she spoke, tears rose in her eyes. "Let him be," she repeated, desperation creeping into her voice.

Morse's gaze shifted from Reese to pin Jayce where she stood.

"My honor means nothing," she proclaimed. "Just don't hurt him."

"You," Morse growled. He lifted the blade above his head. "I would gladly take your life instead of my brother's."

Jayce winced, stepping back, lifting her hands to block the blow.

Suddenly, another sword shot forward to intercept Morse's death blow. Jayce turned to find Reese on his feet, sword clutched in his hand. His blue eyes twinkled at her for a moment before he shifted his gaze to Morse. His hand encircled Jayce's arm and gently set her aside.

Morse moved forward with a lightning reaction, arcing his blade high over his head. Reese caught the blow easily, grabbing Morse's arm. They locked blades, and the sunlight reflected off the crossed weapons and into Jayce's eyes.

"Reese," Morse said, through the crossed swords, "if she means anything to you, admit it and I'll lower my weapon."

Reese tensed, his shoulders stiffening. He stared hard at Morse before shoving away from his brother. He cast a quick glance at Nicole on the platform. But never once did he look at Jayce.

"I'm fighting for the respect owed my family, Reese. I'm fighting for our honor. It was her father that kidnapped

Nicole! It was her family that forced you into marriage. I don't want to fight my brother."

"There is no one left to defend her. She is now my responsibility."

"So, you don't care for her?"

Jayce tried to close off her emotions. She watched Reese's back. And prayed for the right answer.

"No," he proclaimed.

Jayce hadn't realized she had been holding her breath until she released it in a disappointed rush. Disappointed? She had known he didn't care for her.

"Then why fight me?" Morse demanded. "This is not your fight."

"She is under my protection. She is to be treated as a guest in my castle," he proclaimed.

Humiliation flamed across her cheeks. She wanted to crumple to the ground; she wanted to disappear into the earth so no one could see her. Instead, she stood immobile in the middle of the field of honor, honorless. Alone.

A crack speared the center of her heart like a fracture in the earth.

"Then my fight is with you," Morse replied, and ran at Reese, screaming his rage, his frustration.

Jayce gasped as Reese stepped into the swing, catching his brother's sword with his blade. He grabbed Morse's arm and yanked him to the ground with one pull, stepping on the wrist of his sword arm. Reese pressed the tip of his blade to his brother's neck. "How many times do I have to warn you about rushing someone in anger without thinking? It's amazing you've survived this long."

Morse struggled in frustration.

"Yield," Reese urged, pressing the sword closer to Morse's throat.

Morse's fight left him, and he glared at Reese. "I yield to you," he ground out between clenched teeth.

"Apologize to Lady Jayce," Reese encouraged.

Morse's dark eyes danced with flames of anger and defiance, as he snarled, "I apologize."

Reese withdrew his sword and offered Morse his hand.

Morse clasped his arm, and Reese pulled him to his feet. Reese shook his head. "After all those years of training, I can't believe you forgot what I taught you."

Morse sneered at Reese, then stormed off toward the castle. Reese watched his brother go, then slowly followed in his footsteps.

Jayce saw Reese pause once to glance over his shoulder at her. She felt his eyes on her like the heated sun, felt the confusion in his gaze.

Around the field of honor, the crowd broke up, heading back to work or returning to the castle. She stood like a statue, willing their sympathetic stares to bounce off her. But somehow they didn't seem to bounce; she absorbed them, each slashing her heart until it was left in tatters.

A warm arm draped around her shoulder. "Come on," Nicole whispered.

Jayce shrugged off her arm, shaking her head. "No," she answered, trying to keep the quivering out of her voice. "I think I'll stay out here for a while."

Nicole nodded and moved past her toward the castle, casting Jayce a commiserating look.

Morse stomped into his room, ripping the gauntlets from his hands and throwing them on the bed. He had thought this time that he could defeat his brother, give Reese a taste of the humiliation that had filled his life. Instead, his brother embarrassed him in front of everyone! He took that little wench's side over his own kin!

Morse shook his head, pulling the dust-filled tunic over his head and tossing it to the floor. Well, Morse vowed silently, gazing at the flickering flame of the torchlight on the wall, I will see to it that the girl will never be a Harrington.

Jayce wandered through the fields closest to the castle. She avoided the peasants and knights, avoided the sympathetic looks they cast her way. Not a wife. Not a guest. She was caught in a tormented limbo.

As the sun set, Jayce sat beside a wooden fence. She wasn't exactly sure where she was and didn't really care. Could it be any less welcoming than the castle she could see in the distance? Than the husband who would never accept her as a wife? And what of the tender touch he had bestowed on her? Jayce was beginning to believe she had imagined it. After all, how could he be so gentle one moment and proclaim to all within earshot that she meant nothing to him the next?

Jayce sighed and leaned back against the fence. What had her father done to her? Why had he forced her on a man who didn't want her? Surely there had been other lords willing to marry her. She and her father had not been as wealthy or as powerful as Lord Harrington, but they were not poor either.

Suddenly, behind her, a horse whinnied and a man's stern voice rang out. Jayce turned her head, peeking through the slats in the fence to see a beautiful black warhorse. The animal snorted and reared slightly. A man, small compared to the horse, yanked on a rope around the horse's neck.

Slowly, Jayce climbed to her feet. The horse snorted again, its thick black mane tossing as it rebelled against the rope. The man pulled hard on the rope, cursing. He raised his hand and Jayce saw a black coiled whip clutched in his fingers. He drew his hand back and the whip unfurled like a thick black snake.

Jayce jumped as the man brought the whip down hard

across the animal's shoulders. She had believed he was going to crack it in the air, not over the poor animal's hide!

"No!" Jayce screamed, and raced for the man. She rounded the fence just as the horse reared, and the man brought the whip down over the animal's back again.

The man drew his hand back to deliver yet another blow. Jayce reached out and grabbed the man's wrist. "No!" she shouted again. "That's not the way to tame an animal!"

The man turned angry eyes on her. "Then you tame him," he commanded, shoving the whip at her.

Jayce stared at the ugly black coil of rope, then pushed it away in disgust.

"Lord Reese is going to have him put down soon anyway. No one can tame this one. Not even Lord Reese," the man told her. "He's as wild as a ragin' river."

"What's his name?" Jayce wondered, staring the horse in the eye. It whinnied and tossed its head.

"Satan," the man answered with a curt nod. "And not a more befitting name could there be." The man turned his back on her and moved away.

Jayce watched the horse as it stared down at her with the blackest eyes she had ever seen, eyes that were round with fright. "You alone, too, boy?" she asked softly, trying to calm the animal. "They just don't understand, do they? It takes time, that's all. You can't just go in and demand that an animal as grand as you behave." She smiled gently and looked down at her hands. "Did Reese tell you, too, that you mean nothing to him? Or does he reserve that humiliation for me?"

The horse nickered and pranced a few steps away before turning his back to her.

Jayce sighed slightly. "I won't give up on you so easily," she whispered.

Ten

Reese sat on the bed in the guest room he planned to occupy until the situation with Jayce was worked out. James bent over at his side, probing a bruise with his fingers. "I told you I'm fine," Reese growled.

"Far be it from me to argue, sir," James mumbled. He straightened and presented Reese with his white tunic.

Reese snatched it from his hands just as a knock came at the door.

James moved to answer the knock, but before he reached the door it swung open, and Nicole swept into the room. "Well done, Reese," Nicole ridiculed.

Reese grunted.

"You've humiliated both your brother and your wife in one afternoon."

"Humiliated?" Reese exploded, pulling the tunic into place. "What has Jayce got to be humiliated about? I gave her a place of honor! She is a guest here."

"She is your wife," Nicole fumed. "She deserves to be recognized as such."

"I don't have a wife." Yet, even as he said it, he saw a vision of an angel. A chivalrous, brave angel, rushing to save him on the field of honor. *Even though I didn't need saving,* a stubborn voice inside him reminded. Still, what a brave, unselfish act, branding herself honorless to save him.

"Oh, please. Not that argument again! You treated Jayce deplorably," Nicole said, intruding on his thoughts.

He straightened off of the bed. "I protected her honor," Reese countered. "Even against my own brother."

"She gave up her honor because she saw you were hurt. She lied to protect you."

"Lied?"

"You don't truly think she planned my kidnapping? Don't be a fool. She knew nothing about it."

"She told you this?"

Nicole shook her head sadly. "She doesn't need to. And all you could do was embarrass her."

"I did not embarrass her."

"You said she meant nothing to you."

"She doesn't," Reese grumbled, but could not meet Nicole's eyes. He moved to the window to stare out at the darkening sky. *Can Nicole be right?* Reese wondered. *In attempting to make Jayce welcome as a guest at Castle Harrington, have I made matters worse?* "Where is she?"

Nicole raised an eyebrow. "I don't know."

Reese whirled on Nicole. "What do you mean you don't know?"

"I haven't seen her since the joust."

Reese marched past his sister and moved toward the door. He threw it open with such force that it slammed against the stone wall with a thunderous, "Boom!" He strode through the hallways like an ominous storm cloud. Two servants pressed themselves tightly against the wall to give him plenty of room to pass. One of the castle hounds quickly slunk into a side hallway at his approach.

How dare she twist his generosity into something he should feel guilty about? What did she expect of him? Or was it Nicole making him feel this way? When he found Jayce, he would make it very clear to her that he would never be forced into marriage with a woman he didn't love. He wanted a happy life, a happy and devoted wife.

Someone to cherish him and their children. He would make it clear to Jayce that he would not feel guilty about his position anymore. And he would make it very clear that she should not look at him with those deep, innocent blue eyes any longer.

After a quick, fruitless search of the great hall, he headed toward the master bedroom. Jayce must have returned there after the joust. He threw open the door and entered. "I would speak with you—" His voice died like a wavering candle extinguished by a whiplash breeze. The torchlight from the wall flickered over the undisturbed bed. The room was empty.

The shutters framing the window banged in the breeze, drawing his attention. He moved to the window to gaze out on his lands. Darkness had claimed his domain. An uneasiness snaked its way through his body. She was out there. In unfamiliar lands. Unprotected.

Reese dashed from the room and raced out into the courtyard, his usual calm gait turning to a run as he sped toward the stables. He reached the building just as the stablemaster was locking the animals up for the night. With a curt command from Reese, the old man quickly fumbled with his keys and reopened the doors. Reese brushed by him without a word and moved quickly into the stables. He guided his horse from its stall and pulled himself up onto his back, wasting no time in trying to saddle the animal. He had often ridden bareback when he was a child, enjoying the freedom it gave him. But there was no enjoyment now, only a slowly building panic.

His stomach twisted as he imagined Jayce lying on the road somewhere, hurt and bleeding. He quickly pushed the thought aside, telling himself that this was his village, and no one would dare to harm her. Still, Morse's hurtful words rose in his mind, and he knew that it was not only physical things that could wound her. Guilt rose in Reese's heart, and he knew that if anyone had hurt her, it had been him.

He spurred the horse on. As he raced toward the village, riding past the enclosure that housed Satan, Reese wondered where to start his search. But then the eerie silence caught his attention. Satan's incessant snorts and whinnies of disapproval were nowhere to be heard.

Reese reined in his horse, his gaze scanning the moon-kissed pasture. *Where is that infernal beast?* he wondered.

Then, he saw an apparition bathed in the glow of the moon, an angel floating above the fence that surrounded the grazing land. The night's breeze ruffled her dress and danced through the silken strands of her hair.

Reese squinted and blinked. The spirit abruptly vanished, and in its place he saw Jayce standing precariously on the fence. She held something in her hand that flapped in the breeze. It took a moment for Reese to realize that it was a blanket. Then, he heard her calling to the beast.

Reese spurred his steed toward her as she sat on the top plank of the fence, beginning to ease herself over the side of the wooden barricade. Outrage and disbelief flashed through Reese. She was going into Satan's pen! Didn't she know how dangerous and unpredictable the warhorse was?

Before she could climb fully into the pen, Reese reached around her tiny waist and hauled her from the fence onto his own steed. "Are you out of your mind?" he demanded. His reprimand died in his throat as she turned those brilliant eyes on him. Those dangerous eyes. Eyes that captured the pale light of the moon and radiated its energy back tenfold. Eyes that were capable of capturing much more than just the moon's glow.

"What are you doing here?" she asked.

Her bottom pressing against his thighs caught him off guard, and for a brief moment he imagined what she would look like lying beneath him in the throes of ecstasy.

He silently shook himself and frowned, trying to regain control of the situation. "I might ask the same of you."

"Where am I supposed to be?" she wondered.

The innocence of her question, the pure, untainted honesty of it, touched his heart. *Where indeed?* he queried. "Well, certainly not near this beast," Reese retorted, glancing at Satan. The horse snorted once, indignantly, its dark eyes absorbing the moonlight but giving nothing back but blackness. "What in heaven's name were you thinking climbing over the gate into his pen? Don't you know that he could have trampled you?"

"It's chilly," she replied. "I was going to put this blanket on him." She held up a worn cover.

Reese's gaze shifted from the blanket clutched in her delicate hands to her eyes. "He has never worn a blanket at night. He won't let anyone close enough to put one on."

"You can hardly blame him after the whipping the groom gave him."

"He wouldn't need a whipping if he were not so uncontrollable."

"You don't tame an animal by whipping it and bullying it into subservience."

She was gazing at the wretched beast with admiration. A slow grin curved Reese's lips as he stared down at the woman in his arms. He still held her close, his arm wrapped around her waist, his hand splayed against her flat stomach. Was he gazing at her with as much admiration as she was bestowing on the horse? Then he shook himself, and resolve sealed off the fracture she had begun to create in the stone wall he had built around his heart.

"He needs to be loved," she added softly.

He felt his resolve melting. The words pried the fracture open wider. He knew that the woman he held in his arms was unlike any he had known before. Brave and kind and beautiful. And thrust upon him by evil coercion. The thought that she had somehow worked her way into his mind, infiltrated his body like an invader, angered him. "Stay away from him," Reese growled. "He'll cause you nothing but misery."

Jayce turned her eyes to his. Again, he felt that wash of affection overtake him and race through his veins, filling his very blood with the spirit of her being.

Her eyes were large and trusting, her nose pert and turned up just a bit, her cheekbones high and well-defined. But it was her lips that attracted his attention. They were red and full and parted. Wisps of her hair curled forward, framing her face. A lovelier portrait of a woman could never be painted. Reese found himself lowering his head to hers, moving his own lips closer to hers, as if caught in some kind of magical bliss.

Satan pawed the ground, snorting, white puffs of steam erupting from his nostrils. The spell broken, Reese jerked back from Jayce, startling his horse, who lurched forward, slamming Jayce against his body.

Was that disappointment that filled her eyes? Or relief?

"I'll take you back to the castle," he said, and spurred the horse on.

But Jayce slipped from his grasp and his fingers brushed her breasts, sending a jolt of desire flaming through his body. She landed smoothly on the ground. "I have to put the blanket on Satan," she insisted.

Her determination made Reese furious. Hadn't he just told her that the creature wouldn't let anyone near it? Didn't he just tell her it was dangerous? Reese quickly dismounted and stormed over to her, ripping the blanket from her hands. "You will stay away from that monster," he commanded. With a single leap, he almost hurdled the fence, cursing silently as he landed just inside the pen.

How had he gotten himself into this position? He gritted his teeth as the warhorse turned surprised eyes to him.

"Come here, you damned beast," he snarled, unfurling the blanket before him.

"No," Jayce urged from behind him. "Speak softly to him. As if he were a friend."

"I would speak softly to no friend of mine," he growled, approaching the horse. Out of the corner of his eye, he saw her pulling herself onto the gate. "All right!" Reese called, holding his hand out to stop her. He locked gazes with Satan. "Wretched beast," he grumbled. He cleared his throat. "Ummm. It appears to be a chilly night." Reese scratched at his cheek. He glanced back at Jayce to see her watching him expectantly.

He felt ridiculous.

She urged him on with a gentle wave of her hand.

Reese turned back to the horse. "Why don't you wear this?"

The horse snorted and took a step away from him, pawing the ground.

"This isn't working," Reese growled immediately.

"Yes, it is," Jayce answered in a soft, coaxing voice. "You're doing fine. Try again."

Reese looked at the horse. "We wouldn't want you to catch your death, now would we?" There was thick sarcasm in his voice. "Now just stay put and we'll have this on you in a—" He took a step closer.

The animal whinnied and reared slightly. Reese stubbornly refused to move as the horse pranced closer to him.

"Not this time," he warned. "I won't tolerate your temperament. I know you don't much like me, and I could care even less for you. But it's for Jayce. Just stay still a moment longer and let me put this on you." He took a step closer, mumbling so only he and the horse could hear, "You wretched beast."

The warhorse swung his snout forward and hit Reese hard in the stomach. The air exploded out of his lungs and he fell backward onto his backside. Reese looked up to see the horse's sharp hooves pawing the air above him, kicking wildly just above his head. He thought for sure the damned animal was going to trample him.

Eleven

Satan's hooves slashed the air. But then the beast was gone, and in his place was the angel Reese had seen on the fence. He lay still for a moment, a stunned grogginess clouding his thoughts. The angel was standing very close to the horse. The angel was—

Jayce! The thought of her in the demon's pen sent tremors of terror racing through Reese's body. His mind cleared instantly, and he lunged forward, pulling her against his chest, rolling away from the monster. When his momentum stopped, Reese lifted his head to find Satan at the other side of the pen.

"I guess you're all right," Jayce murmured.

His gaze was drawn to her. She was trapped beneath him, and Reese became instantly aware of the press of her breasts against his chest. Desire flared in his veins. He scowled, angry that any woman could arouse his passion so completely and uncontrollably. "I told you to stay out of the pen," he growled after catching his breath.

"You were in trouble," she replied. "I—"

"I didn't need your help," he answered. Reese pushed himself from the ground and held a hand out to her.

Jayce sat up. Reese could see the same agony etched over her features as he had seen on the field of honor. She ignored his hand and stood, dusting her palms on her dress.

"Looks like your horse will have to go cold tonight," Reese said.

Jayce headed for the fence. "No he won't," she answered.

Confused, Reese glanced toward Satan. The blanket was draped over his back. Astonished, Reese turned back to Jayce to see her climbing over the fence.

"You dropped the blanket when he shoved you," she said. She eased her feet to the ground and headed toward the castle, leaving Reese standing alone in Satan's pen.

"I don't believe this," Reese muttered, absently rubbing his sore stomach.

Unable to sleep that night because of deep blue eyes that hovered in his mind and red, parted lips that called to him and spoke his name, Reese went to the study to bury his mind in work, to try to exorcise his demons.

He stood and strode to the window to gaze out at the chilly evening sky. The sun had fled beneath the invading blackness, and the evening was peppered with small glistening stars. Reese felt an anxiousness stir his soul.

Tendrils of cold blew in from the open window to wrap icy fingers around his strong form. Perhaps he felt so restless because he and Nicole had been arguing since she had returned.

Suddenly, the door swung open on silent hinges, and he turned to see the woman who had haunted his dreams enter the room. Jayce paused in the middle of the open doorway, her hands folded before her, her small frame dwarfed by the wide entranceway. Reese's breath caught in his throat, and his gaze traveled slowly over her; her hair was hidden beneath a sheer blue fabric, her figure curvaceous and regal, her shapely hips accented by a belt of rich velvet fabric that hung to the floor.

Reese stepped closer, thinking he must be imagining

such beauty. But the closer he got, the lovlier she looked. Her blue eyes shone like beacons; her full lips were as red as cherries. He might just want to taste those cherries. He stopped immediately, realizing what the little nymph was doing to his senses.

"Oh, I'm sorry," she apologized. "I didn't know anyone was here. I saw the light and I was coming in to douse the candle." With her hands folded demurely, Jayce looked as innocent and pure and righteous as a damned saint.

Reese approached her, but moved around to the back of the table before he came too near her.

She stepped up to the table, her eyes scanning the parchment that lay scattered across it. "What are you doing?"

"There is a problem in the fields. Some of the men have been stricken with a fever and are unable to work."

"Is it serious?" Jayce wondered.

He shook his head. "The ones who have had the fever have recovered fully in about a week. If the fields are not fully seeded in two weeks' time, it will be too late."

"How many men are still ill?"

"Ten." His eyes swept her unwillingly. "But that's my concern." She was quite comely. Her petite figure was curvy, alluring and inviting. Her brown hair was neatly tucked under the coif, but Reese remembered the rebellious curls that had framed her face. And her face! God's blood! Her deep blue eyes reminded him of the ocean, the deepest part of it. The part you had to be careful you didn't drown in. He forced his gaze from her and his jaw clenched. He was angry for being forced to marry a woman he didn't love. He was angry with her for being so damned beautiful. "Had you no suitors?" he inquired suddenly.

"Suitors?"

"Men asking for your hand in marriage," he clarified dryly.

One dainty eyebrow rose. "Many," she replied defiantly.

Of course she did. How could she not have had men lining up to wed and bed her? Then, another thought occurred to him, and he clenched his fists. "Does a babe grow in your belly?"

Jayce straightened indignantly. Heat suffused her cheeks. "No," she retorted stiffly.

"Then why would your father go to such extremes to have me wed you?" he demanded. "It makes no sense."

"I don't know," she admitted, turning to glance at the parchment.

Reese swore he heard agony in her tone. "Jayce," he called. When she lifted those blue eyes to him, he forgot his words. He stood with his mouth open for a moment before shaking himself. "I cannot help but think I would never do this to a daughter of mine. She would be happy in her life, with her husband."

"Are you so sure I am not happy?" Jayce wondered.

Reese studied the simple dignity of her face. The honesty that shone from her eyes touched his heart. He shook his head. "You cannot be. You know nothing of me."

"I know you're an honorable man."

"A rich man," he added in a biting, accusing voice.

Her chin rose a notch. "Yes," she said. "A wealthy man."

"Perhaps that was why your father did this," he said. "To make sure you were well established, well taken care of. My wife will have luxuries you were never used to. Luxuries—"

"Well taken care of," she repeated, as if to herself. "Perhaps. And perhaps he didn't see you as a liar."

Reese stiffened to his full height, towering above her like a stone tower. "I am not a liar."

She reached across the table to touch his arm meaningfully. "You lied to my father."

He stared at her, trying desperately not to be moved by her touch. "You lied, too," he accused.

"I was protecting my husband," she answered. He began

to shake his head, but she continued undaunted. "It was my duty to stand by you."

Reese's gaze was drawn by her parted lips. Any words she was about to say died as his gaze devoured her mouth as thoroughly as if he were kissing her. He turned away quickly and found his stare occupied by the ledgers of his farms.

"Perhaps you can use the alewives for the time being," Jayce suggested.

"What?" Reese asked.

Jayce pointed to the ledgers. "The alewives. Take some of them to work in the fields until the men are well. They won't be as skilled as the field workers, but they'll do for the time being."

"Women?" Reese asked dubiously.

"Their backs and arms might be sore because they're unused to the work, but give them a day of rest, and they won't protest as much."

"A day of rest?" Reese echoed with distaste. "Women are not made to do the job of men," he added imperiously.

Jayce shrugged and turned to move out the door, calling over her shoulder, "It will solve your problem."

Reese watched her go, staring at the empty doorway for a moment, then turned back to study his ledgers. "Alewives," he muttered incredulously under his breath.

Early the next morning, Jayce leaned over the gate to Satan's pen, waving a carrot at the proud stallion who haughtily eyed the offered food. She dropped her arm in disappointment and lifted her eyes. Beyond the pen, out in the fields, Jayce noticed six alewives working alongside the men. She smiled in amazement.

She turned back to Satan, again offering him the carrot. The horse snorted, refusing the food. Finally, frustrated by the horse's disregard for her gift, Jayce straightened.

"He's not as easily fooled by your pretense at innocence."

Jayce whirled to find Morse approaching from a nearby barn. She clutched her hands before her, trying to still the unease that raced through her body.

Morse eyed the horse, then the gate. "How fitting to find you at the gate to hell."

Jayce scowled. "What do you want?"

Morse took a step toward her. "I should ask you that question."

Jayce tilted her head slightly in confusion. "I don't know what you mean."

"Tell me why you've come to Castle Harrington," Morse demanded. "Are you here to destroy my family?"

"Destroy . . . ? No!" Jayce answered emphatically. "I came to wed Reese."

"By kidnapping Nicole?" Morse demanded.

"Do you think I would have come if I had known what my father had done? How do you think this makes me look? Do you think I wanted to live like this? A husband who wants nothing to do with me. No chance for a loving family, no chance for children." She looked away from him, blinking back the tears of remorse that suddenly rose before her eyes.

"Such a touching act," he cooed richly. "I could almost believe you. Tell me, how long have you practiced that speech?"

Jayce straightened her back, her eyes narrowing. "I don't want your sympathy. What's done is done. And I, for one, intend to make the best of it."

"Make the best of what?" Morse asked. "By Reese's own words you are nothing more than a guest here at Castle Harrington."

"I am Reese's wife in the eyes of God."

Morse laughed sharply, his snicker spitting out from his mouth like a snake's venom. "Nowadays that doesn't count for much. Not with an annulment so easily paid for. And that is one thing we do not lack—coin, as you well know." He turned his back on her, his ugly chortle of contempt lingering in the air as he walked away.

Annulment. The word sent shivers down Jayce's spine. What would she do if Reese decided to annul their marriage? Where would she go?

She felt a warm wetness brush her hand, then she heard a crunch. She looked down to see that she still held the carrot tightly in her fist but a large bite had been taken from the end of it. Jayce raised her eyes to see the black warhorse towering above her, munching noisily on the carrot. A grim grin came to her lips as she held the rest of the carrot out to him.

When Jayce returned to her room, she was smiling softly to herself. She patted the pocket that held the few carrots left over from her victorious excursion, pleased with her little victory, then pushed the door open. And froze.

Reese stood in the middle of the room, filling it with his presence like a sculptured god. His bronzed skin glistened in a ray of sunlight; dust particles shifted around him in the light, showering him in what looked like a splash of magical powder. His black hair just barely caressed his shoulders in a touch that made Jayce feel envious. His shirt was off, and he held a piece of material in his hands.

Jayce didn't realize until a moment later that the cloth was his leggings.

Her eyes dipped past his waist to his buttocks. They were rounded and firm. His long legs were well muscled. Her gaze traveled back up his body. His torso was strong, and she saw his shoulder muscles release as he drew himself up taller.

He slowly turned to face her. "Come in." His voice rumbled through her like a tremor. "And close the door."

Twelve

Jayce obeyed Reese without question, stepping into the room and closing the door behind her. It was only when she heard the soft "thump" that she realized with a start what she had done. Shut herself in with a naked man. Not any naked man, but her husband.

She swallowed hard and pressed herself back against the wall.

A smile curved his lips before Reese moved to the bed and sat down, pulling on his leggings.

"I'm sorry," she whispered. "I didn't realize you were here."

"It's my room," he replied.

She swallowed again and could do no more than nod in agreement.

He pulled a white tunic over his head. "Where were you?" he demanded.

Jayce watched with a pang of remorse as his beautiful body disappeared beneath his tunic. "I didn't know you were looking for me," she responded.

"That wasn't my question," he said, picking up a string to thread through the "V" in the neck of his tunic.

Without thinking, Jayce stepped forward, taking the string from his hand. She stood before him, feeding the string through the first loop. "I was out walking. It's a beautiful morning, and I wanted to see it before the village woke. I—" She paused, realizing what she was doing. She lifted her gaze to meet his amused blue eyes. "Sorry." She dropped the string into his hand.

Reese eyed her, and Jayce had to drop her gaze beneath his intense perusal. "You were with Satan again, weren't you?"

"You told me to stay away from him." Nervously, she took a step back.

Reese's hand shot out, ensnaring her wrist. He rose before her like a god casting judgment and finding her lacking. He pulled her close to him.

Jayce's heart raced at his nearness. He was so strong. He smelled like leather and musk. His chest just barely touched the tips of her breasts and it sent swirls of desire and anticipation coursing through her. She stared into his blue eyes and found them smoldering like the blue at the center of a flame. For a breathless moment she waited. She felt his hand skim her waist to her thigh.

"Then what's this?" he asked softly, and patted her pocket.

"My leg," she whispered.

A low rumble sounded from his throat, and his eyes lit up. Jayce had never seen a more wondrous sight. Her heart melted into a pool of contentment.

Reese pulled a carrot out of her pocket and displayed it before her eyes.

For a moment, Jayce frowned in confusion, her foggy mind refusing to relinquish the tenderness in his eyes. Then the cold realization of where the carrot had come from jarred her. She fumbled for a coherent thought. "I—I happen to like carrots," she bridled. She grabbed the carrot from him and took a bite.

"What a strange coincidence. So does Satan."

"He's a wonderful horse, Reese. It would be such a shame to destroy him. He's so smart and spirited and beautiful. I know he can be tamed. You're just going about it all the wrong way. I—"

Reese lifted a finger and touched it to her lips, silencing her. His finger trailed the shape of her lips and moved over her cheek to her jaw. "Satan will live. But only until you tire of him."

Jayce's lips tingled where he had caressed them. She stared into his eyes, wanting more, but unsure of what.

Reese stepped back from her, pulling his hand away. "But I don't want you near him unless I'm with you."

As he moved away, Jayce felt the contentment in her heart drain away. "Reese!" Jayce called, suddenly very desperate for him to remain at her side.

Reese paused at the doorway.

She fumbled with her whirling thoughts for a moment before asking, "If my father hadn't taken Nicole, would you have courted me?"

A sad smile curved the corners of his lips. "I would not have known you then." He turned and was gone.

Two days later, Reese found himself once again outside Satan's pen, leaning against the fence, his arms resting on the top rail. He saw the impetuous girl grin as the horrid creature took another carrot from her hand. She reached out and actually patted the beast's nose. Reese snorted. He had owned Satan for six months and couldn't even get near the fiend.

He shook his head in complete disbelief as the horse nuzzled its head against Jayce's hand. "Wretched beast," Reese grumbled, and looked away from the touching scene. Something in it disturbed him. Something that had nothing to do with the horse. He had watched her work with the animal, cooing and talking to it for an hour and a half. One might think he had nothing better to do than to watch her handle Satan. One might think he was slack in his care of his lands when all he could do was stand at the fence and stare at Jayce.

He envied the damn horse. And that thought disturbed him much more than what others might think.

"Try it."

Reese lifted his head to see Jayce holding a carrot out to him, an encouraging grin on her red lips. He almost reached out and took the carrot, enchanted enough to do her bidding. But then the animal snickered, and Reese turned his gaze to it. A snarl curled his lips. "I don't think so."

"You have to try someday," Jayce said.

"I do not bribe animals into becoming tame," he proclaimed, crossing his arms over his chest.

"No, you whip them and beat them into submission. That's no way to gain loyalty."

Reese opened his mouth to object, a scowl crossing his dark brow.

"Let me show you something," Jayce said, overriding his objection.

To his horror, the little imp ducked beneath the rails and moved into the pen. "What do you think you're doing?" Reese demanded. "Leave there at once."

"Don't worry," Jayce assured him. "Satan won't hurt me."

"That remains to be seen," Reese warned. "Get out of there now."

"Most creatures respond better to kindness than to a whipping." She approached Satan with her hand outstretched.

The horse whinnied and raised his hoof, smashing the ground and splaying up a cloud of dirt. A thunderous panic rang in Reese's ears. He gripped the fence so tightly that his knuckles turned white. "Jayce, don't."

She moved up to the horse and it towered over her, steam coming from its nostrils, fire from its mouth. Reese boosted himself up onto the fence, ready to bolt over it to save Jayce.

Jayce reached over the horse, stroking its mane. She grabbed a handful of its hair and in one movement, hauled herself onto the animal's back.

Reese's heart lurched into his throat and he leapt the fence, racing toward Jayce only to find her staring down at him from atop the creature. It suddenly became clear as daylight to Reese. They were cohorts. She had been here many times before, talking to the beast, selling her soul to ride the demon.

Reese gritted his teeth. "I told you not to come here without me."

"I never would have gotten to this point with you brooding at the gate and glowering when I tried to do anything. Besides," she said, calmly stroking the horse's mane, "you make Satan nervous."

"I—!" That was the final straw. He approached her with a dark look. But Satan pawed the earth in warning, and Reese came up short, knowing the animal could trample him in a moment. "Get down from there," he called.

Jayce lifted her eyes to him. Those blue orbs shone at him, and Reese realized that the nervousness he felt in the pit of his stomach was for her safety. He would have done anything to get the girl from the devil's back. He would have battled a thousand men to see her safe. But he knew that his grim resolve would not get her from the beast's back. He gritted his teeth again. "Please," he said begrudgingly.

Jayce slid down Satan's side, and Reese grabbed her hand, pulling her away from the horse. "Are you mad?" he demanded. "He could have trampled you! He could have thrown you, and you could have broken your neck!"

Jayce stared at him sympathetically. "You don't have to be afraid of Satan."

"Afraid?" Reese snorted. "I'm not afraid."

She grabbed a blanket off the fence and shoved it into his arms. Reese stared down at it. Then, with determination, he lifted his gaze to Satan. The horse stared at Reese, watching him out of distrustful eyes.

Reese opened the blanket, cautiously approaching.

"Talk to him," Jayce encouraged.

"What do you say to an arrogant, willful—"

"Reese," Jayce warned.

Reese grimaced. "Traitor," he murmured at the horse. "How could you let a woman tame you?" But Reese knew how. He had to but look into Jayce's eyes to be captured by the spell of her beauty. Perhaps he had more in common with the horse than he realized. "Easy," Reese whispered. "I won't hurt you. All I have to do is slip this over your back."

Reese carefully stepped up beside the horse. The animal nickered softly as Reese slowly, painfully slowly, eased the blanket onto his back. "That's a good boy," he soothed. "You're doing fine." He stood for a long moment, unable to move. Finally, he straightened a corner of the blanket and quietly stepped away from the horse.

Reese backed to the gate, refusing to take his eyes from the horse, sure that at any moment he would charge him and try to trample him beneath his hooves. But the horse didn't move. It stood absolutely still, just watching Reese with dark eyes that mirrored the sun in their depths.

Reese joined Jayce at the fence. He shook his head in bemusement, casting one last glance over his shoulder at Satan. When he looked down at Jayce, he found her beaming a smile up at him. It was a smile filled with pride. "Come on," he commanded, and headed back toward the castle.

Jayce quickly took up step beside him. In all the time Reese had owned the damned beast, he hadn't been able to get within five steps of the animal. Satan had knocked him to the ground more than once. But under Jayce's guidance, he had actually put a blanket on the stubborn horse. Reese smiled in disbelief.

"Now you're ready to ride him," Jayce commented.

He looked at Jayce in wonderment, then shook his head. "I don't think so. Putting a blanket on him is one thing. Riding the monster is another."

Jayce gazed out into the black night, content for the first time since she had arrived. Perhaps, just perhaps, there was hope yet. Reese didn't hate her as he had when she had first arrived. A fond smile touched her lips. And she wasn't quite so afraid of him.

A rumble of thunder jarred her out of her reverie and she stumbled away from the window, staring into the darkness outside the castle. It was mere seconds before lightning lit the sky like a torch.

Jayce grabbed a blanket from the bed and raced from the room toward the great hall. It was late at night, and she knew that there would be hardly anyone there. But there would be a fire in the hearth. Perhaps its warmth would ease the chill that cocooned her body.

As she descended the stairs, all but running, she drew the blanket tightly around her shoulders. A crash of thunder spurred her on to a frantic pace and she almost tripped, but caught herself on the stone wall of the castle. She ran the rest of the way to the great hall, bursting through the doors.

The room was empty and she padded across the hall toward the inviting flames. She heard the wind pick up outside, howling its fury, and rushed toward the protective warmth of the hearth. She didn't see the man sitting before the flames until she was almost beside him.

Reese looked up as she skidded to a halt. Those blue eyes swept her, and he was out of his chair, seizing her shoulders before she could think coherently.

"What's wrong?" he demanded.

She swallowed hard, trying to find comfort in his eyes. For a long moment, she couldn't speak, couldn't move. She wanted to curl into his embrace.

Thunder boomed around her and the castle seemed to shake. She glanced up at the ceiling, half-expecting the walls to come tumbling down around her.

"Jayce?"

She returned her frightened gaze to Reese, pulling the blanket tightly around her throat.

"You're trembling," he observed.

Jayce opened her mouth to reply, but there was nothing to tell him. No words came out.

Another grumble of thunder filled the night, and she instinctively stepped closer to Reese.

He took her elbow and led her to a chair near his. He set her into it and knelt before her. "Are you all right?"

Jayce nodded tentatively.

Reese reached up and brushed a lock of hair from her cheek.

At the soft caress, Jayce lowered her gaze from the ceiling to his face. He gently disentangled her hands from the blanket and held them in his own. His hands were so much larger than hers; they covered hers completely, engulfing them in a sheltered warmth. She watched his hands enfold her own. "I'm sorry," she whispered. "You must think I'm a horribly weak person."

"No," he whispered, leaning toward her.

Thunder rumbled in the air, and her grip tightened around his. "I've been afraid of storms all my life," she said softly. "The thunder, the wind, the rain. It's so loud . . ."

Reese leaned forward and brushed a kiss against her lips, quieting her words. When he pulled back, it wasn't far. His blue eyes filled her vision. Their noses touched, and his breath fanned across her mouth. Jayce parted her lips to speak, but nothing came out.

Reese leaned toward her, pressing his lips to hers in a more demanding kiss. He covered her mouth with his, and she was shocked at the desire that flamed to life inside her. Her stomach swirled as did her world.

She felt his hands move up her arms, pulling her closer. She was suddenly so lost in the tumult of emotions that raged through her that she didn't even hear the loud crack of thunder that filled the castle.

Thirteen

Reese crushed Jayce to him, enticing her to open to his exploration. When she parted her lips tentatively, he took the invitation and thrust his tongue into her mouth, tasting her sweetness. His hands cupped her face, tilting her chin up to meet his desperate kiss. He groaned softly. She was heavenly. She tasted of warm honey and sweet innocence. He kissed her chin and trailed kisses down her neck. He wanted her like he had never wanted anything before.

She was his world, the center of his universe. She was . . . his wife. The recollection shattered the shell of deception he was immersing himself in. He froze, then pulled away from her.

He saw the confusion in her priceless eyes, saw the hurt. He looked away from her and stood. "Jayce," he said, the word like a groan of denial. "I'm sorry . . . but I can't take you as my wife."

He chanced a look at her. She was nestled in the chair, wrapped in a warm blanket, her lips swollen from his heated kiss.

Jayce rose stiffly. He could see the pain he was causing her in her trembling lower lip. If she were any other woman, he knew she would burst into tears and flee from him. But not his Jayce. She stood righteously before him, her chin angled in a brilliant show of determination.

"Why are you doing this to me?" she whispered harshly. "If you despise me so, then—"

"I don't despise you," he interrupted, and was shocked at the tenderness in his voice. He stepped toward her, meaning to comfort her.

But she took a step away from him, banging into the chair, sending it toppling to the floor. "But you can't love me. And if you can't, then what future is there for us?"

Love? Reese wondered. Future? What future did they have together? Hadn't he asked himself that question time and again? A loveless marriage. His father's agonized visage rose before his mind's eye. It was not a life he would submit himself to. His wife would be devoted to him completely, so in love with him that she would not think of looking at another man. Jayce already commanded Dylan's devotion. Who else would fall victim to her charm?

Reese turned away from her.

Thunder growled through the castle like a stalking lion. A log in the fire crackled and popped. The wind whistled outside the fortress.

Reese heard her footsteps and whirled, finding her fleeing toward the kitchens, the blanket still wrapped about her shoulders. Her long dark hair whipped out behind her like a flag.

Reese knew he should go after her. She was frightened of the storm, with no one to turn to. His heart began to hammer in his chest. Alone. He knew what it was like to be alone. Truly alone. He had lain in his bed after his mother had died, heir to Castle Harrington, frightened, overwhelmed. And very much alone.

Thunder scolded him from the heavens.

Reese shot out of the chair and found himself running toward the kitchens.

* * *

Jayce wasn't really sure where she was going. She fled through the castle, searching for a safe spot where she could sit out the storm. But her vision kept blurring and the rumble of thunder was growing louder, confusing her senses. As a flash of lightning lit the hallway, Jayce ducked into a room, covering her ears against the crash of thunder. She pressed her back to the wooden door, waiting and praying, pulling the blanket tighter around her.

"Sweetheart," her father had said. "Your mother . . . she can't be with you anymore."

A fierce crash resounded around the castle, and Jayce swore she felt the stone structure tremble.

"Father," she whispered, "how could you leave me here? Why would you give me to a man who wants nothing to do with me? A man who can't love me?"

The warmth of a single candle fluttered briefly, drawing her gaze. Jayce stepped toward the heat, hoping that somehow it would erase the sudden chill that engulfed her body.

"Perhaps your father didn't want you, either," a voice mocked from the doorway.

Jayce turned unsteadily, recognizing the voice. She swiped at the tears on her cheeks and faced Morse as bravely as her trembling limbs would allow.

Morse leaned against the door frame, eyeing her with an icy disdain. "Perhaps I was wrong as to how seductive you can be," he snarled, taking a step toward her. "I thought that my brother's heart was dead. I thought that he was made of stronger stuff. But when I saw the two of you locked in that sinful kiss, I knew he had succumbed to your wiles." He circled her like a panther eyeing a frightened rabbit.

Jayce stepped forward to leave the room, but Morse moved to block her path and she pulled back.

"I think it's time to end this farce, my lady," he said bitterly.

Jayce watched him warily.

"Reese can't love you," he told her, "and he never will."

"It doesn't matter whether he loves me or not," Jayce insisted, knowing that it was a lie. She realized with a jolt that she had begun to care for Reese. To look at him as a friend. As more than just her husband. "I am his wife," she said out loud, with more conviction than she had ever felt.

Morse chuckled at her. "For the time being anyway."

Her confidence slipped a notch and she watched him warily.

Morse walked around her to the desk. She didn't turn to watch him, but heard the shuffling of papers. Dread slithered up her spine.

Suddenly, he shoved a piece of parchment at her from behind. Jayce jumped, stifling a scream. She pulled the blanket around her neck, trying to seal off the chill that crept through her body, even as she reached for the parchment. She scanned the quickly stenciled letter . . . and froze. Her heart refused to beat. Her breath refused to come.

"You see, Reese never intended to honor your marriage," Morse hissed in her ear. "He doesn't love you. He never will."

The castle rocked with a crash of thunder as Jayce's heart shattered.

The parchment she held was a letter to the king, requesting an annulment of their marriage.

She crumpled the parchment in her fist, lifting tear-filled eyes to Morse. Her entire body was shaking, but it had nothing to do with fear. She tossed the balled-up parchment at him and the paper bounced off Morse's chest, then rolled across the floor to rest back at her feet.

Morse grinned a terrible grin.

Jayce fled from the room, afraid that her pounding heart would burst from her chest if she didn't move, if she didn't do something. Anything. She just knew she had to get away from Morse, from Reese, from the castle.

Morse's horrible laughter followed her down the hallway.

Fourteen

Reese raced through the castle, his search growing desperate. He pushed open the door to his study, his frantic hunt encompassing every room. He came to a halt as he entered the room, his eyes narrowing on his brother like pinpoints of light. Morse sat behind the large wooden table, his feet crossed on top of a pile of parchment. He had a strange grin on his face that set a sinking feeling pulling his insides down into the pit of Reese's stomach. Reese's fists clenched; every muscle in his body tensed.

Morse tossed a balled-up piece of parchment up and down in the air, catching it deftly with one hand. "All our problems have been solved, brother," he said casually, laughing.

Reese launched himself at Morse, grabbing his tunic and pulling him to his feet. The sheets of parchment on the table scattered in every direction. "Where is she?" he demanded.

"Reese—" Morse began, the laughter gone from his face. "I—"

Reese shook him hard. "If you've hurt her, I'll kill you, you bastard."

Morse's eyes rounded in shocked disbelief. "You said you didn't care about her!" he exclaimed. "You said she meant nothing to you!"

Reese shoved his snarling visage at his brother. "Where is she?"

Morse gaped at him for a long moment, unable to speak. Finally, he said, "She left."

"Where, damn you?" Reese growled.

"I don't know," Morse answered quickly.

"What did you do to her?" Reese demanded. "Did you hurt her?"

"No, I—"

Reese shook him again. "What did you do?"

Morse's hand rose, palm up, displaying the crumpled ball of parchment.

Reese's eyes shifted to the paper. In the wadded-up mess that the parchment had become, Reese made out some of the words . . . imploring . . . kindly . . . annulment.

Complete and utter dread swept through him. God's blood! He lifted enraged eyes to his brother. Morse had shown Jayce the letter! An unbelievable rage consumed him, blinding him with its lashing ferocity. With a furious howl, Reese tossed Morse aside and raced out of the room.

The storm outside had continued to lash the lands, only intensifying Reese's sense of urgency. He ran to the main doors of the castle and threw them open. He stood stiffly as the rain pelted his face and the wind whipped his hair about his shoulders. His fingers curled into his palms. She was out there. Terrified. Alone. He had driven her away with his cold denials, his firm resolve against a loveless marriage. He cursed himself for a fool. He could never have thought that a woman forced on him could come to mean as much to him as Jayce did. Reese clenched his teeth and tossed his head back. "JAYCE!!" he shouted, as lightning ripped the sky.

He moved forward, his tense gait turning into a full-fledged run by the time he reached the outer gatehouse. As he reached the road into the village, he paused to scan the countryside. The rain splashed his face, soaked his tunic. *Where can she have gone?* he wondered. *She could be anywhere.* He needed to search the surrounding lands quickly.

Thunder boomed through the air. Then, his gaze settled on the fenced area that housed Satan. He was racing toward the beast's lair before he had formed the thought to do it.

He reached the fence, wiping the blinding rain from his eyes. But the gate was closed. His eyes searched the yard for the monster. The warhorse stood in the middle of the yard, the rain seeming to have no effect on him. His black mane was saturated, hanging down in thick strands. It was the first time he had ever been glad to see the beast.

Reese climbed the fence, all but throwing himself over the top. He landed on his feet in the pen and approached the horse, determination clenching his fists. He needed a horse, and he needed one fast. The stables were back inside the castle grounds, locked up for the night. He would have to rouse the stablemaster and then the old man would have to fumble for his key . . . He had no time for such nonsense.

Satan snorted and shook his head as Reese approached, water sloshing from his wet mane.

Every instinct told Reese to make a fist and club the animal in the snout, demanding his obedience. But the memory of Jayce stroking the animal and speaking gently to it came to the forefront of his thoughts. Reese reached out to the horse's mane, expecting the animal to try to bite him. But Satan didn't move. "Good boy," Reese told him. "Jayce is out there, and I have to find her."

Thunder exploded overhead and Satan skittered nervously, rearing back from Reese. "Easy, boy," Reese quickly said, stroking the nervous animal's hide. The horse calmed under his touch and Reese pulled himself up onto the horse's bare back.

Satan moved beneath his direction, toward the closed

gate. Reese reached out and slid the rope off the end, kicking the gate door open with his foot. With a tug on his mane, and a gentle nudge with his foot, Reese guided Satan out of the fenced yard and onto the road.

"Now let's go find my wife," he told Satan, and spurred the animal on.

Nicole passed the study and saw Morse sitting at the table, his head buried in his hands. Parchment littered the floor. She paused in the doorway until he lifted distraught eyes to her. Apprehension swept through Nicole, and she entered the room, moving quickly to the table. "What is it, Morse?" she demanded. "What's happened?"

Morse shook his head and turned away from her. "I did what I felt was right."

Nicole scowled. *What can he possibly be speaking of?* she wondered. *Did he and Reese have another fight?* "Morse," she said kindly. "You know Reese loves you."

Morse pushed the chair back and rose. "It has nothing to do with that." He looked at her, and Nicole was shocked at the suffering she saw in his eyes. "I thought he didn't care for her. I didn't know." He dropped his chin to his chest. "I didn't know."

"What did you do?" Nicole gasped, understanding instantly who he was speaking of.

Morse didn't look at her. "I showed her an annulment letter Reese had written."

Nicole's mouth dropped open. "Oh Morse!" she exploded. "What happened?"

Morse shook his head. "She left."

"Left? Where?" Nicole's stomach dropped. She grabbed his tunic in her fist. "Where did she go?"

Morse shrugged. "I'm not sure. I don't know."

Nicole released him and raced for the door, cursing his interference. If she had only had a little more time!

"Reese went after her." Morse's words halted her.

Slowly, Nicole turned to him. "Are you sure?"

Morse nodded.

Nicole returned to stand before him, nervously worrying her lip with her teeth. She sighed desperately. "This is all my fault," she murmured.

Morse's brows furrowed. "It's not your fault you were kidnapped."

Nicole began to chew on one of her fingernails.

"It's not your fault that Reese was forced into marriage," Morse added.

Nicole ripped off the tip of her nail with her teeth, glancing at him. She spit the fingernail on the floor. "This is all his fault," she whispered to herself. "If he wasn't such a brute, there would have been dozens of women lining up to marry him."

Morse studied his sister dubiously. "What are you talking about, Nicole?"

She stopped and faced him. "I wasn't kidnapped," she admitted.

Morse frowned. "What do you mean you weren't kidnapped? Reese received a ransom note. Specific instructions that if he didn't marry Jayce—"

"It was my idea. Cullen and I set up the whole thing."

Morse shot up out of his chair. "What?!"

"We met a year ago at Tournament," Nicole rushed on. "Cullen pointed Jayce out to me as she sat in the stands. She was beautiful and lively. When he told me she was spirited, too, I told him that it was exactly someone like Jayce that Reese needed to keep him in line. That's when Cullen mentioned he was looking for a husband for her. Well, at first I thought that for sure all Cullen needed to do was petition Reese to marry Jayce. But when that failed, Cullen and I came up with the kidnapping plan." Nicole stared at Morse desperately. "I never intended anyone to get hurt."

Morse shook his head. "Oh, Nicole," he gasped. "Reese is going to kill you."

She straightened slightly, indignantly. "Only after he kills you." Nicole closed her eyes in anguish. "What did you have to show her that letter for?"

"I thought I was doing us all a favor. Apparently I was mistaken," he grumbled, lifting his eyes to meet Nicole's. "Gravely mistaken."

Jayce huddled beneath a tree, her knees drawn up to her chest, her hands wrapped tightly around herself. She shivered as the wind picked up and whipped around her like a cold cape. Her body was saturated from the continuous rain. Her clothing hung heavily to her. Her dark hair was wet and weighty, forming a curtain of damp strands around her face.

She sniffed again. She had wanted her marriage to work. She had done everything in her power to be loyal to Reese and . . . Her body shook again, but it had nothing to do with the cold. She remembered the smile that lit his face, a smile that had melted her heart. She recalled the admiration in his eyes when she had stood before him on the field of honor. But despite all this, he still did not love her. He still did not want to be her husband.

Her trembling fingertips brushed her lips. His kiss had transported her to a realm of safety; his arms had encompassed her in a shelter of strength. It had been the only time that the storm was completely out of her mind.

Thunder ripped the sky and Jayce jumped, crying out. Sobs tore at her body; fear ate what was left of her heart.

Lightning speared the ground nearby, and Jayce bolted to her feet. As she raced blindly through the night, the rain pelted her body like stones being thrown at an outcast criminal. Her dress hung on her, pulling at her shoulders. She tried to lift her skirt so she could run, but her hands were trembling so fiercely that she couldn't manage to keep hold of it. The material slipped from her hands and she tripped over the hem, plummeting to the earth amidst the crack of thunder. Her hands skidded along the ground through the slick mud, and she went down on her stomach. Jayce lay with her cheek to the wet earth, sobbing.

Reese, her mind called. But she knew he would not come.

She pushed herself to her feet, struggling to regain her footing. The wind lashed at her, sending strands of her wet hair whipping into her face, her eyes. She raised her hands to block the lashing of her hair and the rain.

Suddenly, a roar filled her ears. The wind grew to Herculean proportions, pushing her around like a puppet. Jayce whirled to see a barrage of twisted, torn branches come flying through the air toward her as if nature herself had decided to attack with a swarm of arrows.

Jayce screamed and covered her face with her arms.

Fifteen

"NO!" Reese cried out as he saw Jayce fall beneath the barrage of twisted, gnarled branches. He leapt from Satan, fighting the massive winds to race to her side. He scooped her into his arms, sheltering her from the roaring winds and battering branches. He held her tightly, clenching his eyes shut. With every beat of his heart, he prayed she was all right. He was afraid to look down into her face, afraid the little whirlwind of life would be gone.

He held her against his heart. How blind had he been? How foolish that he couldn't see how much she meant to him? That he couldn't realize what a perfect wife she would make? That he couldn't understand how much he loved her? A growl of anguish tore loose from his throat.

"Oh, Jayce," he whispered. "Forgive me. Please forgive me." He kissed her cheek and her eyes. "I've been so stupid. So blind. I love you," he moaned. "I love you." He pressed a kiss to the side of her throat, to her chin, to her cheek.

Then he felt her move. Her hand slid over his back, around his shoulder.

Reese pulled away, gazing down into her face. Her skin was wet, and Reese tried to dry it with his tunic sleeve, but he quickly realized how useless that was a second after he ran the rain-soaked fabric across her cheeks.

Jayce's eyelids fluttered and then, like the sun emerging

from a dark cloud, her eyes opened. She stared at him for a long moment with those deep blue eyes, her gaze moving over his face. Reese's agonized stare drank in her beauty, her glorious lips, her wondrous eyes; he drank like a man who had been stranded in the desert and was suddenly given a flask of cool water to quench his parched throat. He bent and pressed a kiss to her forehead, then to her lips, murmuring, "Jayce. Oh, Jayce." His arms engulfed her, drawing her closer. He coaxed her to open to his kiss and she obeyed. As he tasted the sweet recesses of her mouth, his blood pounded through his veins. His relief and frustration gave way to a fierce and fiery passion that consumed him.

Her kiss swept him like the lashing winds of a storm; her hands swirled around him, pulling at his shoulders. But the fury of these winds was something he never wanted to abate.

Frantically, Reese pushed at her dress, sweeping it aside to reveal her glorious breast. He lowered his lips to the tip, licking and sucking it with an intensity that was beyond reason, beyond comprehension.

Lightning flashed and sizzled all around them.

Reese's other hand traced the curve of her back, down to her rounded bottom, pulling her tight against him.

Jayce groaned beneath his touches, running her hands through his wet hair, over his strong shoulders.

Rain cascaded around them, splashing through the trees, drenching them.

Reese eased her dress up, higher and higher until he touched her naked thigh and she gasped, touching his hand. The rain made the path slick and smooth, enflaming his already uncontrollable passion.

He blazed a trail of hot kisses down her neck, over the soft ridge of her collarbone. In the next instant his passion rose to tidal-wave heights as he reached down and unlaced his leggings, freeing his manhood. He was burning with a raw want, a desire so desperate, that it boiled his blood, searing his very skin. He barely heard the clap of thunder, didn't see anything but two round pools of blue staring at him with the same desire, the same passion. It was as if they were one.

His hand moved across her womanly curves to the opposite thigh, reveling in the feel of her body. She instinctively arched toward his hand. Reese lowered himself to her, claiming her kiss-swollen, rain-wet lips in a final attempt at control.

She groaned and squirmed beneath him.

He felt her wetness against his manhood and moved forward to feel the heat of her core. He clenched his teeth, fighting a losing battle against the raging want that threatened to sweep him away before he had claimed her. Then he thrust forward, driving into her. He felt her stiffen beneath him, felt the pain that pierced her body.

Reese groaned softly in anguish at having caused her further hurt.

Jayce moved her hips in a slow, tentative movement.

Reese couldn't help himself. He moved with her, and, like a summer storm, the tempo built until Jayce matched his thrusts, raising her hips to welcome him. Reese kissed her savagely, hungrily devouring her.

As Reese watched, her face blossomed beneath the rain, and contented joy spread across her features. Thunder boomed in the sky, rocking her body with its might. Reese heard Jayce cry out as the heavens shattered around her.

Lightning lit up the sky, illuminating Jayce's face. Reese had never witnessed a more captivating sight, a more wondrously glorious vision. Then, thunder rocked the ground, and he stiffened, exploding into her.

When Jayce opened her eyes, she found herself lying beneath Reese, sheltered from the pelting rain by his body.

He wore a grin on his face and a dark look in his eyes that promised much, much more.

A shy smile curved Jayce's lips.

He scooped her up into his arms and trapped her tightly against his body. "Are you hurt?" he asked.

She shook her head.

As he bent over her, drops of water fell from his face and trailed down her cheek like tears. "I'm so sorry, Jayce," Reese whispered. "I've been a brute to you. There's no reason for it. I've treated you horribly. I'm sorry."

Jayce stared up at him and he averted his eyes.

"I never intended to have our marriage annulled," Reese told her. "I wrote that letter before you arrived at Castle Harrington. But once I laid eyes on you I knew . . ."

"Knew what?" Jayce wondered.

Reese swallowed hard and lifted his gaze to lock with hers. "I knew I wasn't going to have our marriage annulled," he admitted.

"But you said—"

"I've been a fool. The biggest fool there is."

"No," Jayce stopped his confession, pressing her fingertips to his lips. "Not a fool. A man trying to live by his honor. It was unforgivable what my father did to you. Had I known—"

"I owe him everything. Had he not kidnapped Nicole, had he not forced me to marry you, I never would have known you. And that would have been the greatest loss of my life." He swept her up into his arms, pressing his lips to hers.

Thunder quaked in the sky, but Jayce was no longer frightened. Now, the memory of thunder would not be linked to her mother's death, but would be wedded to a new beginning.

Reese walked to his horse and gently placed her on Satan.

Jayce gasped. "You rode Satan!"

"I'm just full of surprises," he murmured, still holding her hand tightly in his own. He gazed up at her adoringly. "You are now truly the lady of Castle Harrington," Reese proclaimed softly. "I would like nothing more than the honor of your hand in marriage."

The smile that filled her heart and soul and face was unquenchable. "Oh, Reese," she sighed. "You've had my hand and my heart since the day we met."

As Jayce gazed into her husband's contented eyes, she knew that she had tamed her brute.

A Bride for Gideon

Patricia Werner

One

Julesburg, Colorado Territory
June, 1861

Lou Farland rode like a bandit past the Lodgepole Bluffs and down the sand hills toward the South Platte River. Her time across the short-grass prairie from the last way station had been good. And the last twelve miles on a fresh horse always went faster. Both rider and horse knew they were coming into a home station, one where both horse and rider were changed.

Lou would hand over the *mochila,* the leather skirt that fit over her saddle and which contained four compartments used for the mail. In the eight months she'd been riding for the pony express, not once had she failed to arrive on time and safely and do her part in the fast mail service that linked the Union to California, Utah, and Oregon.

Her horse dashed down the slope to the crossing down-river of the mouth of Lodgepole Creek, where it emptied into the South Platte. The river was up from spring runoff in the Rocky Mountains far to the west, so the horse splashed into the muddy water and plunged across the swift-flowing current. Lou squeezed her knees around the apron of the waterproof *mochila,* in case the current tried to play tricks with them. In such fine weather, she didn't mind getting splashed in the cold water because she'd be able to dry off in moments at the station.

Horse and rider emerged at water's edge, both shaking themselves, and then she urged the horse up the sandy bank and onto the short grass above. She barely had to touch her bootheels to the spirited pinto, who knew that the ragged collection of log buildings ahead meant a stable and food.

Lou galloped into Julesburg. The rough little hamlet hung on to its original name by local custom in spite of lofty attempts to rename the place Overland City.

Before she hit the wide space in the road with a half dozen log buildings on either side, she heard bystanders ahead shout, "Rider comin' in."

They stepped aside as she galloped to the relay point at the end of the street where young Josh Benson waited beside a fleet chestnut Morgan horse. He was small and wiry as she was, dressed in a buckskin vest, cloth hunting shirt, and cloth trousers tucked into high boots. A slouch hat and red bandanna around his neck protected his face and neck from the prairie sun.

The pinto pranced to a stop, and Lou slid to the ground. In a flash, she lifted the *mochila* down from her saddle. Her aunt Sarah had come across the station yard and reached out to open the one unlocked compartment for the Julesburg mail.

"Welcome home, Lou," she said. Her deep blue eyes focused on her job.

In seconds Sarah had the mail out, refastened the *mochila* compartment, and stepped back.

"Thanks," replied Lou. And she tossed the leather *mochila* over to Josh, who fitted it over his saddle.

Then he turned to grin at Lou and Sarah. "See you in two days."

He mounted, flicked the ends of the reins to the chestnut's neck, pressed in his heels, and was off, leaving the dust behind him. One of the young stableboys came to take Lou's pinto to the livery stable.

Lou untied her own slouch hat and mopped her perspiring brow, lifting hunks of wet, medium blond hair away from the back of her neck, where it was plastered under her collar from sweat and the river.

"Have a good ride?" asked her aunt Sarah.

"Real fine," answered Lou.

The other woman stood hands on hips, looking composed and refreshed in her blue-print gingham dress in spite of the warm June sun. Sarah always managed to look that way even after long back-breaking hours cooking and serving food at the way station to travelers who disembarked from the Central Overland Stage on their way from Leavenworth, Kansas, to Denver City.

The whisper of a mocking grin touched Sarah's blue eyes. She didn't smile exactly. One didn't smile in a place as rough as Julesburg. It was a place that demanded constant effort and quick reflexes if one were to survive Indian raids and frequent shoot-outs between the quick-tempered men who inhabited these parts. Sarah Farland got a living from providing food and shelter to those still trickling westward on the Oregon Trail.

Sarah and Lou had been on the way to Oregon a year ago, but Sarah's husband, Lou's uncle Chad, had died from a festered wound. They'd stopped here to bury him, and Sarah had not wanted to continue. When Lou saw the stop was permanent, she'd decided Julesburg wasn't exactly a place she could live in every day and got the job with the pony express.

Girls weren't supposed to be riding for the outfit, but they hadn't known she was a girl when they'd hired her on. Some of the bosses still didn't. She was seventeen, an expert rider with little family, ready to face the dangers of the ride, and that was all they'd needed to know.

Sarah was only six years older than Lou was but had

carved out a place for herself helping to run things for the station manager, Jonathan Kingsley.

"Everything all right here?" Lou asked her aunt.

They walked together to the log way station. It stretched along toward the livery stable and had three glass-paned sash windows and one door in front. This was a home station for the pony express riders, and a bunkhouse sat across the yard at right angles to the livery stable. But Sarah insisted that Lou share the big attic room with her in the log building that served as way station. They had a room at the top of the stairs that they'd fixed up for some comfort, which Sarah got as partial payment for fixing the meals.

Sarah's lack of an answer to Lou's question told her that there was some trouble afoot, even if Sarah prided herself on being able to handle it. But before they could pursue it, a tall blond man stepped into the opening of the way-station door and paused with one hand on the doorframe. And what a man.

He was tall and solidly built. His loose linen shirt with a double row of buttons hung from confident shoulders and was tucked into a wide leather belt and trousers that allowed for flat torso and slim hips. Muscled thighs pressed against the material. Lou noticed the ivory-handled pistol stuffed into the gun belt slung over those hips.

When she lifted her face to take in his glinty hazel eyes and chiseled cheekbones, she felt her mouth drop open. His expression made him look tough enough to take on the scoundrels that had given Julesburg its unsavory repu-tation, but his golden hair, almost aristocratic nose, and pleasing mouth stunned her into breathless silence.

Sarah seemed to have no such notions and stepped right up to the gorgeous and imposing figure of a man and made introductions.

"Lou, this is U.S. Deputy Marshal Gideon Preston. He's been in town for a while on federal business."

Lou was instantly aware of her muddy clothes, plastered

hair, and face burning from the sun. She wished she'd had time to wash up at least before having to meet a man so important, and so . . . *clean.*

She took his big hand and gave it a shake, clearing her throat and squinting downward. "Pleased to meet you, Deputy Marshal."

Having not spoken much for some hours, her voice sounded hoarse and squawky to her. When she cocked her head to peek at him, she saw that he gave her a small grin.

"Likewise. Your aunt has mentioned you."

Then his face returned to a relaxed, but wary look, the kind lawmen and other officials wore as if letting it be known that they were on their guard and wouldn't be taken unawares.

Lou scuffed a boot in the dirt. "Well, uh, if you'll excuse me, I'd best wash up."

And she fled around the corner of the way station to the pump at the back. There, she splashed off the worst of the dirt before going inside. She passed through the large well-equipped kitchen and dining room and up the stairs. The second landing led down a short hallway to some crude rooms where overnight travelers could rest.

She took the wooden staircase upward to their attic retreat. She hung her hat on the peg, then sat down on the camelback trunk to tug off boots and peel off the rest of her clothes. Doing the best that she could with the towel and basin of water Sarah had left on the dresser they shared, she sponged off another layer of dirt and sweat.

While she washed, she listened out the open window cut into their log room as Sarah continued to talk to the fancy lawman still standing in the station yard below. In the background were the sounds coming from the other dozen buildings that had arisen around this way station a few years ago. She wondered what the deputy marshal was doing hereabouts.

And why her foolish heart was still hammering after her

exertion. Her blood usually pulsed from the wild ride until she got her breath. But she ought to be breathing normally by now.

When she was stripped down to nothing, she opened the trunk and pulled out a dry suit of masculine, knitted drawers and climbed into them. She rode like a boy and dressed like one, even if she didn't pretend anymore. Rough clothing was still the most handy for the kind of work she did. And sometimes she had to ride at a moment's notice, if one of the other riders were delayed for some reason. It was best to be ready.

She sat down on the quilted cover of the bed Sarah kept made for her and stretched out her weary bones. The voices from the outside drifted in, and she just let everything float over her. She didn't have to ride again for two days. Maybe a little rest . . .

When she woke up, she gave a shake and glanced up. The cotton-print curtains drifted inward on a breeze, and the fading dusk told her she'd slept hard for hours. Her stomach growled, and she got up, feeling better than when she'd ridden in. With enthusiasm, she finished dressing. Sarah was sure to have something hot and tasty downstairs on the cookstove.

As she headed for the open staircase in the middle of the attic room, she paused. Better listen first. She doubted that deputy marshal was still around, but he made her feel unusually shy, and she didn't want to just barge in if he happened to be passing the time in the common room downstairs.

She tiptoed down the staircase. Nobody on the guest floor. As she reached the bottom she saw some of the usual crowd stretched out around a potbellied stove in the common room. Tall, skinny George Dabney, who worked the stables, lifted his hand in a wave. Arthur Ramsey, who ran the trading post, sat gossiping with the way-station manager, plump, spectacled Jonathan Kingsley.

Arthur broke off from their conversation and twisted his rangy body sideways to grunt at her, peering over the top of his pipe. "Howdy, Lou."

"Howdy, Arthur," she replied.

Then she tipped her head to the man who kept Sarah employed since they'd decided to stay in Julesberg.

"Jonathan."

The station manager turned his balding head toward her. A gold watch chain gleamed on his leather vest.

"Howdy, Lou. Safe ride?"

"Safe enough," she said.

Even though the common room was filled with crudely built chairs and benches, the warmth from the potbellied stove and the horseshoes, rifles, and few pictures that hung from nails on the split-log walls gave the place a homey feel. And Sarah's feminine touch had graced it with curtains and two hooked rugs, some of the fine things she'd brought in the covered wagon.

Lou continued on through the dining room, which was just two long tables with benches, and through the door cut into the wall to the kitchen. This was the best-equipped room, with a big iron cookstove, worktable, pots and pans hanging from pegs in a dish rail at eye level. There was a pantry behind that held their stores, and the pump out back brought water from a well.

Sarah's help, Addie, a young Negress who'd escaped from the South, was washing dishes in a big tub. Lou greeted her warmly.

Sarah's normally stern expression, worn from all her hard work, relaxed when she gave Lou an appraising look.

"Hungry?" she asked, lifting one dark eyebrow.

Lou grinned. "Need you ask?"

She seated herself at the small round table in the corner that she and Sarah preferred when they were eating alone. And where Addie and Sam, the hired man, took their

meals afterward. That way they could talk privately, away
from any guests.

Soon Lou was digging into a plate of fresh stew accompanied by hot bread with melted butter. It was a meal fit
for a king . . . or a federal deputy marshal. When Sarah
brought coffee for both of them, Lou felt enough strength
return to ask her questions.

"So what's happened around here, and how did you
meet this deputy?"

Sarah seated herself at the little table and gave her niece
an ironic look. "Those are two different questions."

"Well, all right," said Lou, after gulping some of the
fresh, strong coffee. "You didn't answer me this afternoon
when I asked if everything was all right. So I take it to
mean there's been some trouble. What's worryin' you?"

Sarah gave a little huff. "I'm not always sure just who's
doing the lookin' after in this place. Me or you?"

Lou beamed. "Well now, you known durn well it takes
two of us to do that. We knew that when we came west."

Her smile faded a little. She hadn't meant to remind
her aunt of Uncle Chad's death. But Sarah seemed to understand and nodded seriously. Then she sighed.

"It's the cattle again. I don't know whether to blame
Indian raids or rustlers."

Defensive anger flared in Lou's chest. "How many this
time?"

"A dozen. Sam counted 'em this morning."

It was a small herd, and Sarah had lucked into it when
one of the British ranchers had sold out after losing most
of his herd to blizzards and Indians during the winter.
Jonathan had bought some steers to butcher for meat, but
Sarah had spent the last of her money on fifty head, thinking that if she and Lou could homestead, they might be
able to make a real home for themselves.

The cattle grew fat on the prairie grasses of the open
range. But the Cheyenne and Arapahoe Indians still didn't

like the fact that so many white folks were migrating west-ward. And they took their share of cattle and horses when-ever the chance came.

Everyone who tried to run cattle tried to help fight off the raids, but Sarah only had Black Sam, her hired help who'd come with them from Illinois. And she wasn't really sure it was Indians. The tribes had been leaving the little settlement alone lately.

Sarah fixed Lou with her steady blue-eyed gaze.

"Acton Burns came around again, asking to buy the herd."

Lou paused in gulping down her coffee. Her eyes nar-rowed, and she looked at her aunt's hardened gaze with a suspicious one of her own.

"Did he, now?"

Sarah's mouth drew into a hard line as she started to clear the dishes. She gestured for Lou not to get up. "There's a pie just cooled from the oven."

Addie had finished up, and Sarah told her to go out and have the night to herself. Addie skedaddled to sit on the back steps in the cooler air.

Lou leaned back and listened to the sounds of convivi-ality coming from the common room. She wished she felt like relaxing herself, but her aunt's mention of Acton Burns gave her an ill feeling. She didn't like the man.

"Is Burns still determined to start a cattlemen's associa-tion around here?" Lou asked Sarah.

Sarah uncovered the pie and was cutting into it slowly, making sure that all the pieces were even. She dished up pieces for Lou and herself and brought them to the table.

The straight line of her mouth hadn't lost its grim irri-tation, and her blue eyes glinted with the hardness that came from working in what some called the Great Ameri-can Desert. She shoved a piece of pie at Lou.

"They talk about it. But you can be sure Burns will make

sure any small-time homesteaders like us are left out in the cold."

Lou lowered her voice. "Do you think he stole the cattle?"

Sarah's chin went up. "I can't prove it. And I can't have Black Sam working all day for me and stayin' up all night to keep watch."

Lou crammed pie in her mouth. When she could speak she sat up straighter. "I'll be home for two days now. I can watch the herd at night."

Sarah looked doubtful, flicking her eyes toward the opening to the common room as if watchful that someone would decide to come into the kitchen and hear their conversation.

"You need your sleep."

Lou shrugged her thin shoulders. "I'll get enough."

There was a stir in the front part of the building, and even from their vantage point in the kitchen they could both tell that there were new arrivals coming in the front door. But before Sarah could scrape back her chair and wipe her hands on her apron to go see, footsteps on the floorboards announced a customer's approach.

Then, the tall, handsome Deputy Marshal Gideon Preston appeared in the doorway and looked around the cozy kitchen. In one glance, Lou saw the interest in his glimmering hazel eyes. He wore that look of yearning you saw on so many newcomers to the west, admiration for a home that managed to look comfortable. No small feat for a territory where Indians still threatened from time to time and feuds in the sparsely populated and unorganized territories were normally settled with a gun.

She realized she was staring and looked down. She wondered how long he'd been in town.

Sarah seemed unbothered by his presence and invited him to sit down. He removed his hat and hung it on a peg. She served up some pie and coffee, putting it in front of him without asking.

"Why thank you, ma'am," he said politely.

His voice was mellow like honey, but with an underlying certainty.

He tucked himself into the chair and scooted closer to the table. Lou wanted both to remain near him and to move away. Then she silently rebuked herself for being so dumbstruck by the tall, handsome lawman. So she sat up straighter, thrust out her chin, and took a sip of coffee to do something with her hands.

Sarah and Gideon exchanged a few trivial comments before Lou felt like joining the conversation.

Gideon swallowed a bit of pie, praised Sarah, and cast Lou a grin, making her heart double its beat all over again.

"How long you been riding for the pony?" he asked.

She shrugged her shoulders, glad at least that she had on a clean shirt that Sarah had made.

"Eight months."

Tiny lines creased at the corners of his eyes, and some of his straw-colored hair fell across his tanned brow.

"I didn't know they let girls ride."

"They don't. Not normally anyhow. But I showed 'em how good I could ride."

His eyes swept along her figure as if assessing that she was lean and trim enough to make a fast rider. His assessment seemed approving, and he nodded.

"I don't doubt that. I saw you ride in."

"You did?"

"Hmmm." He munched at the pie and washed it down with coffee. Sarah poured more.

But Lou didn't like being the subject of the conversation. She had a few questions of her own.

"How long you been in town?" she asked him, not quite meeting his eyes.

He was nodding and smiling at Sarah in silent thanks for the second cup of coffee anyway.

"Few days," he answered.

She waited for a moment. No one else said anything, so she decided she might as well.

"Stayin' long?"

It sounded cordial enough, but from the seconds it took for him to frame his answer, she knew he knew that what she was really asking was why was he here?

He leaned back in the creaky chair, stretching the wood joints with his weight.

"Well now, that depends. I have some business for the Union to take care of. Can't say how long that would be."

Lou jerked her chin in a nod. Then her eyes met his again, feeling a mite more comfortable. He didn't seem so intimidating now.

"Well," she drawled, "it can't hurt to have a lawman hereabouts."

He considered her, then stirred his coffee slowly with a spoon. "Been some trouble around here?"

Before saying anything, Lou looked up at Sarah, who took a chair. Her aunt didn't send any warning glances, which meant that she didn't mind if they told the deputy what was going on.

Lou spoke to Gideon but looked at Sarah as she said, "Cattle rustling. Probably Indians."

She knew better than to point a finger at who they thought was really stealing the cattle. Deputy Marshal Gideon Preston might finish up his business and leave by the end of the week. Lou and Sarah had to live here and make themselves agreeable to everyone, at least on the surface.

But Gideon's interest was piqued. "Rustling, now, is it?"

He looked from one to the other of the women, but neither of them said any more.

"Hmmmm," he said. "Well, if I see anybody doing any rustling, I'll have 'em arrested."

"Doubt you'll see 'em," said Lou. "They work at night."

They all exchanged looks that spoke more than they were saying. But it was enough. Lou knew that Gideon had his own business to attend to. He wouldn't cross a man as powerful as Acton Burns without proof. And Acton had a way of covering his backside.

Gideon got up when it was time to go and thanked them both kindly.

"I'm stayin' at the boardinghouse at the end of the street. You ladies call on me, now, if you need anything."

His slow smile dazzled, then he settled his hat on his head. Lou and Sarah watched him disappear into the next room. His boots on the floorboards mingled with the other sounds of conversation and folks shifting around to get a comfortable spot in the front room.

Black Sam came to the back door, and Sarah let him in.

"Evenin', Miss Sarah," the big, smiling man said as he entered the kitchen. "I got all the chores done."

"Thank you, Sam. Come in and eat your supper."

"Why, hello, Miss Lou." The smile widened in his beaming black face, and Lou grinned at him, making room for him at the table.

"Hello, Sam." Then she turned all business. "I heard there's been some trouble."

He rasped a dejected sigh. "Lost some cattle. Just can't keep my eye on all fifty head all the time, what with the rest of the work to do. Not that I'm complainin', mind you."

"It's not your fault, Sam," said Sarah, bringing a dish of hot stew over to him. She cast her gaze at her niece. "Lou says she wants to help you keep watch the next two nights."

He grunted, then spoke before he dug into his food. "That'd be a help. But Lou's got her own job to do."

"I'm home for a couple of days, Sam. I'll stand watch."

Then in a lower voice. "I don't like to think that powerful cattlemen around here object to a couple of women owning a few head."

He swallowed and met her gaze with his fierce black eyes. "Might be that some don't like two women who keep a Negro hired man to help them."

Lou felt a cold shiver. Acton Burns hailed from Missouri. Could be he was a Southern sympathizer. She didn't say anything. But it made her wary. If Burns were a sympathizer to the Southern states, he would also be dangerous to the pony express, an organization whose owners were dedicated to keeping Oregon and California tied to the Union by fast communication, proof of the feasibility of a stage line across the central route.

She scraped back her chair and stood up. "I'll keep first watch, Sam. You rest. I'll call you if I need any help."

"If you're sure, Lou. I'll just be in the shed."

She gave both of them a stern nod and went upstairs to fetch her gun belt. When she returned, she tied her slouch hat under her chin. Then she crossed the room to reach for one of the rifles on its rack next to the cupboard. It was a .44 caliber Henry repeating-rifle with the new metallic-cased cartridges. Uncle Chad had bought it for the trip west.

"It's been cleaned and oiled," said Sarah quietly. She fetched a box of cartridges, which Lou stuck in one of her vest pockets.

She left the coziness of the kitchen for the dusky evening outside. Behind her in the street, the sounds of the revelers came from the ramshackle buildings in between. A few voices were raised at the saloon, a nightly occurrence everyone was used to. Gunshots might erupt if someone got offended. Then it was best to stay inside.

The settlement of Julesburg had begun a few years ago, named for the scalawag Jules Beni who had established a trading post at the popular Indian crossing. Then the Overland Stage had rattled down the South Platte River, heading for Denver City. But wagon robberies turned out to be perpetrated by Beni himself, his cronies dressed as Indians.

So the branch manager of the stage line came to investigate, confronted Beni, and fired him. Beni ambushed him. But the man survived, tracked down Beni, and shot him. Then he cut off Beni's ears and nailed one to the door as a warning.

Lou was recalling these sordid events as she picked her way around the split-log cow pen they'd built for roundup time. They had herded Sarah's new cattle in and branded them with a Lazy S, an S lying on its right side.

She strolled across the field behind the cow pen and down toward the river. No one would think it odd that she was taking a walk. But in fact, she wanted to approach the open range in some degree of cover. Once she came to where the cattle were grazing, she'd rather not be seen as she set up her watch.

She tramped along the riverbank, enjoying the stiff evening breeze. The sun had finally sunk over the hot, dusty plain, leaving the remnants of a sunset in a burnished western sky. A yellow-bellied kingbird shrilled his bickering call, while a brilliantly colored bluebird sang lively and high in measured summer phrases. In the distance a redtailed hawk glided overhead, circling some prey in the grass.

The tall grasses brushed Lou's trousers as she made her way among the cottonwoods on a path used by Indians and fur traders alike before the settlers came. She'd been out here alone before, and she wasn't afraid. Nature and Indians were things you just had to take your chances on. And you usually knew the Indians were coming long before they got there.

What she was more afraid of was men like Acton Burns, men with power and a grudge. Meanness and greed, that got her back up.

She followed the line of trees until she was a ways from the settlement, then she climbed up a slope leading to the range. Light was fading gradually, but she could see where the herd was grazing. There was nothing to keep them from wandering off or mixing with other herds, nothing except their Lazy S brand. But Lou had gotten to recognize them and she moved in close enough to be able to see the brand.

She talked low to the cattle in a reassuring voice so she wouldn't scatter them. They weren't spooked, so she found a likely spot to watch for a while, sitting cross-legged, the rifle across her lap. A spot where she could see a mile around if there was anyone coming. And she would hear them approach long before that. Besides, there was a silvery moon out. Her eyes would grow accustomed to the darkness.

She sat there alone with the cattle, thinking about Deputy Marshal Gideon Preston. He was a fine figure of a man, no doubt about that. Trouble was, she had trouble looking at his lithe, masculine body. His prowess was quiet, but it was unmistakable. There was some steel in his hazel eyes, masked by his comfortable smile. She wondered just how friendly he'd become with Sarah.

She shivered though it wasn't cold, and the cattle were munching and calling to their calves peacefully. She couldn't help but hope that Gideon Preston would stay around. Julesburg had elected a city marshal, but he was a mealy-mouthed man who would take orders from a man like Acton Burns. No, they needed someone like Gideon Preston to stand for law and order in a tough little town like Julesburg, with its toehold on the plains.

Two

"Ever think about homesteading, Preston?" Acton Burns shoved the bottle of whiskey across the bar toward the deputy marshal.

Gideon leaned on the wooden bar and lifted his glass to his host.

"That would require a home and a wife, now wouldn't it?"

"That and a few animals," replied Acton.

He wore a tailored black coat, white shirt, black vest, and string tie. His polished boots shone beneath the hems of his gray-striped trousers. A silver-handled revolver gleamed in the holster strapped to his leg.

Gideon tossed back his drink and set the glass down. The firewater burned his throat, then suffused his limbs. He smiled congenially.

"I hear you've got yourself quite a herd," he said.

It was casual conversation, nothing to give away Gideon's real intent, which was to find out just what kind of activities Acton Burns was up to and for whom.

"That's right," Burns said. "There's money to be made in cattle out here. Free grass is what it amounts to on the public lands. And the markets east are cryin' for beef."

Gideon rested his elbows on the bar behind him, gazing casually at the other customers gathered in the brightly lit saloon over cards at two round tables.

"What about the South?"

Acton shrugged, as if the Confederate States were no concern of his. "I sell my cattle for the best price I can get come time to drive 'em to Denver City for the miners."

"That's where you take 'em?"

Burns didn't answer.

Both men were gauging each other, and neither was giving anything away. From across the room, the small-of-stature, black-moustached city marshal, John McGee, lifted his eyes from his cards and glanced up at Gideon, whom he'd met when the federal deputy had ridden into town.

Gideon touched his hat in greeting. McGee nodded somberly in acknowledgment, then returned to his cards.

Gideon could see that McGee would have his hands full if there were actually any trouble in Julesburg. He was no doubt the kind of official controlled by the real men who ran the town. Men like Acton Burns and his cattlemen's association. And that made Gideon very curious indeed about this cattlemen's association. It was a subject he had decided to find out more about.

Acton pressed on with his own friendly snooping.

"So what brings you to these parts, stage robberies?"

Gideon gave a noncommittal nod. "You could say that."

Then to further lead Acton away from the truth, he gave a grin and a wink. "Might consider homesteading hereabouts, like you said. Been lookin' for a wife if truth be told."

Acton gave a snort. "You'd do better to look for a woman in Denver City. Things are sparse right here."

Gideon gave a shrug. "Had myself some mighty good pie just now over at the way station."

At the mention of Sarah Farland, Acton's eyes narrowed. His voice took on a thin veil of wariness.

"Have some interest there, do you?"

Gideon gave a disarming smile and poured himself

some more whiskey just to be sociable. He had no intention of getting drunk.

"I didn't say that, now, did I? Just that it was right pleasant to sit in that kitchen and smell home cooking."

Then his gaze drifted off in the direction of the way station as if thinking to himself. "And to keep pleasant company."

He brought his mind back to business. If Acton Burns were doing anything illegal, it was enough to let him know that he wasn't immune to the law. Gideon wouldn't put any pressure on him. Burns would trip up soon enough if he were trying to sneak around. And when he did, Gideon would be there.

He finished his drink, thanked Acton, and ambled across the room to where John McGee had just thrown down his cards in disgust. He was clearly out of the game. Gideon stood beside his chair, and McGee, becoming aware of the federal marshal's presence, finally looked up.

"How 'bout a stroll outside, McGee?" asked Gideon in a friendly way.

McGee flicked an eye at Acton, but the rest of the men at the table studiously avoided his or Gideon's eyes.

McGee smiled thinly. "Why, that sounds like a fine idea. I ain't aimin' to lose my shirt tonight."

The two men left the noticeably quieted saloon before things livened up again.

They strolled to the end of the street and stood peering into the darkness where the road ambled along beside the South Platte River toward Denver City. The wind gusted through the tall grasses, and birds settled down in branches along the river for the night. In the distance came the barely audible sounds of cattle lowing. It was a deceptively quiet night. The kind of night when dark deeds were accomplished out on that eerie rolling prairie.

He suddenly wondered where Lou Farland was. From the moment he'd set eyes on her there was something about her that moved him. Her boy's getup and the mud all over her face hadn't fooled him. She was tough, having to prove herself to do her job. But her liquid green eyes and the warmth he'd seen flow between her and her aunt had spoken volumes. Maybe it was the fact that they were family that struck a poignant chord in Gideon. Family was something he'd been sorely lacking for the last few years.

He let the cool air clear his head and spoke to his companion.

"You get much trouble hereabouts?" he asked.

The little city marshal shook his head.

"Oh, no. The boys get excited once in a while and go on a rampage. But nobody gets hurt mostly. Stage robberies stopped some time ago after Jules Beni got his ears cut off. You could say things go on without any trouble here."

"Hmmm. I suppose the cattlemen's association sees to that."

The comment caught McGee off guard and he sputtered. "Well, Acton Burns don't let no . . ." His words drifted off.

Gideon grunted. "He won't stand for interference, is that it?"

"Well, uh . . ." McGee smacked his lips. "He, uh, formed the association to protect the herds from cattle rustlers."

"Ah, I see."

"Yessir. Seems to be workin'. Cattle rounded up and shipped without any trouble."

Gideon could practically see a large group of men in Burns's pay, standing around with mean-looking rifles to make sure that business deals were transacted the way he wanted them.

Gideon studied the dark shapes near the river. "Well, you're lucky then. No stage robberies. No cattle rustlers. Nice safe town you got here."

McGee cleared his throat as if unsure whether Preston

was sincere or was mocking him. He squared his narrow shoulders, standing up as tall and cocky as he could. He gave a jerk of his narrow chin.

"Got to keep law and order," he said.

"Ummm hmmm, I'm sure you do."

Then Gideon exhaled a long breath as if ready to fill his lungs with the clean night air.

"Have a pleasant evening, McGee. And sleep well. As for myself, I think I'll just take a little ride down by the river. My horse is a mite thirsty."

McGee tried to peer into his face in the moonlight, but evidently gave up trying to figure him out. He turned back to the little collection of buildings that called itself a settlement.

"G'night, then, Deputy."

" 'Night, McGee."

Gideon watched him go, then he went to fetch his piebald horse, Beau. He untied his reins from the rail where he'd been hitched.

"Come on, boy."

The horse whickered softly, nuzzling Gideon, then following, ears forward, as Gideon led him out of town.

For this evening's explorations he wanted to go on foot, rather than on horseback. But he took Beau in case he encountered the need for swiftness. They found the path along the river and walked slowly along. There was another reason for having Beau. Animals knew before humans did if there was trouble about. Many a time Beau had warned Gideon of approaching danger.

But now the horse plodded along, nostrils working to take in the many scents along the riverbank. Beau whickered happily and bumped Gideon's shoulder. No danger here.

After the horse drank from the river, Gideon led him back up the bank, then up the slope toward the lowing cattle on the range. He wasn't looking for anything in particular. Just wanted to get the lay of the land and see what he might discover about Acton Burns's activities.

When they were standing on the little rise where he could see the humped figures of at least a thousand head in the moonlight, Beau's ears strained forward, and he gave a low rumble in his throat, moving his head to the left and listening.

"Something out there, boy?" whispered Gideon.

Out of habit his fingers touched the pistol handle at his hip just in case he should need it.

"Don't come any farther," came a voice that he thought he recognized.

He turned in the direction of the voice, his hands raised, but at first he couldn't see her. Then he heard the soft brush of boots in the grass and saw the outline of the slouched hat and slim hips against the slightly darker background. When she was close enough, he also saw the long end of the rifle pointed at him.

"Don't shoot, Lou," he said, gently. "It's Gideon Preston."

She came forward until she could see his face, then she lowered the rifle, but still kept it angled sideways across the front of her body.

"What're you doing out here?" she asked in a low, careful voice.

Her question struck him with irony and he grinned. "I could ask the same of you. Shall we talk?"

She lowered the rifle farther and glanced at his horse.

"It's all right, Beau," he said, still trying not to make Lou nervous. Then he moved forward, the reins still in his left hand.

He came up to Lou, and she tipped her head back, her face looking particularly pretty in the silvery shadows. He wanted her to take off her hat so he could see her better. *Bless my soul,* he thought to himself. What was it about this girl that so intrigued him?

He cleared his throat and gazed at the quiet herd. What as she doing out here among all these cattle? This was n awfully big herd.

"These your cattle?" he asked.

She eyed him warily, then spoke in a somber voice. "I ink some of them are."

"What do you mean by that?"

"I been watchin' our herd in the next pasture over ere. We told you some of 'em been rustled off. Don't ink it's Indians. No Cheyenne or Arapahoe been seen these parts for a while."

Gideon squinted at the larger herd, the mention of istling priming his interest.

"What do you think happened to them?"

Lou's voice was low and intense. "These here are Acton urns's cattle. But some of ours, too. I know 'em cause I amed 'em."

"You named 'em?"

She nodded. "Fifty head ain't much. I got to know 'em. hat's how I can tell some of 'em are here."

"I hope you branded 'em as well as gave them names." e couldn't resist a little humor in his voice.

"Well, that too. But brands can be altered."

He paused. "So you can't prove by the brands they're ours?"

"Well, I can, if you look and see how the brands've been essed with."

"Show me."

She studied him as if suspicious of any trickery.

Then she made up her mind. "OK, but don't spook em. Leave your horse here."

Gideon dropped the reins and left Beau where he could raze on the tall grass. Then he followed Lou closer to the erd. She talked to the cattle so that they didn't get up or the most part as she and the deputy began to thread etween them. Then she came up to one old steer who gave a loud moo as they approached. Some of the other cattle got up and lumbered away.

"Acton's brand is a figure eight with a bar through it. All he has to do is finish our Lazy S and cross it with a bar and it looks like his. But that mark's been singed recently."

Gideon straightened. "Why would he want to steal your cattle? Looks like he's got plenty of his own."

"If you ask me, I'd say he don't cotton to the idea of a woman running cattle on the grazing lands."

Gideon pondered her words as he let his eyes pierce the darkness. What with blizzards in the winter, some cattlemen lost as much as a third of their herds. The settlers' hold on this territory was still tenuous. He shook his head. There had to be more to Acton's motives than that.

"I'd like to get your cattle back," he told her. "But unless there's witnesses to him stealing the cattle, or altering the brands like you say, I'm afraid I can't arrest him."

"There might be witnesses," she told him, a tone of stubbornness creeping into her voice. "Black Sam and I are keeping watch."

He felt a twinge of admiration for the tenacity of these two women who'd stopped at Julesburg. A town like this needed the civilizing company of women. He just hoped they wouldn't be run off.

And he was noticing more about Lou Farland than he was prepared to say. Her trim body and unmistakable curving bosom under her shirt were mighty appealing. Her voice struck a chord in him and sent a pleasant little tingle through him that made him want to remain here beside her. The darkness was cool, and their whispers out here among the cattle had a clandestine quality about it that made him feel drawn toward her enterprise.

They moved away from the cattle and stopped near where his horse was grazing. He was liking the appearance of Lou's face in the moonlight, too, now that she'd let her hat fall back on her shoulders. Anyone with spunk enough to go up against a powerful cattleman like Acton Burns had to earn Gideon's respect.

"How'd you come to put down roots here?" he asked her, feeling in no hurry to leave.

He saw the way her mouth jerked at the corner, and her eyelids lowered for an instant.

"We were heading for the Oregon country. Me and Sarah, we decided we needed a new kind of life. Uncle Chad was sick. When he died, we stopped to bury him. Sarah just didn't want to go on."

"Sorry."

Lou seemed to be enjoying the company as well and didn't move off.

"You got any other family?" he asked.

She shook her head, her chin lifting in that way he could tell she used to let folks know that she had pride.

"My ma died and Pa couldn't stand it. He got into bad company after that. Went to prison sometime back. My brother is in the Union army, if he's still alive. We only get letters every few months."

"Sorry." They let a moment pass.

Then Gideon said, "So you came west to get a new start."

"Yup. I could ride and shoot as well as any man. So I got hired to ride for the pony express."

"A dangerous job, that. You like sticking your neck out?"

One shoulder went up and back in a shrug. "The pay's good. We need the money."

Her vest had swept back in front and Gideon kept his face neutral. No use mentioning that she looked nothing like a boy with those rounded hips and narrow waist. Her face with those defiant green eyes and feminine mouth looked like it belonged out here in the moonlight. But it was good for something besides standing off cattle rustlers. His mind began to wander into what.

He shook his head. He'd been without a woman for too

long. Long days in the saddle and nights on dirt floors of settlers' cabins had left him aching to rub up against smooth skin. Better to keep his thoughts to himself.

They heard a rustle in the grass and both reached for their weapons. As a shadowy shape came over the rise, Lou relaxed.

"It's just Sam, come to relieve me."

"It's OK, Sam," she said, as the other man approached. "Deputy Marshal Preston's here."

Sam came near enough to see them. "When you weren't over by the herd, I got worried."

"I just came over here to see if I could find any of our cattle. The deputy was out for a moonlight stroll. That's all."

"If you're sure, Lou. Then I'll go back and keep watch."

"Best do that, Sam. We can't leave our herd alone for long."

"Doesn't Acton Burns keep his own guards out here?" asked Gideon.

"Sure does, and they know I'm here. I ran into a couple of 'em the first hour I was out here and hailed 'em before they could shoot me. Told 'em me and Sam would be standin' guard around our herd for the night. They rode off somewhere."

Gideon resettled his hat. "I'll ride you back, then," he said to Lou, half-disappointed that they had to go in. But he didn't want to deprive her of her rest.

"It won't be necessary," she said. But he thought he heard some encouragement in her voice.

"Girl like you'll need your rest."

He picked up his horse's reins and turned Beau around. He slid her rifle into a scabbard tied to his saddle, then waited for her to mount up. She removed her foot from the stirrup so he could get a leg up behind her.

When his strong arms reached around Lou for the reins, she trembled as his warmth surrounded her. His face came near her cheek as he separated the reins and clucked to Beau. She really hadn't ever been so near a man like this. New feelings swam through her as she drank in his masculine protection. And she liked having her back pressed gently against his chest. It felt safe and secure against the wind that rushed across the grasses in little gusts as if someone were walking there.

They didn't have to say anything, and she couldn't have if she'd wanted to. What was passing between them was complemented by the darkness, the loneliness of the rolling plains. She didn't want it to end.

When they reached the way station in town, Gideon rode around to the back, where it was quieter. He slid to the ground.

Lou kicked one leg over Beau's neck and slid down into Gideon's arms. She ducked her head under his chin as he held her shoulders for a moment. Neither of them moved.

Then his voice came softly. "You'll be all right?"

"Sure."

He let her go, and she walked shakily toward the back door. She turned to glance at him before going in. He lifted his hat in the shadows.

"G'night," she mumbled.

"Pleasant dreams, Lou."

She went inside and shut the door, sliding the bolt. Then she leaned there a while, shaken by her newfound feelings. She peeked through the muslin curtains and watched him lead his piebald horse away in the direction of the boardinghouse.

"Don't be foolish," she whispered to herself. "A man like that ain't never gonna' look at you."

She dropped the curtain and replaced her rifle on the rack in the kitchen. Then she tramped up the stairs, walking more softly when she reached the attic landing so as not to wake Sarah.

Three

There weren't any more cattle thefts before Lou had to leave on the Sweetwater Run.

She was dressed for the ride, and a fleet-footed pinto was saddled and waiting in the warm June morning. The horse stood in the shade where he could reach the water trough. Lou rechecked the cinch and saw that her ammunition was dry. So far she hadn't had to use it. The pony express riders counted on their grain-fed animals being able to outrun grass-fed Indian ponies, should the need arise.

She heard the distant pounding of hooves coming over the ground, then the rider appeared at the end of the street.

"Rider comin'," Sarah said from where she waited in the station yard.

She watched Lou settle her hat on her head and mount her horse. They both squinted at the rider dashing in. His horse reared on its heels, then he jumped down, unfastening the *mochila* from his saddle. He crossed to Lou and flung it over her horse's back.

"H'llo, there Lou," said the dirt-covered young man. In spite of the dust plastered on his face and in his hair, she recognized Billy Joe Taylor.

"Hi, Billy Joe. Good ride?"

"No trouble."

As soon as the *mochila* was secure, Billy Joe stepped back.
Lou mounted and turned the horse into the road. Just
before she dug her heels in, heading for the river crossing,
her eyes lit on Gideon, who'd just come out of the false-
fronted general store across the road. He looked up at her
and touched his hat.

Even from that far away, his smile made her heart miss
a beat. She nodded and then flicked her reins, feeling his
eyes on her back. No time to speculate. She had to make
time. But it was a good day. She'd make the first leg of the
run by noon, change horses four times before stopping by
nightfall.

Her horse splashed into the river at the crossing, and
Lou dashed through. It would be a good two days before
she saw Julesberg and Gideon again.

Gideon turned his mind to his job. He'd snooped
enough to know that there was a new fellow in town who
drank with Acton Burns. He needed to find out just what
the two of them were up to. It wasn't easy to sneak up on
two men having a conversation in a place with so little
cover, but Gideon had come up with a way. The two of
them had let drop something about a card game tonight.
Gideon planned to ride out to Burns's place after dark
and listen in on their conversation if he could. The man
fit the description of a Confederate purchasing agent he'd
been told to look for.

After riding part of the way, then going on foot under
cover for the last mile, Gideon hid out behind Burns's log
ranch house that night to no avail. But he was a patient
man. He'd hadn't earned success as a deputy marshal for
nothing. As long as he could keep the purchasing agent
in sight, he would trip Burns up eventually.

* * *

Lou had an uncomfortable feeling when she rode into town again two days later. When she crested the low rise that gave her the first view of Julesburg, she could see that something was wrong. There weren't any cattle in sight on the prairie and none in the new pen that Sam must have got finished while she was away. She burned to take a detour and ride out to see if the cattle had moved off to another pasture to the south or west. But she had to get the mail in first.

So she pushed ahead, fording the stream against the strong current and climbing out to the other side. The thought of Gideon crossed her mind. She'd thought of almost no one else in the time she'd been away. Now as she pounded breathlessly along the road, she half hoped she wouldn't see him in her muddy, windburned state.

She dashed through the crowd that waved their hats like they always did when a pony express rider came through. Then she jolted to a stop at the way station. Josh Benson was ready, and she jumped down, whisking the *mochila* off the saddle and laying it at Sarah's feet.

"Hi, Lou," said Sarah, busying her hands to get out the Julesburg mail before Lou handed the leather *mochila* over to Josh, who slung it onto his saddle.

Once he was off, Lou untied her hat and caught her breath. She looked over Sarah's shoulder, half-expecting Gideon to appear. When he didn't, she wiped her brow with her sleeve and led her horse to the stable.

Instead of the stableboy, Sam appeared out of the shadows to take the horse.

"Howdy, Lou. Good ride?"

She handed him her reins. "All right. How about things here?"

His black face looked anxious, and she could see the anger in the whites of his eyes. Seeing that he must have something to say in private, she followed him to the stall and helped unsaddle so they could talk.

"It's the cattle, ain't it?" she said, when he didn't answer her question.

He took off the horse's bridle and reached for a rag to rub down the wet, sweaty animal. Sam didn't meet Lou's gaze.

"Got stolen, far as I can tell."

"All of them?"

He nodded, working on the horse, who shook his neck in pleasure at the attention it was getting.

"Yup. I checked all the ravines. Couldn't get close enough to Burns's herd for fear I'd be shot by his guards. He's doubled them up. But our cattle ain't anywhere else that they could walk to. They had to be driven off."

Lou clenched her teeth. "That's it, then. We're going to do something about it."

"What do you think we can do? Just you and me and Miss Sarah."

She cleared her throat. "That federal deputy marshal still around?" She tried to make it sound casual.

"That Deputy Preston? Yeah, I think I seen him around."

She shifted her weight from one foot to the other. Foolish to ask if he'd seen Sarah. She loved her aunt, but she was very aware of some strange new feelings that made her self-conscious of the difference between them. In spite of all her hard work, Sarah always looked pretty in a gingham or cotton-print dress she'd made. Her dark hair had natural curls that she kept done up in a loose bun at the back of her head.

Lou had never cared about looking pretty before. There was too much to do to survive out here. But when she saw Gideon Preston, he made her want to look pretty. But she'd die before she told anyone.

She wished he'd help with the cattle, but Gideon had only her word that the cattle he saw had had their brands changed, so he couldn't prove anything.

She waited until Sam was done with the horse, then they crossed the shadowy stables. The other horses were out in the corral. One thing about the pony express, they got the best horseflesh—native mustangs, pintos, and Morgans. The riders' lives depended on them.

Even while she was admiring the horses, a plan was forming in the back of her mind.

"We're gonna' get those cattle back," she said with soft intensity, so that only Sam could hear.

"How we gonna' do that?"

"Let me think about it, Sam. I think I know how."

She went on into the station building. Sarah met her in the kitchen and nodded grimly. "Tub of hot water's in the pantry," she said. "I set up the screen."

"Thanks, Sarah. That sounds good."

Lou fetched clean clothes and then headed down to the kitchen. There was room in the pantry for the round wooden tub, and Sarah had poured hot water into it. A bar of soap and towels were on a three-legged stool nearby. But before she undressed and indulged in the tub bath, she went out for a quick word with Sam and gave him some instructions for what she had in mind this evening.

Back in the pantry, Lou stripped out of her dirty clothes and stepped thankfully into the warm water. It sure felt good after the hard day's ride, and she slid down, resting her head against the rim of the tub.

She almost fell asleep, but then roused herself and dunked her head in to scrub her scalp and wash her hair. The hot bath started to restore her spirits, and she gave some more thought to the cattle problem. They'd have to sneak up on the herd tonight and see what they could do.

Then she heard a voice in the kitchen that made her sit up so suddenly she sloshed water over the edge of the tub. Gideon's unmistakable deep voice was conversing in a most congenial way with Sarah. Lou strained to listen, embarrassed that she was eavesdropping.

"Don't mind if I do," he said.

"I always try to have something fresh-baked when Lou rides in," she heard Sarah explain.

She could almost see him smile.

"Then that's lucky for both of us," he drawled.

Lou hugged herself in the tub, a blush of embarrassment creeping over her. She was stark naked in the tub with nothing to keep prying eyes from seeing should anyone take it into their head to come into the pantry. Sarah would keep them out, of course, but Lou lost her head for a minute imagining the devastatingly handsome Gideon Preston looming around the corner at any moment. It made her finish her bath more quietly and reach for the towel to dry herself without making any noise.

The conversation in the kitchen kept up at a leisurely pace, and she heard Gideon mention that he'd be away for a day or so on government business.

She stubbed her toe getting out of the tub and bit her lip to keep from squealing. Finally, she got into the clean clothes and rubbed her hair as dry as she could, combing it out with her fingers.

It was all silly. What did it matter what she looked like to a man as important as a U.S. deputy marshal? Better that he go away on his business so she could be clear-headed about what she needed to do here.

When she was ready, she stepped around the corner into the cozy kitchen. The gentle evening light made the place inviting after the heat of the day. Gideon broke off mid-sentence and rose out of his chair. Sarah poured a cup of coffee for Lou at the stove, then gestured to their corner table.

"I made corn soup," she said, filling the awkward silence between the other two.

Lou and Gideon stared at each other for a minute, neither saying anything. Then he nodded. She tried to cross the room in normal fashion, but felt weak in the legs. He held out a chair for her, but she decided to sit in the one farthest from him and nodded her thanks.

"Thanks. This here'll do fine."

She was glad that the coffee appeared, so she would have something to do with her hands and her mouth. Still, she couldn't resist peeking at him over the rim of the cup. His golden eyes glimmered at her, and his mouth twitched at the corners. *Bet he does that to all the women he meets,* she thought.

When Sarah rejoined them, Lou glanced at her out of the corner of her eyes. She wondered if Sarah was as smitten by the deputy marshal as she was. If so, then Gideon would be a fool not to come courting her.

Gideon leaned back, hooking his thumbs through his belt.

"Heard you had a problem with your cattle," he said casually.

Lou and Sarah exchanged glances. Lou could tell Sarah wasn't anxious to talk about it. That's how it always was with them. They kept problems to themselves. You didn't know whom to trust. Just because a man wore a badge didn't necessarily mean he was on your side. A lot of times a lawman was just a puppet for somebody bigger and more powerful.

Sarah narrowed her eyes, speaking guardedly. "They seemed to wander off. Black Sam was out lookin' for 'em."

"And?"

"Didn't find 'em. They either got driven off, or the rustlers got to 'em."

Gideon grunted, but he looked at both women with that scrutinizing gaze that seemed to miss nothing.

"Any idea who might have run off with 'em?"

Sarah stuck her chin out. "I got my ideas, but they change the brands so fast, I can't prove it. Maybe it was a mistake to try to run cattle around here. The big herds just seem to swallow them up."

She looked meaningfully at Gideon, then busied herself cutting the pan of corn bread she'd brought to the table.

Lou looked at Gideon, then glanced away. She wasn't about to confide any of her ideas. Better to let things take their course.

His speculative gaze was making her nervous. His eyes glinted, and his expression set on her as if he were thinking. She couldn't help the way her spine tingled at her being in the same room with him again. She'd thought of him while she was away, but she'd forgotten some of the things. Like how his tall, masculine frame seemed to fill the kitchen with his presence. It made Lou's heart quicken and the blood hum through her veins.

His lips curved up in just a bit of a smile. She could tell he was enjoying himself. Who wouldn't with Sarah's cooking and the tidy kitchen? They said there weren't enough women in the West, and you could tell when you walked into a shack that a man lived in alone. None of the comforts and pretty things a woman could do would be found.

Lou shook her head. Funny thing to be thinking about pretty things when she should be thinking about her plans for tonight. But maybe not. She was beginning to wonder if Deputy Marshal Preston was some sort of mind reader. The best lawmen had instincts that normal men hadn't. If he was one of those, best to keep him off her trail. When there was a lull in the conversation, Lou spoke up.

"How long do you reckon you'll be around here?" she asked.

He shrugged. "Hard to say."

"Government work," she commented, as if understanding what he meant.

He nodded. "That's it. Have to find out a few things yet to do my job. When that's done, well, I haven't decided."

She looked up at him shyly. "Guess a man like you is always on the road."

He shifted his weight, his chin coming forward a bit.

"Well, now, that's true. I have a job to do, but someday, things might change. Might buy a piece of land and take up ranching."

Lou paused in her chewing and studied him, trying to picture him a rancher. A lot of men who were used to being in the saddle and using their guns found it hard to settle down in one place. Maybe he was one of those.

She looked away, still feeling his gaze on her, making her face warm. It shouldn't matter anyway.

When Gideon was through with his coffee he thanked Sarah very politely. But he caught Lou's gaze when he got up to leave.

"Guess I'll be seein' you around for a day or two," he said.

She swallowed, trying to hide the flush on her face. "Guess so."

She got up to help clear the table, but she just stood behind her chair, clutching the curved back of it until Gideon settled his hat on his head and left the room. His footsteps blended with the noises of folks conversing in the front room. She heard him laugh at a comment from someone, and then he must have gone.

She let out her breath. Then she helped Sarah do some chores. They didn't talk about anything important until they went upstairs as it began to get dark. Lou sat down on the floor to rummage through the trunk at the foot of the bed. Sarah sat at the small wooden table she used for a dressing table and lit the kerosene lamp. She began to take the pins out of her hair.

Lou couldn't resist asking what she was beginning to be curious about.

"You see much of that deputy marshal?" she said, trying to interest herself in the clothing she was sorting through in the trunk.

Sarah only paused slightly as she picked up her brush.

Her dark brows drew together thoughtfully, then she lifted her chin and began to brush her long, dark tresses.

"Not if you mean do I see him in the sense that he might be after anything from me but my cooking."

Lou made a face. "Well, he ain't exactly ugly to look at."

Sarah's face glinted with a rare touch of humor. Mostly her face betrayed nothing but hard work and determination to keep herself and Lou going.

"Well, he is a good man. Polite, respectful of feelings. But it's not me he's after."

"What do you mean?"

Sarah shrugged one shoulder. "I notice you bein' a little quiet around him yourself. Thought I saw a little blush on your cheek this evening."

Lou ducked her head and cleared her throat. "Well, can't help feelin' a little shy around a man like that. I mean he's seen the world and all."

Sarah gave a small chuckle. "No doubt he has."

Then she lowered the brush to her lap and turned in the chair to study Lou. Her voice was quiet and reassuring.

"There's nothing between the deputy marshal and me, Lou. I can assure you that."

"How can you be so sure?"

Lou pressed her lips together. She hadn't meant it to come out so quick like that.

Sarah's gaze burned into her. "Because I'm not looking for a man. It's too soon after . . ."

Lou's chest tightened. It was only six months since Chad died. They didn't talk about it much. But Sarah went out to the grave a lot to make sure it was tended. Sometimes she'd sit on a log out there by herself for a long time, thinking or maybe talking to Chad's spirit in a private way. Lou figured it wasn't any of her business.

"Sorry."

"No, it's all right. But I mean it. I'm not looking to

marry again right now. Maybe never, maybe someday. But not now. I know that in my heart."

Lou frowned. "If you're sure, then. Does Gideon know that?"

Sarah cocked her head, then turned back to her brushing. "He's seen me out at the grave. I mentioned it. He said he was sorry. That's all I know."

Lou waited for a moment, then tried to form the right words.

"Well, I don't mean to pry, a' course. But he seems like the right kind of man for a woman like you."

"What do you mean like me?"

Lou grinned. "You know, civilized. Someone who can cook and sew. And you always look pretty. A man likes that."

Sarah looked skeptical. "Those aren't the only things a man likes." Her face softened. "And besides, you learned how to sew once. And play the piano."

Old emotions flooded Lou, and she looked at Sarah with her mouth parted. They almost never talked about what life was like way back then before everything happened and before Sarah and Chad had taken Lou into their home and then left for the Oregon country. Hearing Sarah mention it was like a bolt of lightning illuminating a part of their life that she scarcely remembered herself. She blinked twice before she spoke. Then her voice was a whisper.

"That was so long ago." She shook her head. "I almost forgot." She looked into Sarah's eyes. "It seems like another lifetime."

Compassion filled Sarah's soft blue eyes. "I suppose it was," she said.

Another life when things seemed fine. When Lou had grown up in a big house on a corner of a town plot with a big oak shading it. As a little girl she'd learned all those things little girls learn from their mothers, including getting piano lessons on the upright piano. But then her mother got sick.

Lou and her brother did the best they could, walking to school and walking home again. Then their father began his odd behavior. Maybe it was his wife's illness did it. Maybe he couldn't stand to see her all thin and wan like that, barely able to get out of bed. There were few celebrations after that.

She dragged her mind back from the past. It was too painful to dwell on that. She'd turned her back on all of that when she'd gone to live with Sarah and Chad, her father's younger brother. Now here they were. It reminded her about the cattle. It made her more determined to do something about the cattle, but she wasn't going to tell Sarah what.

Sarah looked at Lou in a kind and melancholy way. "You can't ride for the pony express forever, Lou."

Lou stuck out her lower lip in a defensive pout. Her shoulders went back and her chin up. "Why not?"

"You might want to settle down, one day."

"Hmmph. We were going to settle down in the Oregon Country, and we didn't even make it there."

Now it was Sarah's turn to look stubborn. "Maybe Colorado Territory's as good a place as any."

"Maybe, if we can keep our toehold here."

"The railroad's building this way. There'll be opportunities for ranching."

"If we can hang on to our herd," said Lou, getting out a box of cartridges and reloading her pistol. She didn't intend to use it tonight, but she wanted to have it along, just in case.

"Where're you going with that thing?" asked Sarah.

"Just out to look around. Don't worry about me."

Sarah knew better than to say anything more.

"Don't wait up," said Lou as she shut the lid of the trunk.

The two women exchanged looks, but Sarah kept her lips closed. She finished brushing her hair and braided it loosely to keep the tangles out during the night. Lou disappeared down the stairs.

The way station was full. The upstairs rooms had been rented, and travelers were bedded down in the sitting room on pallets they'd unrolled for the purpose. Lou spoke to them as she skirted their feet, so as not to frighten them.

"Evenin'," she murmured when heads lifted to see who was traipsing through.

Outside she approached the livery stable quietly, glancing over her shoulder to make sure there weren't any curious pairs of eyes watching particularly close.

She waited just inside the stable for her vision to adjust to the shadowy shapes. Her favorite horse gave a neigh low in his throat.

"I'm here, Sam," she said softly.

He came out of a stall carrying a pile of old gunnysacks. "I got old Shanda's feet wrapped. These are for you."

She nodded, then applied herself to wrapping her favorite pinto's feet in the gunnysacks and tying them with twine. It was the way to avoid the horses leaving identifiable footprints. She stood up.

"All set."

They led their horses out quietly and headed for the path by the river. They didn't talk until they were far enough from town that their hushed voices wouldn't carry.

"Did you find Acton's herd?"

"Spotted 'em about three miles from here in a pasture other side of the old caves. Out of the way, all right."

"Good job. How many guards?"

"I saw four of 'em. There's an old shack at one end of the pasture. They might be usin' it for themselves."

"Good. Then if our luck holds, we won't run into any trouble. You sure you still want to do this, Sam?"

"I got the nerve if you do," he said. "What we got to lose?"

She grunted. "Our heads, is all."

They rode over the rolling grasslands until they came to a grove of trees against a rise in the ground. There were some old caves in the hilly land where the river cut through behind them. The caves ran a long way underground, but could be dangerous. Most people steered clear of them, fearing that outlaws or Indians might be hiding there.

They turned off and followed the slope downward, getting off their horses while they were still in the trees. Now they could see the herd, and on the other side of the pasture a light came from the old shack.

"We'll have to sneak up there and see what's going on," Lou whispered. "Leave the horses here."

Sam nodded, and they began to thread their way stealthily and slowly around the perimeter of the pasture, going quiet enough not to spook the cattle. When they were close to the cabin, a man's shape appeared at the doorway, and Lou signaled for Sam to draw back.

Her nerves tingled as they watched the cowhand look around. She didn't breathe for a long time. Evidently satisfied with what he saw, the man disappeared inside again. Lou motioned for Sam to stay put, while she moved closer. Creeping up to the cabin, she could see inside the doorway without being seen.

The four of them were crouched around an upturned box, sitting on bedrolls and playing cards. Rifles and six-shooters were in evidence, and she knew that if she and Sam were found out, they'd be shot. She had second thoughts about the enterprise. She was willing to face them down, but Sam was no gunman. If she and Sam both got shot, where would that leave Sarah?

She took a long breath and breathed quietly. She decided it was worth the risk. Her integrity was more important. It just wasn't right to be always under the heel of a man like Acton Burns. She had something to prove tonight.

She noticed the men passing around a bottle of whiskey. Hoping they'd be too busy with their drinking to notice too much, she crept through the trees back to Sam. She whispered into his ear.

"They're in there all right. We'll have to be real quiet and slow."

He nodded. They'd discussed it all before, and he knew what to do.

They began their silent roundup. The cattle's hooves made no sound in the soft bottom land and they didn't drive them along fast enough to start them bawling. Once a man's figure appeared at the doorway again, and Lou stopped breathing. A sound would have alerted him that something was going on. But their luck held. The cattle went where they drove them, out of the pasture through the natural opening between two low hills, then along past the caves and out toward the high grasslands.

After an hour they dared drive them faster, guiding them toward a dried-up creek bottom. The sky was turning to pewter as the last steer disappeared into the dense thickets. The horse's gunnysacks had long since worn off when Lou and Sam sat watching the cattle trample down the tall grasses. In the morning they'd come back and cut out their own cattle and drive them back home, putting them safely in the new pen.

"Guess he won't be gatherin' that bunch inside of a few weeks," grinned Sam.

She turned her horse around in the direction of town again. "We did it, Sam. We'll come back later to cut ours out of there. They'll be safe enough for now."

They galloped for home, crossing the high range before dipping down toward the river, then leading the horses into the livery stables just as the old cock was crowing at the end of the street.

Four

Sarah didn't wake when Lou crept up to bed, and her aunt let her sleep in until the sun was beating insistently through the small window.

But when Lou came downstairs, she heard the oily voice of Acton Burns in the kitchen. She slipped to the side of the dining room so she could hear their conversation, not wanting to see the man she had tricked last night.

"Now Sarah see reason," Acton was saying. "A woman can't defend her land out here all by herself. Your own cattle have a way of walking off when you're not lookin'."

"That so?" said Sarah. "Well, if they walked off, maybe they'll walk back."

He gave a chuckle. "I offered to buy your herd from you before; the offer still stands. But now I'm thinkin' of offering more than that."

Sarah didn't say anything, and Lou could imagine that she was avoiding Acton's eyes. When he spoke, his voice was even oilier and more persuasive.

"Seems to me a woman like you needs a husband. You ever think of marrying again, Sarah?"

Lou put a hand to her mouth to keep from gasping.

"I do just fine as I am, Acton. I got Sam and Addie, and I got Lou to think of. I ain't thinking of remarrying."

"Too bad," said Acton. "If you were, I might come

around myself. You could do worse for a husband. You think about it, Sarah."

Lou nearly choked. In the kitchen, Sarah maintained her poise.

"Thank you, Acton, but I'm not considering it."

A terrible revulsion overcame Lou. How dare that slimy bastard try to worm his way into their family? And just why was he so persistent about trying to keep Sarah out of the ranching business? She only owned fifty head. That could hardly be a threat to a man like Acton Burns, even though he wanted to monopolize the grasslands around the South Platte.

She nearly bumped into him as he exited the kitchen.

"Sorry," she muttered, keeping her head down.

"Morning, there, Lou." He tipped his hat. "Well, you two ladies have a pleasant day. I've business to attend to now."

Lou didn't say anything, just stood with her body sideways to him, lifting her eyes slowly to Sarah, who looked at Acton with a noncommittal gaze. When he'd gone, Sarah poured Lou a mug of fresh coffee. They didn't refer to Acton again.

After breakfast, Lou got up and headed out.

"I'm taking Sam with me to hunt for the herd," she said without meeting Sarah's gaze. "You might leave the gate open to the pen, just in case we find them."

Later that morning, Sam and Lou begin the task of cutting their own cattle out from those they'd run into the creek bottom. It was a hot and sweaty job, but they shouted and laughed every time they spotted one of their own. Acton's cowhands had done a sloppy enough job altering the brands, that the Lazy S was still prominent if one were looking for it.

By evening, they had every last one of their own cattle

cut out and rounded up. Then they waved their hats and shouted as their fast ponies drove the cattle back toward home. Sarah had left the gate open, and pretty soon the cows were all herded into the fence, bawling their announcement that they had arrived.

Sarah came out to watch, and to Lou's surprise and consternation, Gideon Preston followed her out the back door. The two of them stood at the fence as Lou and Sam herded the last of the cattle in. Then Lou got down to shut the gate.

She was covered with dirt from head to foot and used her bandanna to wipe off her face. She knew it would only smear worse. The sweat under her hat was salty and gritty. Why was it every time she saw the deputy marshal she looked like she'd just been rolling in the dirt?

She watched him from across the fifty-foot pen where he leaned against the fence. His hat covered part of his face, but the golden hair glinted in the sunset coming from the west. The rays caught the silver of his badge on his vest and sent a reflection. The way he stood, tall and easy, made you know he was a man of the law.

She followed Sam, leading her horse at a walk until they were almost within hearing distance of Gideon and Sarah. Then another more unwelcome visitor rode around the way station on his black horse, accompanied by two other men with rifles across their saddles. Lou stopped a few feet from Gideon and Sarah.

"Well, well," said Acton, getting down. He was still dressed in the black suit and black hat he'd had on this morning. "What have we here?"

He approached the cow pen, and Gideon leaned back on the fence, one arm along the fence, the other hand resting on his hip near his six-shooter. Lou stepped up angrily.

"Just our own cattle, Acton. We rounded 'em up and brought 'em home. Anything wrong with that?"

"Well, now, I don't know," he replied. "Deputy, I'd like to take a look at those brands, if you don't mind. From this distance those brands look like my own Bar 8. I'd just like to satisfy myself."

Lou got right between Acton and the cattle pen, forgetting what she looked like. Forgetting anything except her hatred of this slimy bastard.

"They ain't your brands, Acton. They're our brands, changed to look like yours. But not well enough that those with eyes can't see the truth."

He paused and gave her a look that said she was being a nuisance. Then he gave a false-looking smile and laughed.

"Do I hear right? Is this young lady accusing me of wrongdoing? And without any proof? Let me just see."

He jerked his head at the two men, who got off their horses, bringing their rifles with them. But Lou faced them off, her hands on her hips.

"This is our property. You'll be trespassing if you set one foot inside that fence."

Acton raised his hands in a helpless gesture.

"Deputy Marshal, I appeal to your good sense and your authority as a man of the law. All I wish to do is examine the cattle brands. What harm is there in that?"

Gideon narrowed his eyes and looked at all of them. Then he directed his question at Lou.

"You got that gate secure so the cattle won't get spooked?" he asked her.

She swallowed and nodded. "Yup."

"All right, Burns. Let your men go in nice and slow and look at the brands. No funny business."

He nodded and the other two men climbed between the bars and walked over to where they could see the brands better. They'd barely had time to look before they turned around.

"It's the Bar 8, all right," said the sour-looking snub-nosed one.

Acton nodded, still standing with his hands clasped in front of him.

"See there, Deputy? I'm afraid I'll have to file a complaint."

"Now wait a minute," shouted Lou, stomping over to where Acton faced Gideon. "I can testify as well as Sam and Sarah that those brands have been changed. The Lazy S is clear as daylight. The crossbar is newly singed. Anyone with eyes can see it."

She didn't miss the lift of Gideon's lips. He looked at the cattle, then back at Lou and Acton.

"Guess I'd better take a look."

He walked to the fence and slung one leg over the bottom rail and ducked his head under. He spoke softly to the cattle and walked among them, looking at the brands. Everyone else waited. Then he walked back and staying inside the pen, he leaned his arms chest level on the top rail.

"I'm not making any accusations," he said slowly. "But it could be like Lou says. The crossbar on that brand and part of the figure eight isn't as deep as the S lying on its side. I wouldn't like to accuse anyone present of cattle rustling. But I'd agree that the first brand applied to those cattle was the Farland brand. It appears that someone, I'm not saying who, has messed with them. Any arguments, gentlemen?"

He said it pleasantly, as if they were just having a conversation. Acton's men scuffed in the dirt, but Acton lifted a hand to indicate they should stay put. Finally, he gave his thin, sleazy smile.

"Well now, I guess I see how it is. You ain't gonna' support my notion that these are my cattle, Deputy, is that it?"

"That's how it is, Burns," said Gideon, politely. "If I were you, I'd help make sure that nothing further happens to these cattle, or further investigations might be necessary."

Lou could see Acton simmer, but he didn't argue. In another few seconds, he glowered a warning at Sarah and Gideon and stalked back over to his horse. His men followed him. They mounted, then Acton turned to face them all.

"You mind your business," he said to Gideon, who had come back to stand on this side of the fence. "And I'll mind mine."

"That sounds like a good idea," replied Gideon.

Acton jerked his head, and the three men turned and rode off.

Lou's sputtering anger at Acton mixed with gratitude for Gideon. As she reached for her horse's reins to lead him away from the trough, where he'd gone to drink, she suddenly felt self-conscious. Her heart swelled at the sight of Gideon, and her hands actually shook as she started to guide the horse toward the stables. Gideon's smile stopped her.

She tried to find some words to thank him. It was hard, wanting to meet that dazzling smile and at the same time wishing she didn't look like she'd just been dragged through the dirt. Finally, she was able to utter a few words.

"Thanks, for what you did."

"My pleasure," he said. "Can't have a man like that intimidating ladies like yourselves."

The fact that he was calling her a lady coaxed a smile and a blush to her face, but she still ducked her head so her hat might hide some of the grime on her face. Gideon carried on as Sarah and Sam gathered around.

"I always say, a man who threatens his neighbors like that must have something to hide. It just might be that Acton Burns isn't going to have everything the way he wants in this territory."

Sarah glanced in the direction Acton had gone. "I'd be careful, if I were you," she warned Gideon. "He might put up a fight."

Gideon followed her gaze, but his quiet words brooked no argument. "I got the law on my side."

Lou thought her heart would burst, the way she was feeling. Better get into the stables before she made a fool of herself over the handsome deputy marshal.

Lou led her horse off, followed by Sam. Behind them, she heard Sarah invite Gideon in for supper.

"Come on inside," Sarah told him. "I got food for the hungry."

"Well now," replied Gideon, "I never say no to a good meal."

Inside the stables, Sam said, "I'll care for the horses, Miss Lou. Why don't you go on in and get cleaned up."

Embarrassment flooded her. "That ain't fair, Sam. I'll do my share."

"Sure it's fair, Lou. I'll come along shortly for my supper. I think you better get in there and help entertain that deputy marshal." He gave her a wink.

She was chagrined that even Sam might have figured out how the deputy marshal was causing her to feel. She half wanted to stay and rub down her horse just to prove that no man was going to make her want to shirk her duties. But the other half of her was ready to seize the opportunity to be with Gideon again.

"All right," she conceded. "If you're sure."

"Go on, go on."

She nodded her thanks and went out. First, she pumped water at the trough and splashed it over her face and hair, getting the worst of the dirt washed off. In the pantry she hung up her hat and wet bandanna, then went through the kitchen, sniffing the aromas. Gideon wasn't there, but she could hear his voice as he visited with Jonathan Kingsley and Arthur Ramsey in the sitting room.

Lou hurried upstairs and undressed, then washed the rest of herself with the soap and water from a full ewer sitting next to the basin they kept on the dresser. When she was rubbed clean and had her hair pulled back smooth, she threw open the trunk of clothing. Maybe it would be too obvious to do what she was thinking of doing. But as her hands dug deep into the trunk, she knew she wasn't going to stop herself. She was going to put on a dress.

She climbed into the cotton drawers with ruffles of eyelet and slipped into an equally delicate camisole. Since being in the West she'd had no need for such clothing, but now she was thankful she still had them.

She unfolded and held out the long-sleeved cotton dress with ruffled collar. Then she pressed the print material to her face. It brought back old memories of home, bittersweet. But there wasn't time to dwell on the past. Instead, she shook out the wrinkles and climbed into the dress. It still fit.

It was hard to do up the fastenings at the back without any help, but she managed. Then she sat at Sarah's dresser and looked into the hand mirror.

She pinched her lips together to give them some color, then she combed through her hair and tied it at the base of her neck with one of Sarah's blue ribbons. She noticed how her eyes looked big, her eyelashes fanning them attractively.

"I look like a girl," she whispered to herself.

Riding for the pony express for so long had made her forget about her feminine side. It sent a little thrill through her heart to wonder how people would look at her now. Maybe she wasn't as plain as she'd thought.

She half considered taking off the dress and appearing downstairs in her normal shirt and trousers with suspenders, but she'd already gone to all the trouble of fastening the dress. They'd be holding supper for her.

She found a pair of slippers that buttoned up the ankle and put them on. Then she straightened her back and started downstairs.

At the bottom, heads turned from the parlor. Billy Joe Taylor was there, and he broke off his conversation.

"Lookie there, Miss Lou. What's the occasion? You look mighty pretty."

She shook her head. "Aw, shucks, Billy Joe. I don't have to go around in trousers all the time. Not when I don't have to go out for the express tonight."

She grinned at him and headed through the dining room, where Addie was just picking up the supper dishes she and Sarah had served. The black woman gaped at Lou, the whites of her eyes standing out against her dark face.

"Land sakes, Miss Lou. I ain't never seen you in a dress. Might a' not recognized you."

Lou grinned. "Had to wear it sometime, I guess."

Lou passed on through to find Gideon already seated. He stood up and stared at her as she entered the room. Sarah only paused for a moment in her slicing of corn bread.

Lou lowered her gaze shyly, but Gideon's eyes seemed to cut right through the thin material of her dress. She felt the warm glow of his smile as he slid a chair out for her, and she dared glance at him out of the corner of her eyes.

She sat down and his hand seemed to linger on the back of her chair. She actually felt it touch the strands of her hair as he moved to sit down again. A tingle sliced through her.

"You look mighty nice," he said in a voice that seemed to go just between them.

"Thanks," she replied.

She wanted to look at his eyes, but she kept her face averted. When she got braver she allowed herself to look at his hands, his arms, his relaxed torso slouched against the chair. So as to fill the silence, Gideon commented on the food as Sarah brought it over, and they busied themselves eating.

Lou half listened as they talked about events in Julesburg. Gideon alluded to things he was here to find out, but never said exactly what. She could hear the darkened tones of his voice when he mentioned Acton Burns.

"Then you think we're right to hang on to our cattle," Lou finally said. "Not give in to his offers to sell out. Things might get nasty if we don't do things his way."

She looked at Sarah, but didn't say anything about Acton's ridiculous offer of marriage.

"You have to follow your own conscience," said Gideon in a nonjudgmental way. "But if I'm right about the man, he may not trouble you much longer."

Lou chewed thoughtfully on her corn bread, washing it down with coffee.

They finished eating, and Addie came in to clear up the dishes. Gideon had wandered out through the pantry and out to the back steps.

"You go on," Sarah said in a low voice, nodding her head in the direction Gideon had gone.

Lou pressed her lips together, but she wiped her hands on a dish towel and smoothed her skirt. She tried to tell herself there wasn't anything unusual about passing the evening time with their guest.

Gideon had wandered out to the cattle pen and was resting his arms across the top rail. Lou joined him there, and for a minute they just watched the cattle milling about.

Her nervousness settled down a little, and she could just enjoy being there, looking at the peaceful scene. The evening sky was still light, and the twilight sounds floated up from the river. From the yard behind the boardinghouse down the street, children's laughter carried on the air. Gideon seemed affected by it, too.

"Back home, this was always my favorite time of day," he murmured.

"Where was back home?"

"West Virginia, but that was a long time ago."

"Yeah, me too. I mean, back home seems like another life."

"Guess that's true for a lot of us."

"Yeah, I guess."

They stood silently for a moment, then, without saying anything, they began to stroll along the fence. They turned the corner and followed it toward the river. It was a pleasant walk; a path had been worn away that led to the stand of cottonwoods along the bank. The muddy water cut a swath below them on its way to irrigate the plains.

Gideon leaned against a cottonwood while Lou stood a little distance off, reaching for a branch to twist off a twig.

"Sarah tells me you were bound for the Oregon Country," said Gideon, gazing at the landscape about them.

She sighed. "Never got that far."

"And now?"

She shrugged. "Ain't goin' there now, seems like. Too much happening here."

"You like it here?"

"It's a place to be, I guess."

He nodded. "For those that can make a go of it here, it is."

She looked at him. "What about you?"

One corner of his mouth pulled back in a grin. "You mean where am I bound for?"

She shrugged, looked away. "Once your job here is done."

Her pulse ricocheted uncomfortably. She didn't mean to give away any feelings.

"I know what you mean. Do you care?"

She paused. "How do you mean?"

"I mean if I left, would you care?"

Heat fanned her face again.

"Wouldn't everyone? We don't have that much law and order around here. That city marshal ain't got any spine. The army talks about building a fort down the river, but 'til they do, if the outlaws don't get us, then the Indians will.''

She was rambling, but she wasn't ready to answer such a personal question. Gideon took a few steps closer to her and touched her shoulder. It made her stop talking. She wasn't facing him, but his nearness burned through her.

"You're very pretty," he murmured in a honeyed voice that made her knees wobble.

She didn't feel anything but his presence beside her. She just closed her eyes, feeling his breath fan her hair. Finally, she swallowed the lump in her throat.

"No one ever said that since . . ."

"Since when?"

"Since my daddy and mama used to tell me that when I was a little girl. I almost forgot it."

"I imagine they were right. I imagine you were as pretty then as you are now. You've just been hiding it under those clothes you wear."

"There's a reason for that," she said shakily.

"I know, and I admire it. I'm just sayin' there's another side to you."

That he was awakening her other side there was no doubt. She longed for the pleasant feelings to linger, but she was scared, too. Scared of letting anyone get so close to her it might hurt.

"Why're you telling me this?" she said in a small voice.

She heard the deep chuckle in his voice. "I think I'm falling in love with you, Lou Farland."

Tears formed suddenly in the corners of her eyes. Why such a statement should make her cry was beyond her, but to have a man like Gideon Preston pay her all these compliments was too much to bear after the austere life she'd been leading.

"I, uh . . ." She didn't know what to say.

His hand slid along her back and snaked around her

waist. He pulled her gently against him, his chin resting against her head.

They stood that way for a long time until she felt comfortable enough to rest the back of her head against his shoulder. His arm around her waist was an unbelievable sensation, one she could enjoy for a long time. But her heart hammered wildly, and it still frightened her. She'd loved a family once and lost it. It was too dangerous to love. She pressed her trembling lips together.

Gideon seemed aware of her conflicting emotions. Finally, he turned her into him and held her in a gentle embrace.

"You're a beautiful woman, Lou," he said in a husky voice. "A man who can't see that is a fool."

She shook her head. "What good is it? A woman's place out here ain't any good. You have to know how to ride fast and shoot straight."

He grinned, his fingers tracing her cheek. "You know how to do all that. Maybe you're right. The frontier isn't a tame enough place for everyday women. Not yet."

He sighed, stroking her hair. "Sure would be nice though." His voice had a dreamy quality to it.

"What do you mean?"

"Tame the wild frontier. Homes for decent folks. The war in the States over. Make places like this a good place to live."

She lifted her chin, her head still nestled under his. "Do you think it will ever happen?"

"I'd like to see it so. Guess that's why I'm doin' what I'm doin'." He tightened his grip on her body in emphasis.

"You mean you're fightin' for law and order so that folks can make a home out here?"

He gazed down at her eyes. "Yeah, that's what I'm doin'. I guess I'm hoping I can have a home myself to return to one day."

She made a sound of skepticism in her throat. "Seems like a long time away."

"Maybe."

Her face had inched up, and his had lowered. She felt his lips brush her forehead and make it burn. But she didn't pull away. Then his lips were kissing her cheeks, the bridge of her nose and finally met her mouth. It was a gentle kiss, as if he sensed that Lou had not ever really kissed a man.

But their lips met as if they were meant for each other. She would have sunk to the ground from weakness if he hadn't been holding her up. The sensations were almost too much to bear, and she clung to him tightly, drinking him in, her head dizzy.

When he raised his mouth to let her breathe again, he held her tight, and they swayed against each other. Lou couldn't speak, as she fought back bittersweet tears. It was too wonderful to last. She had been kissed, really kissed.

Finally, he set her gently away, but tucked her under his arm, supporting her with his hand around her waist as they walked a few paces back. She clung to his waist, unsure she could walk steady, thrilled anyway to be holding onto his firm, strong frame.

They stopped at the far corner of the cattle pen. He turned her to face him, and he lifted his hand to touch her jaw. It was all too overwhelming, and Lou just stared at him until it made her feel shy, and she dropped her gaze. She was still trembling.

"You leaving again tomorrow?" he asked.

The question jolted her back to reality. She gave a nod. "Gotta' do the Sweetwater Run."

Dammit. For the first time ever she didn't want to go. She wanted to stay here with Gideon.

"You'll be careful then, won't you?" His voice warmed her like a caring caress.

She nodded, wishing he wouldn't take his hand away from her cheek, ever.

"Sure. The horses are faster than anything out there."

He slipped his arm around her shoulders then and kissed her cheek, near her mouth.

"I'll be waiting for you to come back, Lou Farland," he murmured.

Her heart overflowed. Would he really? She couldn't believe that. It was only as they were almost to the house and he dropped his arm to his side that she thought about his own work. She stopped on the back step to face him.

"You never did say how long you planned to be in these parts yourself."

He grinned mysteriously. "Well now, I do have some business that will take me away from here for a little while. But there's always after that."

"Is there?"

She hadn't meant it to sound accusatory, but the old skepticism born of life being hard and unpredictable came out. Lou lived from day to day. The vague notion of Gideon coming back someday had little meaning for her. A lot could happen in between. She tried to steel herself to the certain disappointment.

Why would a man like Gideon, who could go anywhere, choose to come back here?

He gave her a smile and touched her chin with his finger, lifting it to look into her face. He dropped another kiss on her lips, then touched her back in gentlemanly fashion to urge her inside, accompanying her.

Sarah had gone upstairs, and Lou walked through the kitchen, glad she didn't have to speak to anyone. Gideon paused at the bottom of the stairs and lifted his hat. While she clung to the wooden railing, he turned and crossed to the front door and went out.

She would have given in to the weakness in her knees and sat on the stairs, but someone behind her reminded her she was still in a public place. So she climbed upward to the attic bedroom, her cheeks burning, hardly knowing what she'd say to Sarah.

Sarah smiled calmly when Lou emerged at the top, but didn't say anything. Lou started to undo the fastenings of the dress and Sarah got up to help her.

She folded the dress, feeling foolish to have put it on at all. Tomorrow she would be back in her trousers and slouch hat. If she saw Gideon then, perhaps he would realize that she wasn't the sylvan nymph he'd seen in the placid summer evening. And he'd forget his errant kiss.

She put on her plain nightshirt and slipped between the sheets covering her horsehair mattress. Sarah extinguished the kerosene lamp and rustled into her own bed. Lou lay with her eyes open, watching the moonlit sky out the window where the curtains were pulled back. She knew Sarah wasn't asleep yet.

"What do you suppose Gideon's trying to find out, Sarah?"

Sarah stirred. "Don't know. He didn't tell you?"

Lou shook her head to herself. "No, just that he might have to go away for a while."

"Hmmmm. Did he say he'd come back?"

"He said he might."

Lou turned on her side and stuffed an arm under her pillow. "But you can't count on anything like that."

Sarah understood that Lou meant that you couldn't listen to promises. If you did, you were setting yourself up for disappointment.

Five

Gideon's slipping around Acton Burns's property paid off. From various conversations he wasn't supposed to hear late at night, he learned when Acton's herd was going to move out. Then he spent three days riding to Denver City and deputizing some help to set up their ambush.

He placed his men in thickets of trees along a butte where Burns's herd would be headed. They'd follow the South Platte as far as they could before turning south to avoid getting too close to Denver City. No one would question a herd traveling south. Gideon had overheard the men discussing how they would say they were taking the cattle to Bent's Fort if anyone asked.

In reality, they would swing eastward around it before they got there, then turn southwest again to meet their Confederate party farther south at Santa Fe. For a Confederate army was marching across the Southwestern deserts in an attempt to wrest the area from the Union.

Gideon gave his final instructions to his men before they fanned out to take up positions to wait.

"Sims, you and Dugan stay over there on the far right. Barnes and Shipley stay in those rocks and cover us as we ride down. The rest of you men follow me out onto the plains at my signal. Hold your fire unless Burns's men start trouble. Try not to spook the herd. If we have a battle on our hands, we'll turn the cattle east and north. Any questions?"

The men, all experienced veterans, nodded and rode off to take the positions they were assigned. Then it was only a matter of waiting. Gideon and his longtime friend, Bud Johnson, waited by an outcropping of rocks where they could see the trail he expected Acton to use, following Sand Creek. They didn't have long to wait.

When the first head of cattle appeared over the rise of the rolling plain, Gideon and Johnson crouched down. Johnson shook his head in amazement.

"You were right, I reckon. Can't figure anybody else drivin' cattle south."

Information had always been one of Gideon's specialties, first in the Union army and now as a federal lawman. He nodded, squinting to be able to see more clearly the men riding with the herd. The herd bellowed its way along the flat grasslands below them. And sure enough, out ahead was trail boss Acton Burns. And he was not alone.

Riding alongside him was a little group of six men armed for a confrontation. Gideon counted. The two point men at the head of the herd would probably join in the fight, while the cowboys riding swing and flank would probably try to turn it. Then the boys riding drag might try to get behind Gideon's men. But he had thought of all of this and had brought enough skilled deputies to do the job. And they had surprise on their side. He stood up and spoke to Johnson.

"You make sure everything back here stays nice and quiet. I'm going to ride out alone."

A single man approaching Acton on horseback would not be seen as a threat until they knew what he wanted. And the men knew to wait for his signal before they started anything. Still, Gideon doubted that Acton was going to come along nicely.

He mounted up and moved out at a walk, coming down

the hill in time to intercept Acton, but well ahead of the herd. He saw the glower of recognition as soon as he got close enough, and Acton reined in, his men a few feet behind him.

"Well now, look a' here. What could you be doing this far south, Deputy?" asked Acton.

Gideon glanced over the other man's shoulder at the herd coming behind him. "I could ask the same of you."

"What I do is none of your business, Deputy. Now if you'll kindly move out of the way so that my men and my cattle can be on our way."

"I hope they are your cattle," said Gideon.

Acton gave him a nasty look that did not try to hide the malice in his eyes.

"I know you've been spending your time with the Farland skirts in Julesburg, Preston. But I'm surprised chivalry brings you so far."

Gideon let the slur on his personal interests pass in order to serve the bigger picture.

"Cattle rustling is a crime, to be sure," he responded. "But I have a warrant in my pocket that says you're under arrest for a bigger crime."

Acton gave a sharp laugh. "And what might that be?"

"Trading with Confederates. These cattle are meant for a Texas army on its way to take Santa Fe. Only problem is, I don't think your herd is going to get that far, at least not this year."

"Says who?" said Acton in his snide tone.

Gideon cocked his head to the west. "Says a posse of fifty deputy marshals in those hills."

Acton and his men gave a suspicious look in the direction Gideon indicated, and Gideon could see the questions in the other men's eyes. He knew that Acton Burns was not a courageous man. He would put himself in danger only when he knew his back was covered by the men whose loyalty he had bought and paid for. Now Gideon could see him doing a mental calculation.

Gideon had stretched the number of men he really had in the hills. It was part of calling Acton's bluff.

"I'm serious, Burns," said Gideon in his final warning. "If any of your men touch their guns, my men will shoot. I ask you if this herd is worth risking your life over."

He could see the indecision in the other man's eyes. Then Acton set his jaw and glared at Gideon.

"I think you're bluffing."

He reached for his firearm, but Gideon was faster. His bullet hit Acton in the arm.

He didn't wait for Acton to reach for his rifle with his left hand. Gideon fired at the next man who aimed at him, then the guns blazed from the trees, giving Gideon time to wheel to the right and away. The confused point rider on this side had his gun out and fired at Gideon, who returned fire. But a shot from the trees had the man out of his saddle, his horse rearing.

Gideon continued to fire at those of Acton's men putting up a fight while racing in to help turn the roused cattle eastward. A shot from the chuck wagon almost took him by surprise, and he returned fire. Out of the corner of his eye, he saw two of the deputies ride out behind him, guns blazing.

Several of Acton's men threw down their guns. Gideon's men rode up and took them prisoner.

Gideon circled the chuck wagon, returning the fire that came from there. He finally saw the man stick out a white rag on the end of the rifle.

"Throw out your weapons," he yelled, as the herd began to thunder past them.

The frightened cook did as he was told and stepped out with his hands up.

A few more shots told Gideon it wasn't over yet. And he saw Acton riding for his life back along the herd. Two of

Gideon's men started out after him. One of them took a hit from Acton's bullet and slid off his horse to the ground. The other man kept after Acton, but Gideon could see from this distance that Acton had the faster horse.

His men were taking up the positions of the cowboys that had surrendered and were turning the stampeding herd back east and north. Gideon jumped down and shouted at the cook.

"Walk ten paces away from the wagon and lie facedown on the ground. No funny business."

The cattle were still bawling, but Gideon's riders had them moving together in the direction they wanted. At least they wouldn't have to waste time rounding up strays.

Keeping his gun on the cook, he bent down and searched the man for other weapons with his left hand.

"All right, get up."

Then he marched the man over to where the rest of the prisoners were gathered.

"Everyone accounted for except for the ringleader," reported Deputy Bud Johnson. "Dugan took a bullet in his shoulder, but he'll be all right. Shipley took off after Burns over that rise."

"All right," Gideon told Johnson. "I'm leaving you in charge of the prisoners. Take two men with you and get them back to Denver City for questioning. We'll drive the herd back north and turn 'em over to the Union army. At least we'll prevent that Confederate army from eating this beef. Well-done, boys."

"Where're you going?" asked Johnson.

"After Shipley and Burns."

Bill Sims had assumed the position of trail boss. Sims grinned. "Smart of you to bring along plenty of boys used to driving these herds. We should have no trouble getting them to Fort Kearney."

"All right then. Keep a sharp lookout for Indians. I'm going to see what happened to Shipley."

He could trust Bud Johnson to handle the prisoners, so he rode off in pursuit of Burns.

Sims gave him a wave, and the men separated. Gideon rode over the hill in the direction he'd seen Acton disappear. He should have expected the bastard to flee instead of having the guts to stand and fight.

He dug his heels in and galloped over rolling prairie, keeping his eyes open. It wasn't hard to follow where the two men had ridden before him. Shipley was a good man, and Gideon hoped he hadn't met with treachery.

The farther he rode, the more he wondered. There were two sets of hoofprints for a long way, but he could see nothing on the horizon. Finally, near a clump of trees that led down to a creek, one rider had turned off.

Drawing his gun in case it was Acton instead of Shipley who had gone down to the creek, he rode warily. Then when he saw Shipley's horse grazing alone, he dismounted. Still wary of a trap, he kept his horse between him and the grove.

But then he saw Shipley lying on his side, his head near the water. He holstered his gun and went to help.

Shipley groaned. He was bleeding from one side, and Gideon stripped off his shirt and examined the wound.

"He got away," said Shipley with labored breath.

"Don't worry about him," said Gideon. "Let's take care of this wound. Looks like the bullet went clean through. You'll be all right."

He washed the wound, then found some clean cloth to bind up the deputy. He'd have to wait for another day to catch Acton Burns, for he owed his help to the man who'd chased him this far.

"What about the cattle?" rasped Shipley.

"Got 'em all rounded up. Johnson has the prisoners. You helped the Union army this day. Think you can ride?"

"I can if we don't have to outrun no Indians."

"It's not far to the next settlement, we'll get you some help there."

The town of Julesburg had not seen or heard from Acton Burns, and it was a few days before rumors began to drift in that his big herd had moved off to the south. Lou felt relief that the man was gone, but they still kept a sharp eye on their own cattle. Neither had Gideon been heard from since he'd told her he'd be away for a week or two. But he'd left her with one thing to hold on to. He'd come back, he'd said. That was a promise.

She tried not to think of it as she left for her run on the pony express. She had to keep her wits about her for the ride. You never knew when danger might lurk, and if she was daydreaming, it might mean her life.

So as she galloped over the high plains, she tried to keep her mind on business. She took care to hurry the horses, but not to wear them out. At each way station, she was quick about refreshing herself and changing horses. Still, something about the change Gideon had wrought in her gave her a lift in her view of life.

She felt joy in her heart as she and her horse dashed across prairie and hill. Her eyes feasted on the green of summer, and her heart soared with the hawks that sometimes arched high above her.

The stars twinkling in the night skies made her feel full of the promise of life.

"Maybe someplace out here really can be home," she murmured to herself staring at the diamond sparkles of the indigo sky one night.

Home. The idea she'd stuffed out of reach because she didn't see how she'd ever find it again. Now she began to hope and dream about it, though she didn't let herself be too specific. Home was a feeling of peace and of being loved. It was that sacred place that you'd die to protect.

She hadn't let herself think it, but now she realized that it was the place she longed for most in the world.

At night she slept well on the narrow bunks in the pony express riders' bunkhouses. And then one morning she began the final leg of the journey back to Julesburg.

She had dismounted to check her horse's hoof because he'd stumbled. A rock or sharp object between the shoe and hoof could cause serious damage. She was on her knees, removing what she thought was the source of the problem, when she heard voices coming from the other side of the ridge where she'd stopped near some rocks.

"You stay here," she told the horse, rubbing his nose. "I'll have a look."

She tied him to some bushes and crept up to peer over the ridge. What she saw on the far side of the river she didn't like. She was enough downwind to hear a few of the words being spoken by the three men on the far bank fanning a fire they'd made until the flames caught on the long grasses lining the riverbank.

Alarm filled Lou. The wind would spread that fire down-river in no time. To Julesburg.

It hadn't rained in weeks. They could burn down the town in minutes.

Rage filled her, and she ran back to her horse, mounting, then digging in her heels. Then she galloped the horse as fast as it could run. If she didn't make the crossing before the flames did, she wouldn't get across in time to warn them.

There wasn't much wind, just enough to urge the flames from brush to brush. Off to the right as she raced along, she saw it move through the grass, leaving black smoke to rise above the trees. If the townspeople were looking, they'd see the smoke, but she couldn't bank on it.

The crossing was near and in a heartbeat, she was down the bank.

"Go on, now," she urged the gelding. "Get on across."

Horses didn't like fires, and she prayed he wouldn't shy away from the oncoming blaze. He snorted and tossed his head, but the fire was far enough away that he took them into the water and a little downstream.

She anxiously watched the fire catch as her horse's strong strokes carried them across. They had to make it up the sandy bank before the fire cut them off. If the wind would only hold for another few minutes, they would be there.

She felt the gelding's hooves touch the bottom, and then they slogged up the bank, taking the worn cut in the bank that led to the grassland above. The fire was spreading now, and flames licked the dry branches of the trees farther inland. Black curls of smoke were rising with their signals of danger.

"Giddap," she cried, kicking the horse through the trees.

With a shout, she emerged onto the road, hollering, "Fire, fire."

Julesburg had no volunteer fire department. It would be up to every man, woman, and child to help put out the fire. Lou slowed down to be able to gasp breathlessly and point.

"Fire along the riverbank!" she yelled to everyone she saw. "Get buckets and shovels! Hurry, it's coming this way."

Several people stopped in the middle of the street and pointed at the black smoke visible above the trees.

The townspeople who heard her wasted no time spreading the alarm, and soon the cry of "fire, fire," was spreading through the town. The tinkling of the piano in the saloon stopped as someone burst through the door to arouse the early inhabitants there.

Lou dashed on, slid off the horse, and undid the *mochila*. The other rider, Billy Joe, had heard her cry of alarm, and looked on with concern. But with everyone pouring out of the way station and livery stable to go help, his job was still to carry the mail safely. Lou extracted the packet of local mail and tossed the leather *mochila* at him.

"Was it you who raised the alarm?" he asked as he quickly fastened the mail container to the saddle.

"Saw it from the other side of the river," she said, as she caught her breath. "Heard the men who started it. You go on. I'll help here."

He climbed into his saddle. "If I see anybody on the road, I'll send 'em back to help."

"Thanks."

She raced around the way station and saw Sarah and Sam coming from the livery stable with buckets and shovels. She grabbed the bucket handles from Sarah.

"I'll take those. You bring whatever else we got."

By the time she reached the river, two bucket brigades had formed. From the back of the boardinghouse, women were filling buckets from a pump and handing it along. Some of the taller men were throwing the water up at tree branches that had caught. Ladders had been brought so they could climb up and wet down the roofs of the buildings to prevent their catching, should the wind change.

Lou splashed down into the sandy bank below. Men were passing buckets full of water upward from hand to hand and dousing the fire in the grass. But they needed more water. Lou splashed into the river and began filling her buckets. She didn't even try to watch the fire as she bent her back to the task.

She wondered where Gideon was. What she'd heard coming from the men starting the fire was crucial, and she had to find Gideon and tell him as soon as they had the fire under control. If they could control it.

In the end, they put it out before any of the buildings caught. Trenches were dug along the fire line and the dirt tossed on the remaining sparks. In another hour, they were sure they had it out.

Grimy and sweaty, Lou stood with a group of townspeople where the fire had started, and she described what she'd seen. She noticed that while they'd worked to put out the fire none of Acton Burns's hired men were in evidence. Even the city marshal, John McGee, was conveniently absent. Gone to investigate a stage holdup, someone said.

As Lou was about to mention her suspicions, she saw Gideon ride through the trees on his piebald horse. The group of men and women gazing at the blackened ground looked up and watched him hasten toward them.

When he reined in and got down Lou could see he'd been riding pretty hard himself. Sweat glistened on his face, and then she realized the dark patches on his shirt weren't sweat, but blood, and her heart slammed against her chest.

Her feet moved of their own volition, and he caught her by the shoulders as she moved to look at the blood.

"It's not mine," he said.

He met her gaze with certainty, and she felt relief wash over her. From the strength in the hands that squeezed her shoulders, she could believe he hadn't been hurt.

"One of my men was wounded," he explained. "I bound up the wound and got him onto and off of his horse. After we got help, I rode on back here. They said there was a fire."

Anger burned in his eyes as he surveyed the burned river bank.

She nodded. "It was Acton Burns's men. I saw them start it. They didn't know I was there, so they weren't trying to muffle their words. Said something about circling around to the south to get back to the Bar 8 before anyone saw them."

Gideon's jaw clenched, and he surveyed the charred earth. "Anyone hurt?"

She shook her head.

George Dabney stepped up. "Lou gave the warning, Deputy. She saved the town."

Jeremy Higgins, the big, muscular blacksmith, nodded. "If it hadn't been for Miss Lou, here, we'd be burned to the ground."

She was about to shrug it off, but she caught the pondering twinkle in Gideon's eye, even though his face remained serious. Her heart swelled to think he might be proud of her.

Then he turned back to business. "You said you heard them say something about circling south and making for the Bar 8?"

"That's right," she said.

His gaze narrowed as he looked at the direction they must have followed. Then he turned thoughtfully to the little crowd still standing with them and raised his voice for them all to hear.

"I need some volunteers," he said. "I'm empowered to deputize citizens to help catch a traitor to the Union. I've got a warrant for the arrest of Acton Burns. We already caught his outfit driving a large herd of cattle to a rendezvous with a Confederate army moving to Santa Fe. When they get there, they'll find the beef intended for their provisions can't be had. But Acton Burns, the ringleader in this operation, slipped through our net. Who here would like to catch a traitor?"

All the men, including the other two young pony express riders home from their routes, stepped up. Gideon looked them all over and gestured for the fittest of them to step to his right. He thanked the rest, but assured them that they'd be better off staying home and protecting their families.

He ignored Lou but gave instructions to his instantly deputized posse. When he was finished he sent them to get horses and weapons.

"Meet at this end of the street in a quarter of an hour,"

he said. "Anyone chooses not to go, I'll understand. Acton Burns is a dangerous man."

Lou started off with the rest of them, but his hand on her shoulder stopped her. "Where are you going?"

"To get a fresh horse," she said. "And my guns."

"You're not going, Lou. I didn't appoint you."

"Well, then, appoint me now."

"No."

"Why not?"

"Because you might get killed."

She inched closer to him, looking up into the lean, chiseled face she cared about so dearly.

"You think I'm about to stay here while you go and get yourself killed as well? No sir, I will not, Gideon Preston. Deputized or not, I ain't stayin' behind."

Gideon looked as if he were going to argue. His glinty, golden eyes sparked with the fierce gaze his job demanded of him. Lou's heart thudded against her ribs as their wills battled for dominance. Then his hands grasped her shoulders, and she gave in to the urge to fling her arms around him.

His mouth sought hers for a hungry kiss, and she clung for dear life. When he lifted his mouth for breath, it seemed they had settled little else than that they craved more time alone together. He spoke more gently now.

"Lou, I have one last job to do in the service of the federal marshal's office. If I can bring Acton Burns to justice, we will have caught and prosecuted a Union traitor. It's a job I have to do. But I want to know in my heart there's someone waiting for me to finish the job."

She sighed and leaned against his shoulder, only belatedly realizing how dirty they both were. For a fleeting instant, she imagined a time when they would have leisure to indulge in sweet, lazy evenings together.

"I want to be here when you come back," said Lou. She

clenched a fist against his chest. "But I ain't the waiting type."

He planted his chin on the top of her head. "I don't have time to argue with you. If you come along, you have to promise to stay back and not expose yourself to Acton's fire. Do you promise?"

"I promise," she said, knowing she would say anything to get his agreement.

He gave her one more hasty kiss, his lips lingering just long enough to taste the sweetness and promise of more.

"Be careful," he said when he finally let her go. "And mind what I said."

Lou scampered off to the livery stable behind the way station, pausing long enough to splash water on her face and neck. She found Sam and asked him to saddle her a good horse. Then she raced upstairs to check her guns and ammunition.

When she was ready, she mounted up and rode down the street to meet the posse already assembling. Gideon had a fresh horse, a bay gelding, and trotted up to lead them. He surveyed his little band with a critical eye, noticing with satisfaction that Lou was keeping to the back.

"All right, men," he said—for Lou was the only woman among them. "Keep a sharp eye out. There may be a lookout waiting for us."

He wheeled his gelding, and they thundered off down the road together. The acrid smoke from the fire still hung in the air, but a breeze wafted up from the river to cleanse it away. Lou scanned the countryside for any movement. But there was nothing except waving grasses and a small clump of trees on the horizon.

They slowed to a walk with guns at the ready as they approached the trees in case of trouble. But Burns's men didn't know they were suspected and probably had no idea there was a posse on the way. They left the horses in the trees, then gathered around Gideon as he gave instructions.

The ranch house could be seen some fifty yards off. There were a few trees off to the left and a shed and barn off to the right. If they were seen, they would have to depend on them for cover.

"You men take the left and cover me," Gideon said to some of them. "The rest of you go to the right and cover the back of the house. Watch the roof of the house and the barn. No telling where he's got men staked out."

They bent as low as they could to start for their positions one at a time. Gideon turned to Lou.

"You stay here," he said to her since it was what they'd already agreed. "Make sure the horses don't scatter. We may need them. And watch your back."

"Watch yours," she replied, as he faced her grimly.

He jerked his chin up in a gesture of agreement, then followed the last man off to the right. Everyone in position, Gideon crept up closer to the house. Lou had her gun out and leveled at the house to cover him, though from this distance she didn't think she could hit anything.

"Damn," she cursed. How could she get in on the fight from here?

She gave a quick glance over her shoulder at the horses all tied to tree branches.

"You nags will be all right. I'm going in."

When Gideon reached a tree near the front of the house, he stepped out.

"Come on out, Acton. Hands up. You're surrounded."

A flash and explosion from the open front window was the answer. But Gideon had anticipated it, and he flattened himself against the tree for cover. Lou fired at the window, hunched over, and sprang forward. After covering twenty paces, she threw herself on the ground as explosions erupted on all sides.

Fierce emotions roiled inside her as she returned fire,

inching up on her elbows in between each shot. She'd be damned if they were going to get the man she loved.

"Gideon, stay back," she pleaded in a soft voice, knowing she was talking to herself.

Tears sprang at the corners of her eyes, and she wiped them on her sleeve. She couldn't see to shoot if she was going to be distracted by tears. But she'd never loved anyone like this, and she was willing to die for him.

Out of the corner of her eyes she saw a figure in the door of the hayloft. The man was about to jump down on George Dabney.

"George, look up," she yelled, and got off a shot.

George saw the man and rolled, kicking the gun out of his hand. She returned her attention to the house. Someone was creeping around the corner of the porch.

"Gideon, on your left," she shouted.

She fired and gathered her feet under her to run forward again. When there was a chance she scrambled off to the left and flattened herself again.

Shots fired all over, but so far Acton hadn't shown his face. A body toppled off the porch. One of theirs. Lou gritted her teeth and crawled closer, returning fire at the window of the house.

Gideon ran around the side of the house, and her stomach clenched as she saw him gain the west side of the porch. What was he trying to do, get himself killed?

Then from the direction of the barn, she saw another kind of spark. Someone had lit a torch soaked in kerosene and she saw Jeremy Higgins haul back his mammoth arm and fling the torch at the house. It landed on the porch, where the flames licked the east side of the house.

Lou got closer, oblivious to danger, only intent on covering Gideon, whose back was to the side of the house except when he turned, ducked, and fired at the open window.

Some of Burns's men must have seen the threatening

flames and fled out the back door. She saw two of the posse light out after them. The dry planks of the house went up like tinder, and soon Gideon was coughing every time he took a breath.

"Come out of there, you bastard, or you'll burn alive."

Finally the front door was kicked open. Lou trained her gun on it in case of any trickery. Acton tossed his gun out and stepped into the billowing smoke, hands up.

"Walk down the front steps," shouted Gideon. "Nice and slow. Keep your hands where I can see 'em."

Lou stood up, her gun pointed straight at Acton's head. The other men who hadn't fled had given up the fight and surrendered. The posse relieved them of their weapons and tied them up.

Gideon showed no surprise that Lou was there to cover Acton while he searched the man for any hidden weapons. She stared Acton down. Acton stared belligerently ahead.

When Gideon had Burns's hands tied behind him, he gave him a shove forward.

"Move. We've got a long way to go to Fort Kearney. Much as I'd like you to walk, it'll be faster on a horse."

They took account of the posse and their prisoners while the house burned. Lou couldn't resist one last remark before Gideon made Acton get on a horse without the help of his hands.

"Only fair, seems to me," she said to the traitor. "A person oughta think twice before tryin' to burn our town down."

He didn't deign to look at her, but jutted his chin forward as he sat on the horse that was being led away.

Six

Lou held the wedding dress against her cheek. The hand-made lace cascaded over her arms and down the skirt spread out on the quilt. They were standing in their attic room where Sarah had just brought out her mother's wedding dress from the bottom of her own trunk, which had come from Illinois. Lou was overwhelmed with the gown's beauty.

"It's beautiful, Sarah. I couldn't possibly wear it."

Sarah's lips quivered into a smile. "Why ever not? You have to stand up in something."

"I know, but this . . . It's so lovely and delicate. It should be kept nice."

"Nonsense. Now take off your clothes. Let's get you into camisole, drawers, and corset to see if it fits."

At the mention of a corset, Lou lowered a brow. "Do I have to wear a corset?"

Sarah's wry grin was answer enough. "On this occasion I would think so. It will give the gown the proper appearance. But I promise not to pull the laces too tight."

Lou obliged and disrobed and tried on the delicate things, laughing and choking on emotion at the same time. Sarah even wound up her niece's hair, then draped the veil over her head. When she was finished, she admired her handiwork with a great sigh.

"You'll do fine, Lou. Just fine."

"Do you think so?"

Gideon, who she still could not believe had asked to marry her, wasn't used to seeing her decked out like this. "I know so," said Sarah.

She gave Lou the hand mirror so she could at least see the effects of the veil and neckline. It was just too bad they didn't have a full standing mirror so she could see the way she looked in the gown.

Sarah felt a tug in her heart. Lou was about to begin a new life. And with a man she felt sure would be good to her. Suddenly she grasped her niece's hands, and the two women wept out of nostalgia and happiness.

Lou and Gideon stood up together under a big oak tree on a low hill just east of town. The itinerant preacher read out the ceremony, and they exchanged vows. All the towns-people, decked out in finery, stood on the hillside, witness to the union.

Gideon lifted Lou's veil and kissed his bride to the cheers of the crowd.

Lou beamed in embarrassment for the whole day long as one by one the pony express riders and all those who knew her came by to grasp her hands and kiss her pink cheeks.

Then when enough whiskey had been consumed that the carousing was high, Gideon came to whisper in Lou's ear.

"It's time to go," he said.

"It is?"

For answer, he gave an animal-like grunt. "I want some time with my wife to myself," he murmured, his hand snaking around her waist. "Without neighbors gawking at you."

"Aw, shucks, Gideon. They mean well."

"Hmmmm. I'm sure they do."

Already she was trembling as Gideon took her hand and they strolled away from the merrymaking. Tomorrow they were taking the stage east for their honeymoon, but tonight Gideon had arranged with Mrs. Carter for a special room at the boardinghouse.

When Gideon opened the door to the decorated room, Lou gave a shy gasp. Wildflowers in profusion were set about the room in vases. Garlands of wild purple asters and yellow prairie coneflowers were strung across the canopy of the big rope-sprung double bed, and ruffled pillow shams covered pillows piled high against the tall headboard.

Gideon put his hat on the peg and swung Lou around to look at her once more.

"I just want to remember how you look today," he said.

He looked so fine himself in his handsome suit that she wanted to say so, but found herself too choked up for words. His eyes glistened, and he touched her cheek.

"I'll be gentle, my lovely bride," he said in a soft voice.

Then he cleared his throat and moved awkwardly toward the door. "Mrs. Carter wanted to help you prepare for bed," he said with a touch of embarrassment, and stepped out and shut the door.

In a few moments, the landlady knocked and entered, all smiles and gushing her compliments.

"You are such a lovely bride," she said. "Here, sit down and I'll unpin your veil and help you with that beautiful dress. Such a beautiful dress. I understand it was Sarah's mother's."

"Yes," Lou croaked.

But in truth, Mrs. Carter's effusive chatter helped Lou get through her awkwardness. When she was finally in a frilly nightdress, Mrs. Carter turned down the bedcovers as if there was nothing unusual about it.

"So lovely to be having newlyweds," she went on. "I do hope you and Gideon will return to Julesburg after your honeymoon."

"I don't know," said Lou. "Gideon's been asked to come to Denver City to work for the law there."

"Well now, that isn't so far, is it? We might see you from time to time."

But Lou had stopped listening to Mrs. Carter, for the door had opened, and her husband appeared behind her. Mrs. Carter wished them a good night and then Gideon shut the door and turned the skeleton key.

He undressed slowly, and Lou closed her eyes when he removed his trousers. But she peeked through nearly closed eyelids just the same as he came toward the bed, his long shirttail still covering most of him.

Then he extinguished the kerosene lamp and slid in next to her, sliding one arm under her and pulling her toward him.

"My love," he murmured as he held her gently. "I never thought I would find so lovely a wife."

"Me, lovely?" she said with emotion, as he kissed her face and mouth.

"Very lovely."

Then she drank in the joy of holding him close as he took his time exploring her lithe body, making her gasp with each new experience. The pleasure of intimacy with his strong, masculine body was a hundredfold more than she could ever have imagined. And he was as gentle as his words had been.

And to think, they were embarked on a honeymoon where every night for a week, they could go to a room together and share their love. She stayed awake long after the ache that accompanied her first time with her husband had subsided. It was a new idea and made her bloom with promise.

She loved him more than anyone could know. And maybe someday she would find the words to tell him so. For now, he would see in her blushes and in her embraces and by the shy way she curled her arm around him, even as he lay in slumber, that she was his blushing bride.

She had found home at last.

ROMANCE FROM FERN MICHAELS

DEAR EMILY   (0-8217-4952-8, $5.99)

WISH LIST   (0-8217-5228-6, $6.99)

AND IN HARDCOVER:

VEGAS RICH   (1-57566-057-1, $25.00)

Available wherever paperbacks are sold, or order direct from the Publisher. Send cover price plus 50¢ per copy for mailing and handling to Kensington Publishing Corp., Consumer Orders, or call (toll free) 888-345-BOOK, to place your order using Mastercard or Visa. Residents of New York and Tennessee must include sales tax. DO NOT SEND CASH.